Hiding In Plain Sight

by Jan Hogan

Published by Vegas Vibe Books

ISBN-13: 978-0990361565

Special thanks go to: to Tyler and Tara for keeping it
real; Sami for her computer skills and vibrant energy; Tobie for
being my cheerleader; Lisa Valentine, for understanding my
vacant stare at work because this book, literally, woke me at 3
and 4 a.m. each night as new scenes presented themselves like a
movie and then demanded to be written until it was completely
done.

This book is dedicated to John LY

Hiding In Plain Sight

by Jan Hogan

CHAPTER ONE

Seated on the private jet, she turned her business card over in her hand. "Becca, Painter of Emotions," it read. It was a new name for a new person. She would add her studio information as soon as she was settled in Las Vegas.

She stared out the window, not really seeing the sky but rather the life she was leaving behind. "Jeez, Luke," she said, "what did you get me into?"

"Hide in plain sight," he'd insisted. "Hide in plain sight or they'll hunt you down."

So that was what she was doing, restarting her life – new face, new body, new name - hoping no one would learn her secret and come to abduct her, torture her. For the rest of her days, until her dying breath, she would have to hide in plain sight, all while living a very public life.

FOUR YEARS EARLIER

Laurel Rebecca Trenton raced into her grandmother's San Diego house, hands working to open the letter she'd just snatched from their mailbox. "Oh, my gosh, it's here, it's here," she called out.

"Oh, good, you're home from school," Grams said, hurrying out of the kitchen. "Quick, what did they say?"

The darn flap wouldn't open. Laurel gave up and tore the envelope end to end. She unfolded the letter and scanned it for the only word that mattered: Accepted.

It wasn't there.

Her shoulders dropped. She let the paper fall to the table. "I've been rejected," she said, her voice flat.

Grams retrieved the letter and read it. She put her arm around Laurel. "I'm sorry, honey. Maybe the next art school will accept you."

The next art school? But this one had been her first choice, the one she'd had her heart set on attending right after high school graduation. She had it all planned in her mind, had dreamed of it, made plans for it. Now she had to hope another art school would accept her and put all her hopes on that one? "Sure, I guess. But I really wanted this one to accept me."

Her grandmother gave her a hug. "I know, sweetie, but sometimes things work out differently."

"It's just that I had my heart set on this on, Grams."

"You still have six months before you graduate, maybe your art teacher can suggest a way to make your portfolio really stand out so the next art institution accepts you."

Sure, apply at another school so her hopes could be shot down again? It wasn't fair. All she ever wanted was to paint and create beautiful artwork.

Laurel swung her ancient car, a hand-me-down from her older sister, Theresa, into the community park's entrance. Theresa had left Gram's house right after high school and was now dancing in a touring show. They'd received postcards from her as the show made the rounds – New York, Miami, Costa Rica even. Some people had all the luck.

She parked, spotted Luke, reminding herself to putting on a brave front. What had Grams said? Think of something that makes you happy, like a kitten.

She thought of a kitten and a smile crept onto her face. There, that wasn't so hard. She strolled toward her boyfriend, waving to catch his attention. "Luke, over here."

He came over and hugged her. "The art school in Denver didn't work out?"

How did he know? "Did Grams call and tell you?"

He just sent her a silly smile. "No one had to tell me."

Of course no one had told him, Luke somehow knew things like that. He'd known when her dog was hit by a car. He'd known when she'd gotten pneumonia and was rushed to the hospital. He'd known when her parents had died.

What had he said when they'd met in sixth grade? "I'm more than your friend," he'd said.

And he was right. They'd become inseparable. Best pals, best buddies, the bond growing stronger as they had matured. They were always there for one another. In some crazy way, it was like they were meant to be together.

And now he knew this, her big, no, *huge* disappointment. Her dream shattered. The tears threatened. Damn, she didn't want him to see her cry. Laurel took a deep breath and set aside her emotions. "I just want to be an artist."

"Artists struggle for years, decades even, before their talent is recognized."

"No they don't."

"Sure they do." He shrugged. "Looks like I'll have to take care of you so you can paint."

Like she was, what, incapable of taking care of herself? She pretended to punch his shoulder. "Don't be so sexist."

Luke grabbed his arm, doubled over and moaned in pain. "Jeez, you're strong. There's a million-dollar career for you in the boxing ring if you want it."

He could always lift her mood. "Show me what you've got."

He straightened up, done acting, and pulled something wrapped in aluminum foil from his back pocket. He checked around for spying eyes and sent her a conspiratorial look. "Prepare to be amazed," he said, folding back the flaps.

Something flat and brown was inside.

"What is that?"

"Gum," he said. "And not just any gum, vitamin gum. Here, try some." He peeled off a piece and handed it to her.

This was new. Usually Luke liked to invent things that messed with radio waves or distorted TV signals. Gum? Really?

Laurel popped it in her mouth. A rush of chemical flavor instantly accosted her. Yuck! She spat it out. "This stuff is horrible."

Luke frowned. "Well, it needs a little tweaking."

"A little tweaking? It needs to be condemned."

He folded it back up in the foil, not looking at her.

"I mean, it's the worst –" She stopped. She'd hurt him.

He shrugged. "I understand. You didn't like it."

That was an understatement. "It tastes like some horrible medicine your that your parents make you take, overwhelming."

He looked down at his feet. "OK."

"You're not mad at me?"

"No, not mad."

But he'd been stung.

"Luke, look, I'm sorry," she said, her tone gentle, "but this vitamin gum, not your best idea."

"Like horrible medicine?"

She nodded.

He looked up and brightened. "Actually, I thought so too, but I wanted another opinion."

"What? So, I was your guinea pig? For something you already knew was terrible tasting?" This time, she did punch his shoulder.

The next day at school, she hung around after the last bell and walked into the art room. Good, no other students were there.

Mr. Peterson looked up from his desk. "Laurel? What can I do for you?"

Here went nothing. "The art school in Denver rejected my application," she said. "I was hoping you could give me some advice on re-applying, sending them new art to access my talent."

"You sent them your best pieces, didn't you?"

She nodded. "The Monument Valley one, the cat at the window one." There had been a couple others, but those two had been the pieces she thought would put her at the top of their list. After all, how many high school kids could paint fur? It took real talent to pull that off.

"Yes, I remember them." He paused. "Maybe you should try a new tack, approach a subject with less rigidity."

Less rigidity? He thought her work was rigid, constrained? "But-"

"It's hard for artists to critique their own work," Mr. Peterson said. "*You* know what you were trying to put on canvas, and *you* see it clearly, but not everyone else does."

There was a noise at the door. Jeremy Witherspoon ran in, waving a paper. "I got accepted! I got accepted!" he crowed. "The Colorado Capital Arts School wants me!"

Laurel felt her insides crumble. That was the school she'd pinned her hopes on attending. That should have been her, jumping up and down with joy.

"Let's see that letter," Mr. Peterson said, reaching for it.

The two of them scanned it together and the art teacher clapped Jeremy on the back. "I knew you could do it."

Laurel plastered a smile on her face. "Congratulations, Jeremy. That's great news. I'll just be going." She walked out, feeling numb. Mr. Peterson's words still buzzed in her brain. Less rigidity?

They were stretched out on the couch. The TV was on, but she wasn't watching. Laurel snuggled closer to Luke. They kissed. He tasted of hot chocolate.

"I don't want to go," she confessed.

"You and me both," he murmured and pulled her on top of him. His hands wandered under her skirt, caressed her butt.

He kissed her deeply, urgently. "You've got the greatest ass," he breathed.

He liked her ass, huh? She ground her hips into his crotch and smiled down on at him. "Feel good?"

"It'd feel better if you were naked." He gave her a wicked smiled.

"You're a bad, bad boy," she cooed. Laurel eased herself off his chest, sat up and slowly undid her shirt.

Luke's eyes lit up. "And you're a bad, bad girl." He flipped her over, worked his jeans off and flung them aside. He lay atop her, moving, pushing, grinding his crotch into her as his hands ran up and down her body. "Oh, Laurel, you feel so good."

A streak of longing shot through her, like electricity, straight to her loins. She arched into him, pressing herself against his massive hard on. Enough waiting, enough of being the good girl. "I want it," Laurel panted, grabbed him close. "Don't stop this time."

Her kiss was deep, passionate, demanding.

Luke raised up and pushed down his underwear.

She tore off her panties, the only thing left between them, and grabbed him, pulling him back on top of her. Her tongue sought out his.

He broke from her kiss. "You sure?" he panted.

She was never so sure of anything in her life. She nodded. "Oh, yes."

Marcus Meddevia eased into the coffee shop's booth and set his motorcycle helmet down beside him. He hoped he'd have a chance to enjoy dinner for once, before dispatch called him to investigate an accident or untangle some traffic tie up. Vegas, what a town.

Wendy, his regular waitress, set a cup of coffee down in front of him. "OK if I don't serve you tonight, Marcus?" she said.

"Huh? Isn't this your section?"

"We've got a new girl. Never been a waitress before, so they assigned her to me." She crossed her eyes.

She was that bad, huh? Well, everyone had to start somewhere. "Sure, send her over. I'm ready to order."

A pretty blonde with her hair in a ponytail and a starched new apron approached. She handed him a laminated menu.

"What's this?" Like he didn't know it by heart.

She smiled. "I'm Suzie. I'll be your server."

She had eyes the color of cornflowers. He could get used to cornflower blue eyes. He sat up a little straighter. "Wendy. Suzie. Do you have to have a name that ends in IE or Y to work here?"

She giggled. "We serve breakfast 24-hours if you don't want dinner, officer." She had a sexy way saying "officer", real sexy.

"If you're going to be my server, you'd better call me by my name. Marcus."

"Howdy, Marcus," she said and grinned.

"Is that a Texas accent I detect?"

"Born and raised."

She was cute, about twenty, which made her two years younger than him, and he liked how she filled out the upper portion of her uniform. Yessiree, they sure knew how to grow them big in Texas. "So, what shift did they give you?"

"Late night, I come on duty at eleven p.m."

Good, same as him. This could prove interesting. "I'll have the steak, Suzie. A Texas girl like you knows how to grill up a steak, right? Medium rare?"

"Sure thing, Marcus. I'll make sure the chef knows I've got a hungry officer out here." She gave him a saucy smile.

He eased back in his seat and sipped his coffee as she sashayed away. As nice as her blouse was stretched out where it counted, her back view wasn't bad, either.

Luke fluffed his pillow and leaned back onto it, getting comfortable. The night was quiet, perfect for some introspection. He calmed his mind, shutting out all thoughts from the day. Nothingness. He needed to experience nothingness.

If only Laurel understood this side of him better. She called it his "woo-woo state", making fun of it. But being able to tap into his mind's eye was easy for him. It always had been.

It felt good to have that sense of peace, of clarity. Heck, it even gave him a sense of purpose.

Part of that purpose was Laurel. Ah, Laurel. There was this urge to watch out for her, to protect her.

But that was silly.

Why would Laurel need protection?

CHAPTER TWO

Grams looked up from watching TV when Laurel returned home. "That school in Denver returned your portfolio."

The package was leaning against the banister. She eyed it. Less rigidity?

"There're cookies in the kitchen, fresh from the oven."

"I can smell them, thanks." Leave it to Grams to see she was always fed. "Luke's coming over. He'll probably want some."

She took the package to the kitchen. Since the day that Jeremy had barged in on her talk with Mr. Peterson, all smiles about his big announcement, three other art students had announced that they'd gained admission to schools. They were all state colleges where they could major in art, not private arts schools like she wanted, but still, it was better than being stuck in the lurch like she was.

Laurel pulled the heavy duty tape off the package and opened it up.

Her Monument Valley piece was on top. It had realistic colors, strong vertical lines. She set it across the room and backed up. Hmmm. Maybe they were a bit *too* strong. And the overall essence of the painting, oh, no. Her face fell.

It was practically all one color – the monuments, the desert floor, even the shadows being cast. How could she not have seen that before? How come Mr. Peterson hadn't pointed it out to her?

Wait. He had. That day in class, when Jeremy and his buddies had been cracking jokes the whole period, the art teacher had come by her desk, peered over her shoulder and pointed.

"Maybe you could bring in a stronger color to differentiate things, huh? Give it some contrast. What do you think?"

She'd thought it was a ridiculous suggestion, not that she'd said that to him. She knew what she was doing, and he was out to mess up her beautiful painting. So, she'd ignored him and his senseless suggestion.

What a mistake.

Laurel pulled out the cat at the window piece. Crap. She'd played it safe. The fur on the cat looked like cotton candy. She winced. The art school's admission committee had probably looked at this painting and burst out laughing.

There was a rap on the screen door frame. Luke was watching her. "Somebody's doing some soul searching."

She gestured at the stupid paintings, wanting to burn them. "Now I see why they rejected me," she said, running a hand over her face. "I missed my chance, Luke. I blew it."

Luke stepped over and pulled her into his arms. "There are other schools."

"I'm so stupid."

"Not as stupid as me. I mean, vitamin gum? What was I thinking?"

A smile worked at the corner of her lips. It *had* been a pretty bad attempt. She pulled back to gaze into his eyes. "I can always count on you to cheer me up."

Luke ran the back of his hand gently down one side of her face. "I'm the man in this equation."

OK, so they'd talked about spending their lives together once they were each established in a career, but he was "the man"? Had he honestly said something as domineering as that? "Yes," Laurel said, "but may I remind you that I'm a grown woman?"

"And may I remind you that you're eighteen?"

She shrugged him off, taking back a step back. "I'm a grown woman, and I can take care of myself."

Luke smiled and pulled her back to him. "But you don't need to, not with me here," he said. 'You can believe that."

She gave up. There was no sense arguing about it. Besides, his arms felt so comforting. She cast an eye at the two paintings. Never again would she create such ugly, crass, one dimensional works. She was better than that, and she knew it, damn it.

Marcus pulled up to the apartment complex. Hmmm, it was a decent part of town. He ducked, trying to read the building numbers as he trolled around it in his Mazda sports car. Damn carports, they always blocked the view of the numbers, the scourge of every patrol officer. Good thing he was a Nevada Highway Patrolman and didn't have to deal with that shit on a nightly basis. He grimaced. No, he only got to pull body parts out of mangled car wrecks.

There it was: 3712. Suzie Caminski had said she lived in unit C.

He parked and sauntered up to her door, straightened his shirt and rang the bell.

"Just a sec," she called through the door.

Two minutes ticked by. He checked his watch. Maybe this was her way of telling a guy that she was independent, in no hurry to have a man.

The door opened. Suzie smiled, a big-as-Texas smile.

Marcus caught his breath. She'd filled out her uniform well, but she filled out the tight little top she wore even better. A sight like this was well worth the wait.

She sent him a saucy little grin. "Hey, ya."

He smiled back. "Let's get going."

They talked about mundane things, first date things, on their way to the movie theater. He revved the engine a little at a stop light, and she giggled. She liked that? He chirped the tires, and she laughed out loud, throwing back her head in delight. The action thrust out her chest and, Lordie, but that was one thin bra.

He swerved. Shit, he'd almost hit that curb.

By the time the movie was over, they'd kissed. She'd rested her head on his shoulder. He'd forgotten half the plot, what with that full breast pressed against his arm. Talk about a distraction. But then, he'd always been a breast man.

The film ended and they shuffled out with the crowd.

He caught her hand as they walked back out to his car. He opened the door for her and she slid in smooth as silk. Damn, she was sexy.

He got in, started her up and zoomed out of the parking lot.

Suzie sat canted in the seat so that she faced him. Her fingers traveled up his arm spider style as he drove her home. "Why don't you come in for a nightcap, Marcus?"

No way. She had two roommates. "Let's go to my place instead."

"OK."

He smiled as her hand found its way to his thigh. Looked like this might be his lucky night.

Laurel sat on the park grass, sketching the Raiders spring football practice. It was easier to draw things if you were interested in them, not that the Raiders had a chance at the Super Bowl. The sting of not getting into her school of choice had lessened over the past month, but it still didn't sit well with her.

This damn charcoal, it got everywhere. She wasn't a fan of the messy medium, but Mr. Peterson's assignment had been specific. So, here she was, trying to capture a defensive back outwitting a running back on an outside stretch play.

Luke stirred beside her. "Shit!" he jumped up. "Did you see that?"

What was he talking about?

He pointed skyward. "Those two planes, they almost hit each other."

Laurel shaded her eyes. High up, two commercial planes were streaking away from one another. "They almost collided? Are you sure?"

"Well, from here it sure looked close." He sat back down and jutted his chin at her sketch pad. "What's that for?"

"It's Mr. Peterson's latest assignment." It was due Monday, and she'd put a lot of work into it.

"Not bad. Maybe you should add it to your new portfolio, you know, the one you're about to send off."

"Well, I –" Wait. He knew about that? How? She set it aside. "I never told you I was ready to apply to another school."

Sitting beside her, Luke chuckled.

Those eyes, the way they crinkled when he laughed, she loved that about him, that, and so many other things, too.

"I know you, Laurel," he said. "I know the way you think, the way you react. I know you from your crooked nose to your gangly knocked knees." He pulled her down on the grass so they were lying side by side.

He kissed her, a long, slow kiss.

Whoa. Laurel caught her breath.

His kiss wasn't like anything her former boyfriends had ever bestowed on her, not even close. And this was not the way he usually kissed her. This was a new Luke, slow, sensuous. And serious. Something was up.

"When we're married, Laurel, I will kiss your lips every night and plenty of other places, too."

Laurel felt her heart flutter. "When we're married," she said. She liked the sound of that.

"And we'll start a family."

Wait, she wasn't even sure she *wanted* a family, and here he was, making plans like it was a given.

"But first, you'll have to have a real job, a little job, of course," he said, pulling back with a thoughtful looking expression.

What?

"Oh sure," he continued, "you'll sell a painting now and then, but that's not an income we can really rely on."

What?

"We both know that, right?"

He made it sound like her art was a mere hobby.

"And then, when I'm established and my inventions are patented, which costs a lot of money that I don't have, but when they *are* patented and the checks are rolling in, then you can quit your little job and paint to your heart's content."

So, he had it all figured out, did he? Like her intention to be an artist was some flighty little pipe dream.

She pushed him off and stood up with a huff. "Sometimes you're such a jerk, Luke," she said as she packed up her things. She stormed off.

Laurel stepped outside. Luke was waiting on Grams' porch. "You left so fast, I didn't have a chance to share my news."

"Well, you were planning our lives without consulting me, so what was I supposed to do?" The *nerve* of Luke to belittle her art career that way. "Well, what have you got to say for yourself?"

He shrugged. "I was wrong."

And?

He looked up at her with those puppy dog eyes of his.

Nope, he wasn't getting off that easy. "When people apologize, they normally say more than three words."

"Look, I was speaking out of turn. Of *course* you'll have a career in art. Of *course* I'll support you in that. I just wanted you to understand that it's my duty to take care of you."

"Your duty?"

"That's how I've seen it since the day I transferred out here to California, since the day I met you at school." He reached out and took her hands, pulling her onto the bench beside him. "Don't ask me how, because I could never explain it, but I knew, I mean, deep inside and without any hesitation, I *knew* that we were meant to be together, that I would be your man, that I'd provide for you and look out for you."

He made it sound like he was her Prince Charming, reincarnated for this lifetime. That was silly. What was he really saying? That it was his "duty" to take care of her? He thought she was unable to provide for herself? Were they back to that again? Where had that notion even come from?

But still, he'd never said anything that sounded so sincere to her before. "Luke, listen, I can provide for myself. I'll have my own career. If we get married, then fine, we'll each have our own professions to contribute to our household equally. But don't feel you have to support me. I'll be supporting myself."

"You modern women," he muttered. "Do you forgive me, Laurel?"

She drew him into her arms and kissed him. "I could never stay mad at you."

That night, Laurel tossed and turned.

Making up with Luke had led to deeper kissing, tongue kissing, "never want to stop" kissing. His hand had slipped up her skirt, teased the silk of her panties until her wetness had excited them both to distraction. She'd wanted more, much more.

But they'd stopped. The bushes out front hid them from the street, yes, but Grams was inside. They couldn't risk it.

She'd still been breathing heavy when Luke uttered a pinched goodbye and hurried off the porch. It had taken every inch of control to keep from running after him, throwing herself at him. Damn, that guy was hot.

And what was that talk about knowing they were meant to be together the instant he first saw her? What guy said things like that? What guy even *thought* of things like that?

She glanced at her alarm clock. "Sleep," she ordered her brain and settled in, letting the night take over.

She opened one eye.

Someone was tapping at her bedroom window.

That didn't make sense. She was on the second story. There was no balcony, no nearby tree, just a sheer drop to the ground.

There it was again.

Laurel tiptoed over and pushed the curtain aside. It was Luke, floating there. What? She threw up the sash. "What are you doing here?"

"I meant what I said. You know that we're connected. You felt it too, that day we met."

She thought back, remembered seeing him come into the classroom, looking out of place. In California, everyone dressed in casual clothes. He'd worn khakis with a belt and a button down shirt. Some kids had giggled at his appearance. Not her. She'd stared, trying to get her bearings. She *knew* him from somewhere, deep inside she could feel it. Their eyes had met and locked, and she'd felt the room suddenly start spinning. Her girlfriend had grabbed her arm, given her a "You OK?" kind of look. She'd nodded, glad the spell had been broken, but when she'd looked back at Luke, a whisper of the feeling had remained. But how could she know someone who'd lived in New York City all his life? "Yes. I felt it."

"We're connected, you and I. We go way back, well before this."

Was he taking about other lifetimes? That was just a theory.

He brushed back her hair. "Now we're here again, here to support one another."

There was that term again. Support. "I told you, I'm perfectly capable of supporting my –"

He pressed a finger to her lips. "There are more ways to support someone than just money." He leaned in and kissed her.

Those lips, that tongue. She wanted him, but – "No, we can't," she said, pulling back. "Grams' in the next room, we can't. I can't."

"I'm not here to seduce you," he said, giving her that easy smile. "I just wanted to help you go back to that moment and understand." He looked into her eyes. "You relived it, the moment when you first saw me."

And felt as though she knew him inside and out? "Yes."

"Then that's enough for now. Sweet dreams, Laurel." He disappeared.

Marcus stepped up to the computer at the station and signed off, officially off duty once more. He had two days off and he knew just how to fill them.

His little red Mazda raced over to Suzie's apartment. It was their fourth date. He hoped she had hiking boots.

He rang her doorbell and the door opened almost immediately.

"I'm just finishing packing," Suzie said and gave him a quick peck on the cheek. Their make out session after going to the movies and subsequent dates had garnered him plenty of tongue-to-tongue time, but not much else. Suzie knew how to make a man wait.

He followed her in. "What can I carry for you?"

She pointed. "That bag, that one, that one and, oh, can you carry this one, too?"

She must think his Mazda could expand on command. "It's a sports car, not a tourist van, Suzie. My own tent and camping gear take up almost the whole area behind the seats."

She blinked with those blue eyes, looking hurt. "I just want to look pretty for you. Besides, I packed something kind of, well, naughty."

No way could he argue with that. Maybe this would be his lucky day.

An hour later, they were on their way to Mount Charleston, 45 minutes outside of Las Vegas but a world away. He'd spent his summers here as a teen, helping to build cabins and homes, wishing he could live there. Sure, like he could afford a place up there. He'd be lucky to scrape together enough money to pay for the land, let alone the funds to build a structure.

As they climbed, the desert transformed into a pine forest thick with trees.

"I'm glad you like camping," he said.

"Looking forward to trying it. It sounds like it'd be fun."

Hold on. "Trying" it? He could swear she'd said it was one of her favorite things to do. Had she stretched the truth, maybe?

He glanced over at her. His car hit a bump in the road, and her breasts jiggled up a storm. Her nipples pressed into the fabric. Holy, shit, no bra this time. A streak of urgency surged through his loins.

Who cared if she'd stretched the truth?

Laurel turned a corner at school and bumped straight into Luke. "Oh!"

He smiled at her. "I'll walk you to class."

"OK," she looked over at him. She wanted to know about her dream. It had seemed so real, like he was actually in her bedroom. Did the fact that he'd taken her virginity cause them to be closer somehow? Wait, she didn't even know if this was real or if it had just been a dream. "Luke, something happened last night after you left."

His eyes searched hers, and he gave her a knowing look. "You mean, late at night?"

So, he knew. "Yes."

"I wasn't sure you'd remember." He brightened. "But I'm glad you did."

"Was it, I mean, was it *real?*"

He pulled her over to an alcove where they could talk. He drew her close. "It was real, Laurel, a hint of what we've experienced before."

He was talking about past lives again, something he'd brought up before. She shifted, suddenly uncomfortable. "I don't know if I can believe in that woo-woo stuff."

"Your inner self does, even if you can't admit it," Luke said. "That's why you reacted the way you did when you saw me for the first time. That's why you allowed me to come and talk to you last night."

That's right, she'd thrown up the window sash and let him in, thinking he was about to fall to the ground. There hadn't been any choice to do otherwise. Laurel shook her head. What was she thinking? He hadn't actually been there, it had been all been a dream.

Luke smiled. "It's hard to wrap your mind around it, I understand, but inside you know it's true. Not all communication is face to face, Laurel."

"Well then, what if I wanted to reach out to you?"

He sent her a saucy look. "You can come to my bedroom anytime."

How like a guy to say something like that. "You know what I mean. What if –?"

"Listen to me." He gripped her hands. "We're connected. We were connected no matter how close or far apart we are. We're still connected. Just accept it."

Just accept it. OK, she'd try, but it still seemed a little far out there.

Marcus shifted the pack on his back as they hiked. The smell of pines trees as heavy here, the chatter of chipmunks punctuating the air now and then.

There was movement in the meadow below. "Suzie, stop," he said and pointed. "Look over there," he whispered.

"Where?" she peered in the direction he'd indicated.

"Look just beyond where that patch of grass is." He set the pack down and rummaged inside, pawing blindly. Ah, there they were. He pulled out the binoculars. "Try these."

She peered through the lenses and gasped. "Two deer!" Her breasts pressed against her top as she held the binoculars to her eyes. "They're spectacular!"

"Not as spectacular as you." He couldn't tear his eyes away from those incredible mounds.

"Really?" She set the binoculars aside and pulled him to her.

Now, this was more like it. He tasted those lips with her cherry lip balm, and let his tongue open them so it could play just inside her mouth.

Suzie pulled back and, taking his hand, led him to a shady spot under a tree. "This looks good," she murmured. "Sit down."

Anything you say.

She sat astride him, and pushed him back gently until he was lying down. Her blue eyes blinked innocently. "I just love the freedom of the outdoors, don't you, Marcus?" She yanked off her top in one quick movement, and those bombs jiggled free.

Holy shit, they were spectacular. He reached out, just had to grab them. Copping a feel on previous dates had been a tease. Finally, here they were, totally exposed. His loins reacted. Damn, he couldn't get enough of them.

She leaned into his touch and smiled down at him. "Almost forgot." She pulled something out of her back jeans pocket and held it up with a single raised eyebrow.

It was a condom.

Only one? The way he was feeling, they'd need about a dozen.

CHAPTER THREE

Laurel tossed in her bed. What had Luke meant? He was her protector, he'd said.

Protector from what? Protector for crossing the street? Protector from car accidents? Protector from weird old men who lurked in alleyways and drank cheap whisky still in paper bags?

Each time they'd talked about their futures, about the day they'd be a couple, it had always come up.

She pulled the sheets closer. It had felt so good to be on the same page, and they'd cuddled closer.

But then he'd ruined it. "When we get married, I'll provide for you I'll look after you," he'd said. "That's my *real* job."

News flash, Luke, she didn't need a man, any man, "looking after" her, "taking care of" her, "watching over" her, however he wanted to phrase it. She was an independent woman, able to take care of herself.

He'd just have to accept that, or this relationship would never go anywhere.

Theresa went to call Laurel's number, but disconnected before it went through. Why bother her little sister with this shit?

There was Grams, but how could she help? No, all a seventy-five-year-old woman could do was send her money. She didn't want money. She wanted her husband to stop hanging out with "those people." It was the industry that was the problem. Entertainment could suck the life out of a clean-living girl like her.

All those years growing up, spent dancing, dancing, dancing. She'd perfected her craft, taken extra ballet lessons in high school so she'd have a strong base for any type of dance specialty. She'd delved into yoga and stretch classes, had been delighted the first time she'd been able to lie down and pull her foot all the way up past her ear, her leg straight as an arrow.

All that hard work had really paid off. She was a professional dancer, had traveled the world, been in shows with top-billing singers and actors. Now, she was in New York with Arielle, finishing up on Broadway. And where was her husband, Arielle's father? Not here, not when she needed him to help her pack up for the move to Las Vegas.

No, he was still in L.A., sounding high as a kite when she'd called to ask why he'd missed his flight.

"What?" he'd said. "I was supposed to be there already? Ha, guess I got caught up in something else."

"Where are you?"

There had been a pause. "Um, I really don't know. Somebody's house, I guess. Amazing place, you should see it, right on the ocean. He has all this shit, right out on the coffee table. Anytime you start to come down, you just pick up a straw and go for it. Crazy, huh?"

"Damn you, Dirk," Theresa had said and hung up.

Marcus felt something pressing on his back and woke up. Birds chirped in the dawn light. The scent of pine was strong. That's right, he was camping on Mount Charleston. He turned over. Oh, Lordie. Suzie was lying on her side facing him. Just look at those incredible tits, totally exposed and begging to be sucked. He eased his face down, just wanting a taste.

Her nipple responded immediately to his tongue.

Marcus maneuvered his hands to cup both of her breasts and squeezed them together. His tongue found her nipples, first one and then the other.

Suzie woke up and rolled so she was face up and arched her back, presenting those tits in all their glory. "Hmmm," she moaned. Her hand slipped down between his legs.

Marcus moaned. Man, this girl was hot. Their first dates had been a tease, she'd barely let him brush his hand against his shirt. But up here on the mountain, she wasn't teasing him anymore. Once they'd stopped hiking to view the deer, it had been like a dam breaking loose.

He could still visualize the moment she'd torn off her top and flung it aside, straddling him while his hands ran all over her incredible body. Then she'd worked off his jeans and ducked between his opened knees. Lordie, what a turn on!

They'd done it four times, all out in the open, all in broad daylight. He couldn't get enough of this girl.

She maneuvered him on top of her and ground her hips beneath him.

They needed another condom, like *now*. Shit, where were they? "I can't stop," he panted.

"Too late," Suzie whispered and slipped him inside of her.

There was a letter on the table in the foyer. Laurel set her books down and reached for it. Hold on. Did the return address say what she thought it said? She picked up the letter. There it was: The Marion School of Art in Philly. Only a true art school would get away with putting "Philly" in their name.

This was it, the answer to her application, had to be.

She tore it open. Please, please.

"Thank you for your application … noted certain qualities in your portfolio … pleased to extent enrollment to you -"

She couldn't read any more. They wanted her, and that was all that mattered.

"Grams! Grams! I've been accepted!" Her voice was a squeal, she couldn't help it. This was all too exciting.

Grams peeked around the corner from the den. "Really? That's wonderful, sweetie."

Laurel ran up and threw her arms around her grandmother. "The Marion School of Art in Philly! They accepted me! I'm going to Pennsylvania, Grams!"

Laurel tucked the charcoal assignment into her art folder. Mr. Peterson had said it was her best effort yet. Maybe she should continue developing her sketching skills, he'd said.

Not a chance. She wanted to paint. Paint in sultry, beckoning colors, creating paintings that called to people, that hit a nerve with their inner selves.

She left the high school and drove to the local IHop like Luke's note had directed. Something was going on, but he was being pretty secretive. As soon as she stepped inside, she scanned the room.

"Laurel, over here," Luke called.

He was alone. She headed over to his table. "What's up?"

He held the chair for her. "We're celebrating. Remember my vitamin gum?"

The stuff that had made her gag? "You tweaked it?"

"I sold it."

Wait. He'd only just invented it a few months ago, but he'd already sold it? "I don't understand."

"I was contacted by Switzer's Gum, out of the blue, and they bought my idea." He pulled out a piece of paper, snapped it open and held it out.

It was a check.

Holy cow, it was for $50,000. She threw her hand to her chest. Luke was rich. "So, you got it to taste good?"

"Nope. It still tastes like crap. They just wanted the idea." He shrugged. "I guess they'll have their laboratory guys figure out how to get the vitamin part in there without making it taste so bad." He slid the check back in his pocket. "Anyway, let's celebrate."

Amazing. He'd been paid for an idea, not the product, just the idea. "Sure. I'm starved."

A waiter brought out two plates. Luke must have ordered before she got there.

Laurel dug in. She was so proud of Luke. The guy had only gotten a gazillion school offers. He had his pick of universities. The check he'd just shown her would likely help pay for his education. "Have you decided which college to accept?"

He stiffened. "Actually, um, I have."

She didn't like the way he said that. "And?"

"You know, Laurel, I'd love to go to Philly with you, but I've had enough of East Coast weather. I've decided that I'm going for an engineering degree, out here in California."

Her food was suddenly hard to swallow. He wasn't joining her in Philly? Suddenly, it was like time standing still. "But, but ... I thought we were a team. I thought we were meant to be together. 'Soul mates', that's what you said."

"Your art school is only for two years."

"So go to a university near me for two years and transfer –"

"Engineering students can't just pick up and change schools like that," he said, interrupting her. "I'll be involved in research as an intern. And the school I'm leaning toward is involved with NASA experiments. Do you know the clout that can bring?"

Suddenly clout mattered to Luke? He'd never talked about such things before.

He'd be here, in sunny California, and she'd be all the way across the country. They'd be thousands of miles apart.

Tears threatened. She fought them back. "But I'll miss you. The funny way you look over at me in class when someone says something stupid, the way you touch my hand when I'm going through a tough time – who is going to bring that to my world if we're so far apart?"

Luke looked deep into her eyes. "Souls can cross time and space, Laurel."

Oh, come on. "This shit again? Do you know how stupid that sounds? One day, someone's going to overhear you and they'll throw you in the looney bin."

He gestured. "Look, did I need to be physically beside you when I visited you that night?"

Last night? That's right, she'd dreamed of him last night. "Well, no, but –"

"Shhh. I've thought about this a lot. If I'd said anything before you were all set to go to Marion, then I know you would have switched to a SoCal university and you'd be miserable there. You need that experience of being around your own kind, people who are driven to paint, to create art for galleries, for private collections, be around others like you and feeding off that essence, that collective energy."

There he went again, talking about things people couldn't see, things that most would consider crazy stuff. Still, the experience of having him come to her bedroom window had seemed utterly real.

Luke got her attention. "Do you understand what I'm saying?"

"Yes, I guess." She pushed her plate away. Suddenly, she didn't feel so hungry.

Marcus elbowed his way to the computer and signed out.

"Hey, what's the rush?" protested another officer, who'd been about to sign out, too.

"Hot date," Marcus said with a grin. Suzie was coming to his place to make him dinner. Then they'd watch the game. She wasn't just cute and a knock out in bed, she'd said she liked football. No, more like, she "loved" football. It wasn't often he met a girl who was as big a fanatic for the sport as him.

He raced to her apartment and spotted her carrying out a pan covered in aluminum foil. It must be their dinner. He swung into the parking space beside her mini pickup truck, another thing he liked about her, and jumped out.

"Let me take that for you," he said. "I'll put it in my car." He drew in his breath. Whatever it was, it sure smelled good. He wedged it carefully in the back of his car, turned to see if she had anything else to carry and caught her pouting. "What? What is it?"

Suzie crossed her arms. "You didn't kiss me," she said.

She wanted a kiss? He'd give her a kiss. Marcus scooped her up in his arms like she was a damsel in distress. All those hours at the gym he'd spent each week made her light as a feather. He planted a kiss on her that lingered long and hard. He pulled back. "How's that for starters?"

"OK, OK." Suzie smiled. "Put me down, you scoundrel."

"I'll show you what a scoundrel's really like, later on tonight."

She jumped out of his arms and straightened her dress, shooting him a naughty look. "Maybe you will, maybe you won't." She swung her hips just so.

Damn, she sure knew how to send an open invitation, but two could play this game. "Course, it all depends on how good you are in the kitchen. A man can't survive on half-assed cooking."

Her eyes flashed. "I'll have you know I'm the best cook in my entire family, Marcus Meddevia. You'll take one bite, and you'll swear you've died and gone to Heaven."

An hour later, he pushed away from the dinette in his little house. Damn, but she'd been right. Her pot roast had been so good he'd practically purred like a kitten as he ate. "I confess, he said, wiping his mouth on a napkin. "I *did* die and go to Heaven."

She preened and stood up to take his plate.

"No, you cooked, let me clean."

She batted away his hand. "Won't take but a minute. Now, shoo. Go turn on the TV."

The Dallas game, he'd forgotten all about it. He hunkered deep down in his favorite chair and hit the remote. The Cowboys had just scored. A Texas girl like Suzie would be sorry she missed it. "Hey, sweetie," he called, "your team just made six points."

"How'd they do that?" she called from the kitchen.

Such a kidder. Still, it was odd she didn't hurry in to catch the replay.

Suzie joined him ten minutes later, perching on the arm rest of his big chair. "So, what inning is it?" she asked, getting comfortable.

There she went, clowning around again. Innings were in baseball. He went to laugh at her joke, but her face said she was perfectly serious.

He'd pulled over plenty of speeders. Clocked them at ninety five in a seventy five zone. "Honest officer, I could have sworn I was only going seventy." Sure they were. He could always read the ones who were out to con him.

But right now, Suzie wasn't out to con him. She honestly thought football was played in innings.

"Why, you little –" He tickled her, and she squealed, squirming into him until she was pressed into his side. Nice. Who cared if she'd fibbed about liking to camp or about being a football fan? She'd only done it to impress him.

Luke was at a back table when she got there. The smell of coffee wafted around her as she made her way to him.

"Wow, 'our' table was free? I don't believe it," she said and kissed him hello.

"Actually, I had to chase two girls off."

He was joking. OK, she'd joke, too. "I didn't know you were that attached to it."

He looked sheepish. "Well, it *is* where we started our first official date."

That's right, she hadn't wanted him to know where Gram's house was, in case he turned out to be weird, so she'd met him here instead. It seemed so long ago. "Did you want to catch a movie?" It would be their last for a long time. Graduation was a week away, and she'd be on the road to Philadelphia two days after that.

"I wanted to do something special." He caught the barista's eye and the overhead music suddenly cut off.

The sudden silence was overwhelming.

She looked around. People were staring at them. What was going on? "Luke, did *you* have them turn off-?"

He was on his knee before her. He held out a ring.

Oh, my Lord.

"Laurel, will you marry me?"

She threw her hands to her cheeks and tried not to cry. But she couldn't help it. "Yes!"

His arms felt so strong, so right, as he grabbed her, and they kissed.

All the other coffee house patrons clapped and hooted.

CHAPTER FOUR

Laurel grabbed her art case – it looked more like a stupid tackle box, but that's what her prep letter had told to purchase – and hustled up the stairs. By level two, her legs were burning. Apparently, the Marion School of Art in Philly expected students to be physically fit, lugging all their art equipment up three flights of stairs.

She gained the third landing and huffed up to class room No. 3. A sign proclaiming "Welcome to your future!" was tacked to the door. Here went nothing. She entered and about dozen sets of eyes latched onto her. "Hey," she murmured, and quickly found a seat.

"Now that we're all here," the instructor said, glaring at her, "we can begin."

Great, she was the last one, even though she'd allotted an extra ten minutes to get here. Shit. What a way to make an impression.

Laurel set down her things as quietly as possible.

"Let me introduce myself. I am Peter Sabastian, but you can call me Peter Sabastian." He smiled at his little joke. "I hope you'll find I'm a better artist than comedian."

She'd seen his bio. His paintings were in corporate collections and also hung in galleries from London to Naples. The Marion School hired only the best.

"Seriously, though," he continued, "I'm known by both names, spoken as one. Please remember that."

There was movement to her left. Laurel glanced over.

"Hiya," breathed the girl sitting beside her, a wisp of a thing with long hair in varied colors. She leaned closer, moving like a sloth. "I'm April. So, you got any dope?"

The girl was serious. Laurel shook her head and, just be sure April got the message, shrugged as though she'd totally spaced bringing any drugs with her that day.

"Too bad," April sighed and retreated, only to lean slowly toward the student on her other side. "Hiya," she murmured. "I'm April. April, um ... Vanderhousen. Yeah, Vanderhousen."

Laurel returned her attention to Peter Sebastian and tried to keep a straight face. Hopefully, April was the only stoner in the room.

The instructor continued. "You're here because all your life, you've taken pencil to hand. It's ingrained in you. You've all demonstrated that to us with your portfolio. Now, we want to take things up a notch, a lot of notches. You've got raw talent. We're going to show you how to really bring it forward."

The speech droned on. Laurel doodled on the margins of her supply list.

If Luke were here, he'd probably be cracking jokes about April and her sloth-like movements, and telling her that he was "Luke Sullivan, but you can call me Luke Sullivan" or some such nonsense. She smiled. He was such a clown sometimes, but such a brain-iac when it came to science and electronics. She recalled how he'd make her laugh with the silliest things, when they went out for smoothies or that day they'd gone to the beach and seen the whales – what a day *that* had been. They'd scrambled up to the cliffs to watch the fins break the water, mesmerized each time they'd broken the surface.

His ring glistened on her finger. OK, so the stone wasn't huge, but it was intent behind it that mattered.

He should be out here with her, going to school in Pennsylvania so they could be together, live together. They always had so much fun in one another's company. And they thought alike on so many topics. Sometimes, it was like she could finish his sentences.

If only he'd quit with this "Let me take care of you" talk. Like she couldn't take care of herself, like she would be lost without –

"*Miss Laurel Rebecca Trenton?*" the voice boomed.

Her head snapped up. Shit. Everyone was staring at her.

Peter Sabastian cocked an eyebrow. "If you have something more pressing to do, perhaps you could tell us what it is."

Her face heated up. "I'm sorry, forgive me, Mr. Sebastian."

His expression turned even colder. "It's Peter Sabastian."

Two names, said as one, she'd forgotten. "Sorry." Maybe the chair would swallow her up and she could just disappear.

"It's cool," April breathed.

By the second week of school, Laurel was feeling more settled. She had her little apartment set up. She had a grasp of what was expected of her at school.

She had stronger thighs and ham strings and actually relished taking the three flights to the Marion School. Who would have thought that art school would increase her cardiovascular capacity?

Everyone was turning in their weekend assignment – capturing a bird in flight. She got in line, caught a glimpse of the other's works. Wow, some of them were pretty spectacular. Jeez, some of these students didn't even *need* to be in art school. Peter Sabastian must have thought so, too. He smiled and nodded as he accepted them.

She set her assignment on the desk. She'd gone to the natural history museum and sat before the aviary section, sketching a seagull that the gallery had suspended midair as though winging above a trawler, eyeing his next meal. She'd spent hours in front of the stupid thing, wadding up one attempt after another until she'd finally gotten a pretty good rendition of it. It had only taken her five hours.

Now, Peter Sabastian cast a critical eye over the result. His lips tightened. "Hmmm."

That didn't sound good. She took a seat, aware of every move she made. Maybe turning in a "pretty good rendition" wasn't good enough.

Peter Sabastian took the front of the room. "As you probably learned from this assignment, movement can be hard to translate to a still picture," he said. "Let's look at different ways you could have approached it."

The lecture continued for another hour, then they were told to get out their sketch pads.

April woke up long enough to follow suit and seemed transfixed by the point of her pencil. "Wow," she breathed, staring at it.

Laurel winced. The girl was constantly high as a kite and yet April's weekend assignment had been nothing less than stellar. The instructor had even held it up and called it "spectacular."

Now, Peter Sabastian handed each of them a tear sheet for their next assignment. Laurel took hers and a wave of relief washed over her. It was a magazine ad for Asics running shoes, a side view of a female marathoner caught mid stride. She could do the human body.

"You'll notice all your references were shot with a high-speed camera, not a blurred image in any one of them," Peter Sabastian said. "You'll replicate the picture in color. But here's the trick – I want you to render that image showing movement. However you decide to do it, is up to you. That's this morning's assignment. It's due at the end of class."

What, the end of class? And he wanted it in color, to boot? She glanced at the clock. There was less than an hour to do this, thanks to Peter Sabastian's long, rambling speech, and now he stepped out, probably to get a cup of coffee and relax while they all sweated out this assignment. Shoot, this wasn't going to be easy. Laurel got to work.

Peter Sabastian returned on the stroke of the hour. "Time's up," he called. "Sign your renderings and leave them on my desk."

Everyone crowded to the front of the room to hand in their assignment.

Laurel packed up her supplies for the move to her next class. She made her way to the instructor's desk, against the flow of others, and dropped her artwork on his desk. She turned to hurry away.

"Laurel," he said, gesturing for her to come back.

"Yes?" She approached his desk again.

"Tell me why you did it this way." He pointed to the legs, the lack of strong lines, except for the push-off leg in back and the knee-high leg in front. In between, she'd slurred flesh toned pastels across the paper, suggesting legs, suggesting movement.

"You want to know 'why'?" Because that was how she'd seen it in her head. That was why. "I thought it made sense."

He studied it some more. "Really?"

She edged the picture around so that he was looking at it from a better perspective. "When I think of a runner, I think of the high they feel, the freedom, the inner power. I wasn't going for the actual sight of someone on the outside, but the inner feeling that the runner has."

"I take it you run?"

Not lately, though she wished she had time to. "I used to, in high school."

Peter Sabastian studied her work a little longer. He nodded. It was a nod of approval.

Thank God. She turned away. She'd glimpsed a smile on his lips, she knew she had. Maybe she belonged here after all. Maybe she would start running again, too.

Luke signed his name on the grant application form and handed it back to the secretary, a matronly woman with garish orange hair and too much makeup. Why older women felt the need to do that, he'd never understand. "How long before I know if I get the grant?"

"You just made the deadline, so it'll only be a month before the decision is made."

A month? He couldn't wait that long. "And then the funds will be available immediately?"

She sighed and sent him a look like he was a greedy bastard.

She didn't understand the urgency.

"Yes, immediately." She shuffled some papers and turned away.

"It's just that, I've got this invention. It's going to save lives." For some reason, he'd felt the need to blurt that out.

The receptionist hesitated. "Is yours a medical invention?"

"No. It's one to keep planes from colliding in midair."

She raised one eyebrow as though amused. "That happens often, does it?"

She was mocking him. But if she only knew. He'd done his research, had to dig deep to learn what most of America wasn't told. "More often than the public hears about. Sometimes, it's a 'near miss'– with the pilots making a correction at the last moment. Those don't get reported the same as closer ones. And who knows how many pilots simply don't want such a black mark on their record so they don't report it?"

She paused. "And your invention will prevent these?"

He gave her the layman's explanation of how it worked. "There's a device in planes already," he concluded, "but mine is much more accurate because it cuts out random radio frequencies. It can actually take the controls away from the pilots if they come too close."

"Hold on a sec." Her eyes swept over his application. "Son, you really didn't explain that in your grant application. How about you pull up a seat, and we'll see if we can't beef up your application, give you a better chance at the grant?"

He took back everything he'd thought about her hair color and makeup. She was going to help him have a shot at eight grand.

Laurel watched as Elan – she was such an accomplished painter that she went by a single name – hovered behind the eleven other art students. This was life drawing class and the naked woman on the pedestal before them was getting shaky from holding the pose so long.

Their instructor paused by a big, burly guy whose touch with a paintbrush belied his giant hands. "Nice," Elan murmured, bending close to another student's work to point out something. "This line, you really captured the form."

Laurel pulled back to look at her own drawing. Had she captured the form, too? Or would Elan utter a noncommittal "Hmmm" like she usually did?

Fritz, the top student in the school, got a hand on his shoulder. "Fabulous," Elan told him.

Laurel bumped her chair up closer to her work. Concentrate, concentrate, find the way the core supported the pose. She pulled back and sighed. Damn, she'd tried so hard, really taking her time to "see" the body's shape, its structure, but even *she* could see it wasn't quite working on her paper.

"There's real tension in this pose," Elan said, speaking to the entire class. "Show that in your interpretation."

Interpretation? Wait, she'd stressed realism in the classes before this. Make up your mind, woman. She felt Elan coming closer, gliding in that ethereal way she had. Ethereal - that was something Luke would say.

Elan stepped up behind her shoulder.

Here it comes.

"Hmmm."

Laurel bit her lip. No praise, she should have expected as much.

Elan clapped her hands. "Time for a break, everyone." She stopped Laurel as the students stepped out. "I want a word with you."

They waited until the model had slipped into her robe and left the studio.

Elan paced and passed a hand over her forehead.

Laurel waited. This was bad, she could tell.

The instructor stopped pacing. "Your artwork, I get the feeling that your parents heaped mounds of praise on you for any little scribble you produced."

Before they'd died in that car accident? "Yes, I guess."

"They did you a disservice."

They did?

"You never grew in your art. You were always trying to please mommy and daddy. Time to change that. Art is all about exploring our boundaries. Can you do that?"

"I'll try."

"Do more than try. We'll help you, but you've got to discard your old way of thinking. Tell me, do you meditate?"

She sounded like Luke. Laurel shook her head. "I don't know how to."

"Come to my studio tonight, seven p.m. Here's the address." She handed over a business card. "I'm having a gathering. We'll teach you."

"All right, I'll try to make it."

"That word again. No, don't 'try.' Be there."

All right, already, she'd be there.

"I'm telling you this for your own good. The Marion school only graduates those it feels are, shall we say, up to its high standards. We have a reputation in the world of art to uphold, understand?" Elan said, her eyes piercing.

Holy crap, they were going to kick her out if she didn't start performing up to par? "I understand," Laurel gulped.

Theresa stepped onto the Potenza Hotel's showroom stage and found a spot. There had to be two hundred girls here in Vegas, all vying for ten positions.

The choreographer, Raphael, a guy she'd worked with on a Caribbean cruise ages ago, stepped up and clapped his hands. "Quiet, girls. Now, I'm only going to do this once, so pay attention."

A girl shifted in front of her, blocking her view. OK, she could deal with this. It was an old trick, done out of desperation, no doubt. Everyone needed this job. Theresa shifted out from behind the girl just as the choreographer counted down.

"And one, two, three, four and five, six, seven, eight, spin two, three, four –"

He had to be kidding. This was grade school stuff. Las Vegas shows were *way* more sophisticated than this.

He finished. "OK, ready? Cue the music. Here's the start and one, two, three–"

Theresa let her body go with the music, a snappy little upbeat tempo.

"And one, two, three, four and five, six, seven, eight, spin two, three, four –" Raphael caught her eye and gave a nearly imperceptible nod.

Good, he'd recognized her, acknowledged her talent. She was nearly in.

He put them through their paces three more times, the choreography more involved each time.

Theresa smiled to herself. This was more like it. This stuff cut the so-so dancers from those who could really pull off the tough moves, the intricate timing and the ones who could make the difficult look like a walk along the beach.

Raphael nodded. "OK, these girls stay." He pointed. "You, you, you, you––" He was culling them out, pointing to the ones who would make it. Girls' shoulders dropped as they were dismissed, and they trudged off stage.

Raphael continued until there were perhaps three dozen girls left. He hesitated. "OK, numbers one sixty one, twenty nine, two twelve, forty nine and sixteen, step to the side. You're in."

Her stomach clutched. Why hadn't he called her number? She'd been perfect. He'd nodded at her. Why did she still have to prove herself? Well, at least she was still in the running.

"Let's try this one, girls," he said and launched into another sequence. "It starts off fast, so pay attention. One and two, three and four–"

Behind her blazing smile, Theresa set her jaw. He wanted spectacular? She'd show him spectacular.

The music started and they launched into the sequence. Theresa whipped around, torqued her body, kicked higher than ever and finished with a stunning flourish.

Raphael nodded. "OK, give me a minute."

His assistant rushed over and they compared notes.

Theresa strode off the stage. She had a good sweat going and yanked off her bib with its number. She stayed standing, shaking out her legs, stretching them while they were warm.

Raphael came over, clip board in hand. "OK, ladies, good job. I'd like to hire you all but that'd reduce my salary to nothing."

Everyone twittered politely at his joke, desperate to be named to one of the last four positions.

"These girls can stay: Three sixty-nine, number nine-"

Her number.

"That's me!" a girl beside her cried, snatching a bib off the floor.

Oh, no you don't. "That's *my* number," Theresa growled and snatched it way from the little twit.

Raphael stepped up and glared at the girl. "That's right, that's Theresa Trenton's number." He pointed his pen at the bib thief. "Try that again, and you'll never work in this town, and I mean 'ever.' I'll see to it, honey."

The girl pouted and threw a towel on the floor. "I don't need this stupid job, anyway," she snapped as she stormed off.

Sure she didn't. That's why she'd pulled such a dumb move.

Luke checked his mailbox. It was here – the answer to his grant application. Luke tore open the letter, eyes scanning the lines.

Yes! He'd gotten it!

There was a check for eight thousand dollars.

Thank God.

He'd already spent it in his head. If only he had two thousand more, but those other grant applications were still being considered.

Thank goodness Mrs. Morehead had helped him fill out this one and found others for which he was qualified.

All he needed now were some electronic components and cables and he could get to work building his invention. This was the beginning of something great, he could feel it.

CHAPTER FIVE

Laurel double checked the address on the card before approaching the building. Elan's apartment was in the trendy part of town, a high rise that probably cost big bucks to own. She was greeted by a doorman and gave her name. She followed him to the elevator where he used a key. "This will take you right to her door," he said and bowed as he left her.

She barely felt the elevator lift off, it was so sleek.

The essence of climbing ended and the door whisked open.

Before her was an open concept great room with marble pillars, a chef's kitchen to one side, a living area covered in intricate rugs, leather sofas and a baby grand in one corner. Half a dozen people milled about sipping from wine glasses.

Elan strode over in a caftan of flowing silk. "Laurel, you're here, come in, come in. Would you like white or red wine?"

She really wasn't a drinker, but why not? "White, please."

"Julian, would you pour dear Laurel here a white?"

Julian, a tall man in his forties, slipped behind the bar and found her a Riesling.

Laurel accepted the stemmed glass and sipped. "I'm new to this. Is this how you get into the correct mindset for meditation?"

Julian chuckled. "Maybe in the beginning, it helps but you won't need wine after your get the hang of it. It's more a social affliction." He shot her a look to see if she got his meaning.

Cute. She wandered over to the window. The city sparkled below. What a striking view. Maybe she'd have a home like this one day.

A woman stepped up. "You're new, I heard. My advice: Just throw up a barrier and not let any random thoughts come in."

A man appeared. "I find it easier to visualize sweeping my daily cares into a dustpan and tossing them in the trash."

Barriers? Trash?

Elan clapped her hands to get everyone's attention, just like she did at school. "Settle in, everyone, get comfortable."

Native American flute music filled the room.

Laurel followed the others' lead and grabbed an oversized pillow and found a spot on the carpet. Everyone lay on their back, knees bent. Good thing she'd worn pants. She closed her eyes.

"Deep breath," Elan said, her voice soft. "Now, let it out and all your stress with it. Again."

Laurel let out her breath and felt her body lightening.

"You're going to imagine a white light starting at the center of your body. It starts as a small ball, bright and whiter than anything here on Earth. It's warm and it feels like love in its purest form. Feel the warmth. Feel the love it emits. Now, let it grow, spreading out further and further. While the white light grows, let all the tension out of your body, just accept it and its warm, loving feeling."

All these people were already accomplished at meditating, so Elan was guiding them aloud for her benefit. She hoped she could do this.

Laurel visualized the white light, felt its glow. This felt so good, not hard to do at all.

Elan continued. "Feel yourself relax as you become one with the light. As you accept the light, let all the strain and worry out of your muscles. Just relax and feel every concern slide out of your body."

The sensation was total peace, tranquility. She let the warmth flow throughout her body. This was actually pretty cool.

"Now, we're going to imagine ourselves in our favorite spot. It could be beside a stream or beside the ocean or a spot that you've always wanted to go to."

So, there were mind exercises. She was so relaxed, Elan could instruct her to jump off the building, and she would have obeyed.

Elan's voice became a far off sound. She was atop Mount Everest, the peaks of the Himalayas spread out in the vast scene before her.

The mountain tops were covered with snow and jutted like spikes above the clouds below. She was above the clouds, how cool. And she wasn't freezing cold or gasping for breath in the thin air or anything alarming like that.

Suddenly, Elan appeared beside her. "Art is not just about what we see, it's about what we feel."

"Why are you helping me?" her mind asked.

Elan said, "Don't question, just accept. The mind has many layers. An artist must use more than regular people. We have a gift. You have a gift. You're using that gift right now." She smiled. "It's not so hard, is it? Go on, try it out."

Maybe this was how Luke seemed to know they were connected.

He appeared before her, so quickly that she gave a start. "Luke? Are you really here?"

He was sitting at a desk, poring over a book. He looked up and a ghost of himself seemed to extract itself from his body. The ghostly Luke came over to her. "It's about time you learned how to do it," he said and took her hands. "See? There are no real boundaries. We can cross the miles, you and I."

He was right. She was talking to him, to the essential him, as surely as she was hearing Elan's voice, still guiding them in her high rise apartment. "I think I get it."

"It works better at night," he said.

Better at night, OK, she could remember that. "Anything else?"

"You need to practice, and I mean, a *lot*. Our Earthly selves have a way of clouding this realm out. So, if you don't use it, you lose it."

"I miss you, Luke."

"This way, you can come and talk to me any time."

"I will." She would, too. Now that she knew how to reach him.

Headlights lit up the long stretch of highway. Damn, he hated the night shift.

Marcus jumped down from the eighteen wheeler's runner board. He popped his pen in his uniform breast pocket and snapped his citation book closed. "OK, sir, be careful pulling back into traffic, and keep it safe out there."

"Yes, officer."

He watched the Peterbilt, with its payload of pipes on back churn forward and ease back onto the highway, headed for Vegas, twenty miles ahead.

Sure, it was tough to be a trucker. They put in long hours behind the wheel, trying to maneuver through all kinds of traffic in all kinds of weather, but this one had broken the law.

Speeding was speeding.

He'd given the guy a break and only written the ticket as though he'd gone ten miles above the speed limit when the trucker had been clocked at twenty over. Maybe he'd learn his lesson and slow down.

Luke threw his leg over the saddle of his motorcycle, hit the electric switch to turn it on and felt the raw power of the engine. His sports car had power, but mostly because it was a light car. This baby had power to burn, exponentially more power by ratio than a car, and he loved to cruise in it.

There was a break in traffic, and he hit the gas. Zero to sixty in three seconds, yeah, he loved this machine.

His headset crackled. Now what?

"Unit sixty-four, two-car accident reported on I-15 southbound near Speedway."

"On my way." He went lights and siren and raced off.

A two a.m. crash on a moonless night, man, he hated that. Oncoming traffic could ram into the involved vehicles before he got there to set out flares, crash victims could be lying on the asphalt and get run over, anything could happen.

This could take hours to untangle.

The only good thing was that Suzie would be waiting to serve him breakfast after it was all taken care of, and he got a break. They'd become an item, and it felt right.

Just wait until she saw the surprise he had for her.

Laurel closed her eyes and got comfortable. *Imagine a warm white light at the center of the belly. Let it spread, feel the peace.*

Had she turned off the oven? That silk blouse had to go to the cleaners tomorrow.

Stop. Get back to meditating.

She cleared her thoughts. OK, back to business.

Hold on. Her car needed an oil change soon, didn't it? It was a miracle that it'd made it all the way across the country from San Diego. What a long road trip that had been, mile after mile of highway with no one to talk to.

Her eyes flew open.

Stop it. You're supposed to be meditating.

She closed her eyes. OK, she could do this. *Empty the mind, imagine the warm glow of the white light.*

Nothing.

Hiding In Plain Sight/Hogan

Elan had never said it would be this hard. And Luke said he dropped into mediation within a few minutes. She must be doing something wrong.

OK, she'd try it again. She got comfortable and closed her eyes. *See the white light –*

Her stomach growled. Lunch had been hours ago and she'd spent so much time at her easel, she'd skipped dinner except for some crackers.

She gave up. She'd never get this.

Luke scooted his chair up to the equipment bay, pulled on his headphones and pushed buttons on the console. Defractor: On. Warbler: On. An electronic whining sound filled his ears. He adjusted the volume and jotted down the decibels.

Creating the detector had been easy. Sound waves bouncing off an object, it was a well-established principal. Ensuring it emitted those waves in every possible direction, X, Y and Z axis, had taken a little work, but had been do-able. Being able to alert someone as to *where* the threat was coming from, now, *that* had been the trick.

It had to be instantaneous. It has to be precise.

Thank goodness the university had allowed him to work in the lab on his own time.

The idea for this invention, like most of them, had come to him in a dream. He knew it was a winner the moment he woke up. It would impact the world, ensuring midair collisions never happened again.

But it had to be perfect. His invention had to be created so that it instantly took control from the pilots and changed each plane's direction. He'd spent hours and hours perfecting it.

The only problem was money.

Another prototype had to be built, a unit that would fit in the tight confines of a plane's cockpit. His money from the vitamin gum was gone, used to pay for college, and an education didn't come cheap. He didn't have time to come up with some other wild idea that some company might be willing to buy untested, not with his internship taking up so much of his time.

He'd already gone through the grant money that Mrs. Morehead had helped him secure. Between buying the components, the interfaces and a gyroscope, it hadn't lasted long.

Now, he needed at least another ten grand. There had to be some way to get it.

Marcus swung the Mazda onto the road leading up to Mount Charleston.

"You wouldn't tell me what you had in mind. I would have worn sneakers if you'd told me where we were going, sugar," Suzie said.

"No need."

"Well, I could have at least packed us a lunch."

"No need," he repeated and set his hand on her knee as he drove. This felt so right.

She sent him a little look, like she was trying to figure him out. "This little jaunt is super secret, huh?" She made a conciliatory gesture. "OK. Whatever you have in mind, I'm game."

They reached the summit parking lot, and he pulled into a spot and killed the engine. There was hardly anyone else there. "Let's walk a little bit," he said. "I'll get your door."

She was in sandals, but they didn't need to go far.

Marcus scooted around to her side, opened the door and took her hand to help her out. "Remember our camping trip up here?"

She grinned. "You were trying to be such a gentleman."

"It took all my control."

"That's why I had to speed things up." She stopped and ran her hands down his shirt, playing with the buttons. "It was all I could do, not to tear your clothes off."

There was that teasing voice of hers again, driving him crazy. He grabbed her to him, looking down at her. She was all he'd ever wanted, so sexy, so playful. But was time to get serious, time to make sure this was right. "But we're more than that, more than just attracted to each other for the sex, right?" he pressed her. "We're great in every way, aren't we?"

"Of course we are, sugar. Is that why you wanted to come up here, just to ask me some silly little thing like that?"

This was it, the perfect moment. "No, to ask you this." He reached into his back pocket and pulled out the tiny box.

Suzie gasped as he cracked it open.

Marcus watched her face. "Will you be my wife?"

Suzie threw her arms around his neck. "Let's tie the knot today! Please, sugar?"

"Sure, anything for you."

Laurel groaned. The paint color was all wrong. She'd added too much blue. This assignment was due in two days, and she was messing it up.

Her phone rang. "Hello?"

"Hey, sis." It was Theresa. She'd emailed a few days ago that she'd been hired for a new show, Hot Stuff at the Potenza Hotel in Vegas, hardly a surprise that she'd been snapped up so quickly after the Broadway show concluded. Those long legs of hers and her dance prowess were a producer's dream come true. Plus, she had experience with those heavy headdresses every showgirl had to endure. Laurel put down her paint brush. "How have you been? How's Arielle?"

"Growing like a weed. She'll be three soon, almost ready for preschool."

There was a hesitation in her voice, like something was bothering her. "Theresa? Is everything OK?"

"Dirk and I are calling it quits."

Like they hadn't separated, what, a gazillion times before? "For good this time?"

"Yeah. I hate what it'll do to Arielle, but I can't live like this anymore, Laurel. He's not the same person."

"We all have our demons. Maybe he'll kick the habit."

Theresa scoffed. "Not anytime soon, he won't."

Poor Theresa, how would she handle the demands being a single mother?

They talked a little more – how Theresa needed to find a preschool for Arielle, what part of town they'd be living in. And how it was too bad that Dirk didn't realize how much his daughter needed him.

Laurel let her sister talk until she was all talked out. "Call me if you need a shoulder to cry on."

Theresa scoffed. "My tears are all dried up. From here on out, it's full steam ahead, just me and Arielle making our way in the world."

"Atta girl."

Gregor Andrysiak pushed away from his easel. It was done. For four months, he'd labored at it. Now, he'd given birth to it. Next week, he'd ship it off to the art patron, a private collector who'd commissioned the piece.

Half a million dollars, it was a fair price.

Right now, he needed to stretch his muscles. He stepped out on the balcony and braced his hands on the railing. God, the sun felt great on his face and that ocean breeze, the way it wafted against his skin, simply inspirational. Below him, the waves lapped on the beaches of Malaga. It didn't get better than this.

Spain, he'd never planned to end up here. It just called to him, the way other spots in the world had. So he'd lived in them all – Malaysia, Japan, Estonia. Each one had furthered his creativity and expanded his reach into the art world. But it was the tide and the rhythm of the waves, he'd learned, that had furthered his art more than anything. They were , inspiring.

Now, the name Gregor Andrysiak was well known across the world.

"Never underestimate the power of the ocean to bring an artist to his full potential," he said aloud.

For ten years, he'd brought students here, supporting them for a year or two to help them reach their full potential. It wasn't like it was a burden. His home was considered a mansion, with two wings of otherwise empty bedrooms and a separate studio converted from a four-car garage. Besides, his creativity was awakened by being around all the young, emerging talent. It was a win-win situation.

But they'd gone off to open their own studios, create the way their own passions had moved them. The last student had left a couple months ago.

Funny how quiet the house had suddenly gotten with their departure, like a vacuum had descended and sucked the life right out of it.

Now, it was time to find new talent, to bring more art students to Spain and pass along that passion for the paintbrush and the beauty it brought the world.

He'd have to contact various art schools and visit them to see what prodigies he might find. You never knew who would stick out. Sometimes it was a person so well developed, their art only needed to be presented to the world.

Other times, he'd find an emerging talent, someone who needed to be guided, helped along. Gregor rubbed his palms together. Yeah, he couldn't wait to find his next protégé.

CHAPTER SIX

She rolled her carryon luggage behind her, searching the crowd at LAX. There! Luke was waiting at the luggage carousel. Laurel hurried up and flew into his arms. Six months seemed like forever. "Oh, my God, I missed you," she gushed.

His kiss was eager and long, and she was sure she never wanted this lip lock to end.

"You're just in time," he said, releasing her. "I've got it in two planes. They're ready to test my multi-directional traffic identifier and avoidance system."

"The what?"

"I refer to it as the Close Call. Come on, we've got to beat traffic." He grabbed her luggage and pulled her away.

Forty minutes later they were parked at a small, private airfield.

Laurel looked around. "What are we doing here exactly?"

"It's the initial test of my prototype. I wanted you to be here for it."

She'd never expected his invention to be this far along. "This is so exciting."

They got out of the car and approached two single engine planes, parked near one another. Two men in aviator sunglasses and short, military style haircuts were strolling over.

"Oh, look, those must be the pilots," she exclaimed.

They introduced themselves - Floyd Charestimi and Andrew Stanton - but she was too excited to make small talk. "I'll just take pictures," she said, pulling out her phone and clicking away. "We'll want to document this. It's historic."

Luke made last-minute adjustments inside each plane and she clicked away – close up, medium shot, wide angle. One day, they'd look back on these photos and remember how it all started, she just knew it.

Luke went through his checklist. All the cables were connected, all the components checked out.

"We're ready to take off," one of the pilots said.

"Good luck," Luke said. This had better work. Heck, he'd put so much time into it, it *had* to work.

He approached the bench where Laurel was seated. She'd flown all the way out here from Philly to see him. He'd wanted her to experience this triumph with him.

He caught her hand and squeezed it. "I brought binoculars for each of us." He handed her a set.

She patted the seat beside her. "Aren't you going to sit down?"

Sit? Who could sit at a time like this? "Too excited."

The planes went up. He watched through the lenses as they took opposing flight paths and headed intentionally on a collision course.

His pulse raced.

The planes soared straight toward one another. They would hit any second now.

Jeez, look out!

The two planes banked away from one another, one to the north and the other to the south. It had to be his invention taking over. It worked!

The planes both turned and headed toward one another again. Luke held his breath. He wished he could hear what the two pilots were saying to one another on their headsets.

The planes went on a collision course again.

Again, they banked away at the last possible second.

It worked! It worked!

Ten minutes later, he held Laurel's hand as they watched the two planes come in for their landings, one after the other.

There was a chirp of tires as the small planes connected with the asphalt. Then they taxied closer and purred to a stop, parking about twenty feet away from one another.

Luke jumped up and hurried up to the closest plane. "How was it? Did the alarm go off when you expected? It did, didn't it? And when it over the controls, was it smooth enough?"

The first pilot eased out of the cockpit. "See how close we parked?" he said, jutting his chin at the other plane. "That's about how close he was when your device went off." He shook his head. "Too close for my taste."

What?

"Now," the pilot continued, "you take a commercial jetliner going five hundred miles an hour, and you'd have a major disaster on your hands. I wouldn't trust my life to it, son, I'm sorry."

The other pilot emerged from his plane. "We pushed it as close as we could but when my plane didn't react like you said it would, I broke it off. Had to. No sense the two of us should get killed for your fool idea."

Fool idea? His face heated up. Laurel was here, watching and it had failed miserably? No, it couldn't be. "But, but–"

The first pilot, Floyd Charestimi, clapped a hand on Luke's shoulder. "Look, son, the idea was a good one, on paper at least. But you're talking about people's *lives* here. Your device is one piece of crap."

"I don't understand. It worked fine in the lab," Luke said.

"Sure, it did," Floyd said. "Now, disengage that thing and get it far away from my airplane." He shook his head and walked away.

Laurel put her arm around him. "Oh, Luke, I'm sorry."

Of all the people to witness his failure. He ran a hand across his forehead. "I'm sorry. I was so sure it would work. I should have tested it more, run more tests, but I pushed it before it was ready." He clenched his fists. "I just, I just want so badly to make sure we don't have to struggle to make ends meet."

Grams pushed a plate of cookies at her.

"I can't have those," Laurel said. "I'm running in a 5K next week."

"One little cookie won't hurt."

Good old Grams, baking her way into everyone's heart. Speaking of which … "You've been OK? The doctor is still monitoring your blood work?"

"I'm an old woman, these things are to be expected. But I *do* want to make sure you have a copy of my will."

"Grams, no, we don't need to talk about those things at this point. You've got plenty of years left." She *did*, didn't she?

"Just in case. Here's my estate attorney's business card. Now, the cabin stays in the family. You and Theresa will share it, of course, just like your parents decreed. There's a maintenance account set up and one for the insurance coverage, so if after I die, a pipe breaks or–"

"Grams, there's really no need to go into all this."

"I haven't been there in probably ten years, but you girls always loved it when you were little, and we'd all go to Vegas together."

Laurel bit into the cookie and nodded. Those had been fun times. They'd all gone hiking and picnicking and had even found a cave, marveling that less than an hour away was a bone-dry desert while Mount Charleston offered such a varied landscape.

Gram looked content. "Those were good times."

Laurel patted her hand. "The best, Grams." And there would be many more. There had to be. Grams was all she had left for family, her and Theresa.

She glanced at Luke's alarm clock. Eleven p.m. It was their last night together before she had to fly back to Philly. No fair. Vacations shouldn't go by so quickly. Laurel stretched in the bed, satisfied from their last go around.

Luke ran his fingers along her back. "When can you fly out again?"

"Our next school break is in three months." She'd already marked it on her calendar.

He groaned. "A lifetime."

Planes go both ways, you know. But she didn't say it out loud. They were both strapped for cash.

He got up and padded into the bathroom. "Maybe by then I'll have another prototype to test."

That soon? "Wait. I thought you spent all the grant money to get this one up and running."

"I did."

The shower turned on. She raised her voice, "So, how will you raise the money?"

He ducked his head around the door jam and wiggled his eyebrows. "Bank robberies."

The nut. She threw a pillow at him.

"Seriously, I'll find a way, Laurel."

Marcus helped the guy crawl out from his overturned vehicle. "You OK, buddy? Is anything broken?

The driver, about thirty, looked around, eyes big, scared. He grabbed the edge of his minivan. "Hey man, did you see it? Is it still here?"

"Is what still here?"

"Get your gun out. You have to shoot it if it comes after me again."

Damn stoners. This one had hit the wall, which caused a rollover that would tie up traffic for more than an hour. At least it was only his own vehicle that he'd involved. "Sure, bud. Anything comes at us, I'll shoot it dead in its tracks. Can you stand?"

"I guess."

OK, the guy had his legs, wasn't screaming in agony or anything. Too bad the same couldn't be said for his minivan. "Hold still, sir. Let me look at you." He flicked his flashlight over the man. No blood. No bones sticking out. No, the idiot hadn't suffered more than a scratch. Lucky guy.

"Oh, shit, there he is! Shoot it! Shoot it!"

"Calm down."

"There it is. Shoot it!" The stoner dashed out into traffic.

No! He was going to get run over. Marcus launched himself after the guy and tackled him, locking his hands around his knees.

The stoner fell with a grunt.

Oncoming traffic- shit!

Marcus rolled the guy back toward the accident scene.

The traffic whisked by, horn blaring.

They'd barely made it to safety, just inches to spare.

Marcus jumped up, pulse throbbing double time in his ears. "Shit, man, are you crazy?" He'd nearly bought the farm, all for some guy who saw a three-eyed monster or something stupid like. Marcus spat. Sometimes, he hated this stupid job.

The stoner pointed an accusing finger at him. "You never pulled your gun. You nearly let it get me, you bastard!"

The nerve of this guy. Marcus threw up his hands in disbelief and made a rolling eyes face.

"Oh, shit! There he is again!" The guy turned to run off.

Oh, no, you don't. Marcus caught the driver's wrist, cranked it up behind the man's back and spun him around. He whipped out the cuffs and snapped them on in two seconds flat. "I just saved your damn life."

There was a reflection of light on his finger. He glanced at his wedding band. Suzie would not be made a widow this night.

Their art assignments were being handed back. This time, all the instructors had chimed in, citing pros and cons in writing.

Laurel accepted her piece and the sealed critique envelope. She took a deep breath. *Here we go. This is the moment of truth.*

She opened the envelope and scanned the lines.

"Good eye for perspective ... Liked the color choices ... Maybe consider working on it longer. It was like you started something good and then stopped three quarters of the way there."

"... Good drawing skills ... Needs a big more 'je ne sais quoi' ... Apply your knowledge of body mechanics with a little more finesse, and you'll bring the missing sophistication to your painting."

Then there was Elan's assessment, her fluid handwriting recognizable immediately. "You have the talent, definitely. Now, look inside yourself for the truth in what you're trying to convey."

Beside her, April gave a snort. Laurel looked over. Had she gotten less than stellar reviews? "That bad?"

The waif of a girl shrugged. "They loved mine, want to put it on display in the art museum."

"The" art museum, as in the Philadelphia Museum of Art? April's work got into such a prestigious location and yet her work was deemed lacking in 'je ne sais quoi' – that wasn't fair. *Her* work should be in the Philadelphia Museum of Art, not some girl who was high as a kite all day long.

Laurel set her jaw. That was it, the last straw. She was going to practice that meditation shit day and night, even if it killed her.

Luke dialed Anthony's number in New York.

"Yeah?"

"Anthony, hey, it's Luke. How's the old neighborhood?"

"Make it quick. I'm busy."

"Remember how I was always inventing things in junior high? Well, I've come up with a new idea that's really going to fly." He chuckled at his joke.

"And?"

"And, well, to get it tested takes some capital, and I'm reaching out to everyone I know for some help."

"Help?"

"Investment, a small sum, really." He rushed to explain the gist of his device, how it would alert commercial airline pilots to nearby planes. "It's a built-in market. It's a safety requirement."

"What's that? It's required?"

Good, he had Anthony's attention. "New legislation is being passed as we speak."

"How much you need?"

"Only a thousand dollars." Luke held his breath. He hadn't seen Anthony Amalfitano in years, but he came from money. What was a thousand dollars to someone who came from money?

There was silence on the line.

Luke's winced. His childhood friend wasn't going to help out after all. "If you don't want to, I underst–"

"Sure, I'm in. A thousand, huh?"

He was in? Seriously? "You won't regret it."

"Give me your address. I'll send it in the mail."

Most of his family had done an electronic transfer, but he wasn't about to argue. A check was fine. It would be here in a few days. "Got your pen handy? Here's my address."

Laurel turned off the lights of her tiny apartment and settled onto the couch. She'd recorded Elan's latest session and put it on now.

She let her hands relax and cleared her mind. She heard the prompts begin and imagined a white dot at the center of her body.

"See the white light growing larger, encompassing your very essence."

Laurel let her mind follow the voice on the device. Soon, the white light surrounded her, and she was at a beach. A group of horses was thundering toward her, looking wild, looking free. Their manes flowed out behind them as their hooves pounded the wet sand.

She slipped onto the back of one of them and grabbed a handful of mane, locking her legs around the girth of the beast. The horse's legs worked hard beneath her, muscles rippling as it moved. The strength in them was readily apparent, the effort spoke of freedom. The wild abandon in the animal's movements was palpable, infesting.

Laurel let the wind whip her hair around. She gave in to the rhythm and let her body move in synch with the horse. Beside her, she heard the thunder of the waves as they crashed on the shore. No, she didn't just hear the waves, she was living the moment with them, hitting the beach with them, even as she rode the steed.

This was unbelievable! She'd never experienced anything like this before.

She came out of the meditation and grabbed a fresh canvas. She had to paint this.

His NHP motorcycle purred along the 95 freeway. It was 3 a.m. Vegas never slept, but at least traffic was lighter at this time of night.

A set of rear lights flashed past, three lanes over – a speeder. He sped up and got behind the silver compact. It was maintaining its lane, it was just that its speed was excessive, nearly twenty miles over the posted limit. He hit his lights and siren.

The compact braked and pulled over, rolling to a stop. It looked like there was just the driver inside.

Marcus approached as the window powered down. His hands slid to his automatic pistol. It was a young female, late twenties maybe. "Do you know why I pulled you over, miss?"

"Yes sir."

No smell of alcohol, so far, so good. "License and registration, please."

She handed them over. He glanced at the license. Theresa Trenton, Summerlin area residence. "I'll be right back."

He returned to his motorcycle and called in her information. Center came back: Ms. Trenton was clean.

He returned to her door side. Now that he knew she wasn't a repeat criminal, he stood directly by her door. She was pretty, even without makeup. "Miss Trenton, you been partying tonight?"

She blinked in confusion. "Partying?"

"It's kind of late to be out and about."

"No, sir. I just got off work. I'm a dancer at the Potenza Hotel."

"Well, you have no priors. So, do you mind telling me what the rush is?"

"I'm sorry," she blurted, "but my babysitter – she was a last minute substitute for my regular girl – said just before I left the house, she said she'd up and leave if I'm not home by 3 a.m. I don't even get off until 3 a.m. I'm sorry if I was speeding, but I can't have my daughter left alone, officer. I just can't."

CHAPTER SEVEN

Her voice was high pitched. She was scared, stressed.

"I see. "How old is your daughter, miss?"

"Four – way too young to be home alone at an hour like this. Her name is Arielle. I wasn't brought up that way, and I won't bring my child up that way."

It was refreshing to hear someone say something like that, especially in this town. Marcus handed back her cards. "Well, Miss Trenton, you're in luck. I'm low on my quota for helping damsels in distress. I've got your address. I'll give you a police escort. Follow me."

Ten minutes later, they pulled up to her house. He'd killed the siren once they'd hit her neighborhood, but he left the emergency lights on.

Miss Theresa Trenton parked in the driveway, and he came up beside her. She was amazingly tall, all legs. Nice. But he wasn't here to admire the scenery. There was something more he needed to do. "Let's go talk to this babysitter of yours," he said.

"This way." She already had her key out, shoved it in the door and hurried inside. "Arielle? Honey? Are you all right?"

"Mommy?"

The kid was cute, with coltish long legs, just like her mother. No doubt she'd grow up to be just as tall.

A college-age girl with mousey brown hair wandered into the living room. "Finally, you're back," she grumbled.

The little girl frowned. "She woke me up, told me she was taking off."

"Oh, honey, I'm sorry." The mother knelt beside her child and hugged her.

Arielle Trenton began to cry. "I begged her not to."

He'd heard enough. He stepped past Ms. Trenton and her daughter. "May I have a word with you?"

The babysitter caught her breath at the sight of him.

Yeah, you didn't expect a cop to witness this, did you? Not that he had any jurisdiction here, but no one would call him on the carpet for helping out the young mother. "Are you in the habit of leaving a child all alone in the middle of the night?"

"Well, I have to be at class at 9 a.m." She threw her hands on her waist akimbo and eyed the leggy mother. "I have to get some sleep, too, you know."

"No one said that you couldn't sleep," Theresa shot back.

"Whoa, everybody calm down." He had to separate them. The last thing he needed was a cat fight. "Let's step into the kitchen, miss," he said to the babysitter.

The house was older, but clean, with a tiny kitchen. Good. Close quarters made for greater intimidation, and he towered over this mousey-haired girl. Being in uniform didn't hurt, either. "You were about to leave the little girl, Arielle, alone?"

The babysitter huffed. "It's not like she's a baby."

"Leaving a child of any age to fend for herself at 3 a.m. is not the best decision, would you agree?"

She stared at her feet. "I guess."

"Have you been a babysitter for long?"

"I just do it to make some spending money. My parents seem to think I can live on practically nothing," she whined. "So, I pick up a babysitting job now and then."

And obviously, she loved it so much. This girl needed to grow up. "Get a job at Starbucks. You're not cut out to oversee the wellbeing of another human being. Now, gather your things. You're not coming back here."

"You can't tell me what to do."

He raised his voice. "Miss Trenton, would you agree that this young woman cannot set foot on your property ever again?"

"Yes, officer, I agree," she called from the living room.

Smart woman. "You see, it appears that under the law, I *can* tell you what to do."

The babysitter sniffed. "Fine. I'll get my things."

He escorted her outside. She stiffened at the sight of his emergency lights calling attention to the situation and a neighbor peeking out of the window across the street. "I'm, I'm sorry officer, maybe I was tired and I didn't ..." she fumbled for the words.

"Exercise the best judgment?"

"Yes."

She got in her late model Chevy, a present from mommy and daddy no doubt, and he shut her door for her. "Drive safe out there."

She peeled off with a chirp of her tires.

Marcus sighed. He'd bet his last dollar he'd scrape her dead body off the asphalt one of these days.

Theresa Trenton appeared in the doorway. "Thank you, officer," she called out.

"My pleasure." OK, so he'd done his good deed for the night. He cut the lights on his motorcycle and climbed aboard. It sparked to life and powered him away. Too bad there weren't more solid citizens like Ms. Trenton in this world.

The Marion School seemed different. The doors were polished. The supplies were organized on shelves. Laurel entered and took her chair. April dragged herself in and melted into her seat. She was as skinny as ever.

Laurel smiled. "Hi, April. How was your summer?"

"Like," the girl breathed, "did you hear the news?"

"What news?"

April paused, blinked and looked confused, suddenly defeated in her effort to remember. "I forget."

More students sauntered in and took their seats. Some looked tanned and fitter. Some looked exactly the same.

Peter Sabastian took the front of the room. "Attention, everyone. I have great news. Gregor Andrysiak will be visiting the school."

"That." April moved beside her. "That's the news."

"Gotcha." She returned her attention back to Peter Sabastian. The man was positively glowing with the announcement. Gregor Andrysiak was only the most amazing painter in the world. No wonder the school had been spruced up.

"Now, I don't want to get everyone's hopes up, but he'll be critiquing your work. If he makes suggestions, I'd pay close attention. The man knows his stuff, obviously, and it's an honor to have him grace us with his presence."

Everyone murmured in agreement. Gregor Andrysiak. She'd seen his work when she'd taken the train to New York City and visited various art galleries.

The man was, simply put, a genius.

Peter Sabastian continued. "The school will host him for dinner, and it's been determined that ten students will be selected to join us."

Laurel felt a thrill pass through her. Having him whisk through school was one thing, but to be able to spend time with him in a social setting was another. Perhaps he could help her understand what options she should pursue, where she should try to get her work represented.

"When will he be here?" someone asked.

"Tomorrow," Peter Sebastian said. "Now, let's remember why we're here and get to work, shall we?"

Laurel eyed her latest work, still in its early stages. Would the famous artist like it? Would he understand the intent behind the lines, see how it all would eventually blend together in the end?

Luke tossed his keys on the desk of his dorm room. What a long day. At least the applied science test had gone well.

His intercom buzzed.

"Yeah?"

"Luke, my man." It was Bomber, one of the dorm building monitors, who always smelled of high-grade weed. "You got mail down here. A package."

"Be right there." It must be from his parents. Maybe mom had sent some of her double chocolate chip brownies. He hurried down to the front desk of his dorm hall.

Bomber saw him coming and pushed a box toward him. It was compact, about the size of a pencil box, like Laurel used for her paint brushes. There was no way that brownies could be in there. "Thanks, Bomber."

"Hang on." Bomber held out a pen. "You gotta sign, man."

"Right." He scribbled his name and hightailed it back to his dorm room. He took scissors and broke the mailing tape. The box spilt open and money dropped out.

Holy, crap. Anthony hadn't sent a check. He'd sent money – all in one hundred dollar bills.

Luke gathered them up. There had to be - wait. This wasn't a thousand dollars. There were twenty bills here. He'd sent two thousand.

There was a note.

"Luke – I figured if you could use one grand, then you can use two. When you make it big, you'll pay me back." He'd sign it with the letter A.

Luke through his head back and laughed. What a great guy his buddy Anthony was.

A sudden hush fell over the classroom. Something was happening. Laurel looked up from her easel. Gregor Andrysiak was here, escorted by Marilyn Goddall, head of school.

She caught her breath. He was way more handsome in person than in pictures.

Damn, she'd nearly dropped her brush.

"Attention everyone," Peter Sabastian called out, unable to keep a grin from spreading across his face. "Our esteemed guest is here. Students, may I present: Gregor Andrysiak."

Their art instructor even made a sweeping motion with his hand. Laurel groaned internally. What would he do next, bow?

There were polite hellos from all the students, punctuated with nods of acknowledgment.

She stared and squeaked, "Hello." Oh, that sounded pathetic. She racked her brain, trying desperately to think of something that would distinguish her from the others, make him notice her behind all the people crowded around him. Nothing brilliant came to mind.

She turned back to her work. The last thing she needed was to make a fool of herself in front of a world-famous artist.

She dabbed her brush in Windsor & Newton's cadmium red, chosen for the fire in her sunset.

There was movement off her shoulder. April's work was getting the attention of the head of school and their distinguished guest. Great.

"So, April, tell us about your work," Marilyn Goddall said.

There was a sigh. "You know how you feel when you first wake up, and you're not really sure where you are? That, you know, feeling of being kind of, I don't know, lost, and, like," she sighed again. "I don't know. And you look at the ceiling, and your mind kind of takes a moment to adjust, even if you've woken up in that room all your life, you're still not sure? And you look at a crack, and you realize you could crawl inside it if you made yourself, like, really, really small. And then you kind of realize you've been in this situation before and it should make sense, but it doesn't. Because it's sort of like you're an ant in a world that is sooooo much bigger than you but you're sure this is all there is. You know? That kind of thing?" She gestured at her painting. "That's kind of what this is."

Marilyn Goddall's face froze.

Gregor moved back as though to keep his distance from the waif-like April. "Yes, well," he said. "Interesting." He turned away.

Laurel swallowed, hard. Oh, damn, he was looking at her artwork.

He moved closer. "What have we here?"

She nodded. "Hello, Mr. Andrysiak. Thank you for coming to our school." She introduced herself and shook his hand. His photo hadn't done him any at all. Up close, he was handsome in a rugged, he-man kind of way.

"Tell me about this painting," he said, peering at it. "I see you're doing a landscape."

"It's a sunset that it will transition into the deep sky, filled with stars."

He shot her a quick look. "Like 'Starry Night?' "

"As my inspiration? Yes," she said. Oh no, he'd think she was out to copy one of the most famous paintings ever created. "But this will be less post-impressionist and more Claude Monet's 'Beach in Pourville.' "

"Mixing the two? That's quite an undertaking. Yes, I see how you've got it sketched out. But the proof is in how you paint it." He grinned. "I tried something like this way back when I was a young art student."

Sure, like he was that old. He was in his forties, maybe. He sure wore it well.

He took his eyes from her work to lock eyes with her.

Those eyes! He had that manly, seasoned look that sold bourbon and spoke of worldly adventures like rafting exploration parties down the Amazon.

Wait. He was studying her, assessing her just like she was assessing him. Laurel felt her cheeks heat up and broke her gaze.

"I'd like to see it when it's further along," he said.

"Of course. Anytime," she muttered, suddenly unsure of what to do with her hands. She didn't know what was happening here, why she suddenly feel so flustered in front of this man.

Peter Sabastian stepped up. "Everyone," he called out. "We have the results of the drawing to determine who will be at the reception tonight at Marmont's in Rittenhouse Square. I'm delighted to announce that one of those students is from this class."

Laurel caught her breath. *Please let it be me, please.*

"And that person is, –" Peter Sabastian paused for effect, " – April Vanderhousen."

What? April? *April* was going to get to spend time with this enigmatic man? *Noooo.*

Marcus swung his red Mazda into the Lexus dealership. His car seemed so old, so unimpressive, even though he'd bought it new only three years ago.

Suzie shot him a startled look. "What are we doing here?"

He acted nonchalant. "Just looking, you know, for the fun of it."

They parked and a salesman descended on them.

"We're just looking," Suzie said, waving him off. "Oh, look at this one, sugar. This is cute." She trotted off, her heels clicking on the asphalt.

Marcus got the salesman's attention. "Tell Jon that Marcus, the state trooper, is here."

"Will do, sir."

He joined Suzie, now ogling another vehicle. "Oooh, I'd love to get this one."

"Maybe one day when we can afford it," Marcus said. "But today, we're just looking, right?"

She sighed. "Right."

Jon was walking up to them. Marcus left Suzie oohing and aahing over a blue two-door model. "Everything set?"

"It's being pulled up front right now." He pointed.

A gold SUV, gleamed in the sun, came around the corner and slid to a stop in front of the dealership windows. It looked like they'd just washed and waxed her, good.

Marcus nodded. "All the paperwork is set?"

"Signed and sealed." Here's your key."

He pocketed it. He'd always envisioned buying a rugged two-seater Jeep when he was in a position to buy a new vehicle. Well, Suzie couldn't very well be seen in a rough-and-tumble Jeep. She deserved better. "Let's see what my wife thinks of it." He raised his voice. "Suzie, honey, come over here for a minute, will you?"

Suzie trotted over, and he guided her towards the front of the dealership.

"Look at this one," Marcus said. "Why don't you slide behind the wheel?"

"OK, sugar."

Jon opened the door for her, and she plopped her little butt onto the seat.

"Maybe it needs a test drive," Jon suggested.

Good idea. "Yeah, honey, why don't you try it out?"

"I can't reach the pedals," she said.

Jon showed her how to adjust the seat.

"And here," Marcus said, dangling a fob, "is your key."

Suzie took it and went to start the car. "How come you have the keys?"

"Because," he said with a grin, "I just bought it for you."

She turned back, jaw dropped, jumped out of the car and threw her arms around him. "Sugar, you're the best!"

There was a knock on her apartment door. Laurel snatched away the extra paintbrush she'd been holding in her mouth. "Who is it?" she called out.

"It's Elan."

At seven thirty at night? What was she doing here? Laurel opened the door. Elan was in a chic cocktail dress. "Aren't you supposed to be at dinner with –?"

Elan pushed past her and began pacing. "We need you at Marmont's. Do you have a little black dress?"

As in, to wear to the dinner with Gregor Andrysiak? You bet she did. "I can be changed and ready in ten minutes."

Laurel dashed into her bedroom and tore off her clothes. "Why the last minute invitation?" she called through the door.

"April is, shall we say, incapacitated."

A drug party, it had to be. Good old April, high as a kite. "So she's feeling no pain?"

"One of the other students found her unconscious. He called an ambulance."

What? "Oh, my gosh, that's horrible. Is she all right?"

"The hospital said she should be over the worst of it by tomorrow. She had a chance to talk one-on-one with Gregor Andrysiak, and she pissed the chance away."

Well, I won't.

CHAPTER EIGHT

Laurel stepped into Marmont's. It was packed.

Elan took her elbow and steered her to the private room in back.

Marion's upper ranks were grouped around Gregor Andrysiak who was dressed in a linen shirt and black slacks. Off to one side was the table, all set up and waiting for them.

Laurel accepted a glass of wine from a waiter. It was the good stuff. She studied Gregor Andrysiak who was absorbed in something the head of school was saying. He looked sophisticated, worldly. He probably wouldn't even notice she was there. She wandered over to the table. Name cards were at each place setting. April's was at the very end of the long table.

If Gregor Andrysiak was at the head of the table, how could she possibly talk one-on-one with him if she was way down here? She peered around. Good, no one was looking.

Laurel scooped up April's name tent and swapped it so that she was two seats away from the famous painter. She smiled. There now, she should be able to get his attention better up here.

Someone tapped for silence. "Dinner is served."

Laurel took her seat as the others edged over to the table and found their name placards.

Gregor took the seat next to her.

What was he doing? He was supposed to be at the head of the table, not seated on the side like the rest of them.

He smiled, picked up the tent on the place setting before him and inspected it. The head of school's name was written on it. "Gee, I guess I'm Marilyn Goddall tonight," he joked. "Ah, let them figure it out."

Ms. Goddall took the chair at the head of the table.

Laurel smiled at the famous painter. "I'm wondering why you chose our school to visit, Mr. Andrysiak," she said.

"You can call me Gregor," he said to her. "No one else can, just you."

He was a joker. That was clear. "All right, Gregor, why the Marion School of Art in Philly?"

He leaned close. "They paid the most to bring me here." He shot her a conspiratorial smile. "Of course, if you repeat that, I'll deny it."

"Seriously, why Marion?"

He turned serious, looking her straight in the eye. "I like a school where students are hungry, where they get a taste for art but aren't corrupted by teachers who demand they follow a certain criteria, a proven path. Art is not about the perfect stroke of a brush. It's not about what's in vogue. Art comes from our feelings, our emotions." Gregor eyed her name tent. "April, is it?"

"April, um, got sick. I'm Laurel. Laurel Rebecca Trenton."

"My God, that's a mouthful."

The CEO stood up. "May I propose a toast? To our distinguished guest, thank you for coming to our school and furthering Marion's sterling reputation."

Laurel raised her glass to his toast.

Oh, shit.

There was a four inch long paint smear on her wrist. In her haste to get ready, she'd totally missed it.

Laurel jerked her hand down below the table. Too late.

The CEO had noticed and was staring at her, aghast. Gregor had noticed, too. In fact, everyone had noticed.

"Forgive me," she said, blushing madly. This was a semi-formal affair and she showed up covered in paint, wonderful. Just let her disappear into the floor right now.

"No, no," Gregor said, smiling broadly. "Don't be dismayed. That's the mark of a true art student if ever I saw one." He reached down and pulled up her hand. "Cadmium red, unless I miss my guess. I think it's splendid." He turned to the others, soliciting their agreement.

Everyone nodded.

What a gallant way to smooth over her faux pas. "I was working on my next piece when Elan told me April wasn't well, and that I needed to come take her place."

"Excellent," Gregor said, "an artist who is dedicated to creating art day and night." He let go of her hand and picked up his wine glass. "Now, *I* propose a toast, to Miss Laurel Rebecca Trenton."

Laurel sat in class, as the scene from Friday evening played over in her mind, like it had all weekend. Gregor had monopolized her time that night, asking about her background, her interests. And then, right at the end, he'd requested that she send him her latest works, and told her that she could ask him for advice whenever she questioned herself.

The man had even written down his personal email address, no less.

She was going to be approachable that way when she became famous, she decided. She would visit schools, she would troll for up-and-coming talent and mentor them.

She jerked at the sudden movement beside her, the trance broken.

Elan was at her shoulder.

"Stunning, Laurel," the art teacher said. "These poppies, it's like they're right in front of me. I want to reach out and touch them, smell them."

Elan moved off. Laurel smiled. Ever since she'd broken through the barrier and ridden the horse along the beach, her art had taken off. It was like she was *feeling* her art as much as painting it. She took a deep breath. It was time to get back to the poppy fields. She wanted to finish this within a week, so she could get started on her senior art project.

Now that she was in her second and final year at Marion, all assignments were self-directed ones. The only instructions for this project had been to "paint something you'd see in the reception hall of a hospital."

It had been the poem, "Flander's Fields," that had inspired her to begin the painting.

She sat back and studied it.

Her poppies reached their faces to the sun, but there was a touch of sadness there too, sadness at the loss of brave soldiers, fighting for a just, noble cause.

Her final art project was going to be even more emotion driven – the two towers of the World Trade Center, depicted after they'd fallen.

She was still working out how to render that one. But it would come, now that she knew how to get in touch with her inner self and let it direct her.

Luke bit his lip. There was no other way. He had no choice. He dialed.

"Yeah."

"Anthony?"

"Yeah. Who's this?"

"It's Luke, out in L.A. How are things in New York?"

"What do you want?"

What kind of a greeting was that? "Um, my new prototype is ready to be tested again."

"Don't ask me for no more money, bro."

But you're my last resort. "Listen, all I need is ten grand."

"I already gave you two grand. Then I heard that when you tested it, you're little invention didn't measure up. You should of told me that before I gave you the money."

"This time, it's better. I found the problem and not only corrected it, I added an element that will have Boeing and every other aircraft manufacturer desperate for it."

"Dude, they won't buy it if they don't have to. Sorry. Got to go."

"Wait. International law. They have to."

There was a pause. "Huh? I thought you were pulling my leg, bro."

"Nope. It's true. The Europeans just passed it, Africa is following suit. Asian countries are set to follow."

"That so?"

Didn't Anthony watch CNN? PBS? The International News Hour? Or did he keep it tuned to some local channel that just spoon fed him the news? "This means my invention is practically guaranteed to sell."

"Hmm. Tell you what. Because we're old friends, I'll loan you two grand more. But that's it."

Luke grinned. "You won't regret it." He hung up and whooped out loud.

He'd make millions with his invention. Nothing could stop him now, then he and Laurel would get married, and he'd support this art career of hers that she wanted so badly. Then, their lives would be perfect.

Gregor tossed in his sleep. He could see Laurel's face, that funny crook in her nose, those big eyes with their long lashes. Yes, she was beautiful in her own way, but she had more.

When they'd talked, her love of art had been so apparent, she'd reminded him of himself as a struggling art student in his native Poland. Her passion was painting, she'd said, that if she couldn't express herself through art, she would wither up and die. He knew the feeling.

And her work had shown promise. There was passion behind her brush stroke, an earnest sense in her style.

He wanted to take her talent, help her mold it, shape it, to bring out the full potential he saw in her.

Laurel's face appeared again in his thoughts – those lips, those eyes. Something stirred deep in his loins. It wasn't just her talent he wanted to tame.

Luke made the final mark with his pencil. This was it. This was the missing program cue that would make his invention invincible.

"Holy crap, I figured it out," he said. He'd done it. He'd solved the flaw that had doomed his invention. It was such a stupid mistake, but had required him starting at ground zero to figure it out.

Now, it was solved. It was full speed ahead.

Nothing could stop him now. Within five months he'd have this invention ready, and airplane manufacturers would be vying for his product right and left.

Now, all he had to do was secure more money to get it built and get it tested.

He dialed. It rang twice, then …

"Yeah?"

"Anthony, it's Luke. I've got good news. I solved the problem. This thing is going to sell like crazy. As soon as I secure the patents –"

"How much?"

"You won't regret –"

"How much?"

Marcus swung by his house. Sure, it wasn't near his assigned area, but he was on a break, and it didn't hurt to show a police presence to keep his own neighborhood safe.

He rounded the corner. Suzie's Lexus was in the driveway. That was odd. She should be at work.

Maybe she wasn't feeling well. Maybe, did he dare think it, she was finally pregnant and had morning sickness. That would be awesome. They could start a family – one, no, two kids – and be the perfect family.

He let his motorcycle purr up to the curb and killed the engine. Marcus slipped inside. He didn't want to scare her. "I'm home. Sweetie? Are you feeling all right?"

There was a sound in the bedroom. He walked in.

A naked man jumped out of their bed, covering his genitals with his hands, eyes wide.

What the hell?

Suzie sat up with a jerk. "What are *you* doing here?" she demanded with a huff.

LAX was crowded. She spotted Luke and waved, running over to him. She threw herself into his arms. "I've missed you so!" It had been six months, and all she wanted to do was be alone with him.

Luke broke the embrace. "Baby, I have news, real good news."

He could attend her school's art show? "Yes?"

"The Close Call detector."

The what? "Your invention?"

"It's ready to be tested again."

"Now?" Not this again, not when she'd only just arrived. The last time had put a damper over her entire stay. Luke had holed up in his dorm room, trying to figure out what had gone wrong, when they should have been going out, hitting the beach, running together, having fun. "Are you sure it'll work this time?"

"Positive." He shouldered her bag. "Come on, we're due at the field in an hour."

The same two pilots were at the airfield waiting for them. This time, Floyd Charestimi and Andrew Stanton were smiling. "Luke," one of them said, "Why don't you and your lady friend ride along? There's room."

Laurel looked over Luke. He was grinning like a little kid with a secret he could barely contain. This was no test flight. This was a "let's do this for the heck of it" flight. She pretended to punch his arm. "You already tested it, didn't you?"

"A few times," he admitted, taking her hand. "But I wanted you to feel a part of this."

She squeezed his hand. "Let's go up and give it a try."

Ten minutes later they were in the lead plane and had reached altitude. Luke's device was so small it barely poked out from below the instrument panel.

"Here he comes," the pilot said. "It should be going off right about-"

An alarm sounded, filling the plane. It banked instantly.

"How far away was he?" Luke called out, above the sound.

The pilot checked something. "Five thousand feet."

Five thousand? As in, a mile? "But if two airliners were each going 500 miles per hour, they'd cover that amount of space in no time," she said, sitting on the edge of her seat, "Isn't five thousand feet too close?"

"Not for us," the pilot said. "We're small planes. But your boyfriend, we call him 'Genius', rigged it so we can set it for anything within ten miles. That works fine for airliners." He killed the alarm. "Not only that, but, as you saw, it can instantly take over the controls." He laughed. "It just whips the plane to one side or the other before you even know what's happening. We've been checking it out all week long. It's like a thrill ride. Want to give it another try? See how it works if the other plane is climbing and doesn't see you?"

"No, no, no," she said. "I believe you when you say it works." She smiled at Luke. He'd done it. He'd really done it. "What's next?"

"I've got to get a lawyer, make sure the paperwork is in order so that no one can steal my idea, then I approach Boeing." He took her hand. "This thing is ready to take off, literally. Quit art school. Come back here to California and live with me."

Laurel turned over. It was morning. Luke was still sleeping. He looked so handsome, with his dark hair spilling over his forehead.

He wanted her to quit art school, just let it go when she'd worked so hard for it. *Oh, Luke, why is it all right for you to pursue your dream, but I'm supposed to let go of mine?* She'd have to have a heart-to-heart with him and make sure he understood that her goals were as important as his.

Luke stirred and opened his eyes. "Hey, you."

"Hey, you," she said back. She couldn't help reaching for him, pulling him to her. They really did belong together … didn't they?

Laurel watched Luke, seated across from her in the little bistro they liked so much. She picked up her wine. "I propose a toast," she said and held it out. "To the success of the Close Call," she said.

Luke clinked it with his.

A stocky guy with dark hair sauntered up.

Luke jumped up from his chair, acting awkward. "Meet Laurel Rebecca Trenton," he said. "Remember that name. She's going to be a famous artist one day." He turned to her. "This is Anthony Amalfitano. We grew up on the same block."

So, he was from New York City. Laurel held out her hand, and they shook. "Nice to meet you."

Odd, he wasn't letting go of her hand. And she didn't like the way he was crowding her space.

Luke looked uncomfortable. "I'll, uh, get another chair." He stepped away to get the waitress' attention.

No, don't go, Luke.

Anthony smiled as he locked his eyes on hers. "He didn't tell me you was a blonde."

Obviously, this mental giant did not know basic grammar.

He edged even closer, breathing on her. "I have a thing for blondes, natural blondes, I mean." He paused. "You a natural blonde?"

The nerve of this guy.

"You are, aren't ya?" He looked her up and down. "I might just whisk you away. You and me, you'd like that."

Laurel hid the urge to shudder, kept her smile tight, and wiggled her hand free. There was a travel sized sanitizer somewhere in her purse.

Anthony swooped in, invading her space again. "Your last name's Trenton, huh? Makes me think of New Jersey."

If only Luke had introduced her with a fake name. Where was he, anyway?

"Maybe someday I'll be buying a paintin' from ya."

That'd be the day. Even if they had grown up together, she really couldn't see Luke hanging out with a guy like this. She had to get away. "If you'll excuse me …" She didn't wait for a response but jumped up and went to shoulder past him.

Anthony leered at her, looking her up and down. "Tall, lith," he murmured, licking his lips as she passed.

Lith? Lithe was pronounced lyth, you Cretan. Longtime neighbor or not, she wanted nothing to do with this jerk.

CHAPTER NINE

Gregor Andrysiak sat on the patio of his home in Spain and read Laurel's email.

"Latest attempt … Still not happy … It's missing something, but don't know what."

Poor kid, she sounded stuck.

He clicked on the attachment and expanded it full screen. Wolves racing through a thick forest.

Yes, yes, it was good, very good. She'd gotten the fur right, hard to do. But she was right, it lacked that certain something.

Was it the lighting?

Was it the tonal quality of the colors?

He sat back, studied it some more. "It needs to be more chromatic," he said aloud. Yeah, that was it, more chromatic.

He hit "respond" and typed his reply.

"Laurel, Your subject demands more vibrancy. Maybe it's your paint. Try a more concentrated color."

He hesitated and looked out over the railing. God, but the Mediterranean was gorgeous. It was alive, powerful, with a rhythm all its own. He added a post script, "If you could see the ocean from here, you'd know exactly what I'm talking about. Sometimes you have to experience something to be truly be able to paint it."

Luke came up behind her, toweling his hair dry.

"At your computer again?"

"Gregor, I mean, Mr. Andrysiak, has been critiquing my work. He thinks this painting could benefit from using more concentrated colors." She turned the computer screen so he could see.

Luke barely glanced at it. He shrugged. "Color is color."

Hardly. But she couldn't expect him to understand. Most people just looked at a painting and decided whether they liked it or not. They didn't process it in a way that told them *why* they liked it.

He pulled on his shirt. "As soon as you move out here, I'll want you to help me get things together, file the proper papers, all that," he said. "We need to have it at the patent office within the month."

Whoa. She'd never agreed to move out. "Luke, we didn't discuss -"

"I know, I'm making you into my secretary, but this is what's going to determine our future." He winked. "You can't argue with that logic."

Yes, she could and she would. "Luke, we need to talk -"

"I want to be responsible for you. I'm the breadwinner."

This again, he was like a broken record. "I told you before, I can take care of -"

"I know, I know," he said. "It's so cute when you say that."

Cute? She fumed. *Cute?*

Marcus pulled the Mazda into his driveway and sighed. It had been a long night, catching speeders and cleaning up after a pickup truck had plowed into three other vehicles, a case of open beer cans, still on the seat beside him. Idiot.

Time to see if Suzie had cleared out. He got out of the sports car and found his house key.

He'd been staying with his brother for a couple days in his swanky house to give Suzie enough time to move out. Let have her skinny, lily-white lover, he was done with her, the lying bitch.

He went to open the door. The key wouldn't go in the lock. He was overtired, had tried to put it in upside down.

He tried again. What the heck? It didn't work that way, either. The lock was silver. The key was gold.

Shit. Suzie had changed the locks.

He pounded on the door. "Suzie, open up." He paced, hammered on the door again. "Suzie!"

Maybe her car was in the garage. He hurried over, stood on tip toe and peered inside. Sure enough, the gold Lexus was there. So, she was home but just pretending not to be. Damn, her.

He stormed back to the door and pounded on it again. "Suzie! Damn it, I'll break this door down if I have to." Let the neighbors peer out their windows, he didn't give a shit.

There was a sound on the other side. "Go away, Marcus," she said through the door.

Go away? Really? She was the one who needed to go away. "You had two days to move out. Now, get your ass out of my house."

"It's *my* house."

The hell it is. "I've got news for you. It's not your name on the mortgage."

"Maybe not, but possession is nine points of the law," she called through the closed door.

"You're in the wrong, and you know it."

"May I remind you - we were married with no pre-nuptial agreement."

So she was out to soak him for everything he had, was that it? "Fine, play your little game. I'm getting a lawyer. You can't take a lover and then take my house, too."

He stormed back to the Mazda, got in and peeled out. And here he'd thought she was the perfect woman. What a damned fool he'd been. They'd had nothing in common except for the sex.

The waitress set their breakfast plates before Luke and Laurel. "Enjoy."

She breathed in the aroma. Their omelets were served with fresh avocado and mango with salsa on the side. Sometimes she really missed California.

Laurel gazed out over the patio railing. The ocean was a hundred yards away. "Smell that fresh sea air, Luke."

"Uh huh, sure," he said as he attacked his breakfast.

"We'll have to take a walk on the beach." It would, no doubt, stir her creative juices, and she'd fly back to Philly with all kinds of inspiration and begin yet another painting. The three she had in progress were all different, as though she was still deciding her style. But she liked each one for its own qualities. It was like what people said about having children, each one was different, yet a parent loved each of them just as much.

"So, you can tell them when you fly back Sunday and that you're withdrawing from school, right?"

Her fork stopped midair. Who said anything about her quitting school? She was "this close" to graduating. He had to be joking.

But he was looking at her in earnest, as though this was a done deal.

"Our art show is in a month and –"

"There'll be plenty of other art shows."

There he went, interrupting her again. "Besides that, I have three months left before I graduate."

She'd already begun applying for artist retreats and looking into special studies in China and Norway, things she'd written him, if he would only pay attention. That was one thing they needed to get straight. Luke simply didn't listen to her.

She tried again. "I really want to –"

"All that can wait. I need you here."

"For what? I can't design your components. I can't build your devices."

"No, but you can do the footwork, like, check out state regulations for new businesses. California is a *bear* for trying to start a business."

It was time to put her foot down. "I'm not your secretary."

"No, you'll be my wife."

Not yet, I'm not.

Luke watched as Laurel slammed her clothes into her suitcase. "You're being stubborn," he said.

"*I'm* the one who's being stubborn? Really?"

"Don't go. We've still got tomorrow."

"No, Luke, you and your invention have tomorrow. I'm obviously interfering here."

Jealous of an inanimate object, this was just great. Maybe her period was about to begin, maybe that was why she was being so bitchy. "Look," he said, grabbing her arm. "Our future depends on this. Don't you see that?"

She stared into his eyes. "All I see is you being so wrapped up in this Close Call idea, that you've lost sight of everything else. You've pulled out of school, for goodness sake, forsaken getting your degree. I'm sure your parents are proud." She shook him off and returned to packing.

"Of course I quit. The school wasn't supporting me. I showed them my schematics, showed them how it works, and they *still* refused to plug any money into it." Surely, she had to understand what he'd been through. "So I'm doing it all on my own. But now that I need your help, you won't come through for me." And that's what hurt the most. He wasn't asking her not to paint. He was merely asking her to devote time to him, first. After all, they were both going to benefit from this. "Once it's all sold and the money is rolling in, you can return to school, if that's what you want."

She threw up her hands. "You don't get it, do you?"

"Get what?"

"That I have a life, too. That I have dreams that need to be fulfilled."

Crazy talk. "So be fulfilled, just … later. Right now, tell the art school you're quitting, then come back to California and be my assistant."

She groaned and shook her head.

"Laurel, please, I beg you."

She tossed in her toothbrush, zipped up her case and grabbed her purse. "I've called a cab. Goodbye, Luke." She hesitated. "I can't wear this anymore." She twisted off her diamond ring.

What? No! His heart lurched in his chest. "Laurel, don't do this," he pleaded. "We can talk about it."

"We *have* been talking about it. You simply refuse to listen to what I have to say."

"Don't shut me down, not when I need you most."

"Oh, no, Luke, don't try to lay this on me. You made all these plans without consulting me. Like I'd agree to anything you said, be some puppy dog, blindly plodding along behind you. I tried to explain what was going on in my life and you completely ignored me, just barreled over my words, interrupted me, cut me off. All you care about is what *you* have planned. That's not the type of marriage I want to have." She handed the ring back to him and bit her lip.

His heart stopped. "What are you doing?"

"I'm sorry, Luke. I thought you were 'the one', but I was wrong. Goodbye."

He watched her walk toward the door. "No, Laurel, don't go. We can talk about this."

She waved a hand in the air, dismissing him. Then she was in the elevator and the door slipped closed behind her.

Marcus parked across the street from his house, out of the gaze of the street light. Suzie and her *lover* were in there. How dare she do that to him, play with his feelings then play him for a fool.

Damn her. He hit his fist on the steering wheel.

He'd fallen for her, hook, line and sinker. And now she was taking him to the cleaners.

The front door opened. Something was happening.

He crouched lower in the driver's seat, watching.

There she was, now, wearing a dress so tight it ought to be against the law. Her lover followed her out the door. Osh, he was lily white. They were joking about something.

Sure, laugh it up while you're living in my house. Why not, you're not the one paying the mortgage.

Three little kids suddenly ran out the front door.

Marcus powered down his window.

"Mommy, mommy, don't go," the children beseeched her.

Shit. Suzie had children? She'd never mentioned them, ever. She must have had them stashed in Texas somewhere.

Suzie gave them each a hug and sent them back into the house. "The babysitter will give you ice cream but only if you're good," she called after them.

Suzie and Lily-White Lover got in the Lexus and left.

Marcus started his car. He'd seen enough.

Laurel opened the door to her apartment and spotted the wolf painting. She hesitated. Had she really thought it was good?

It was weak. The colors were too muted. The way she'd rendered the faces, they lacked the hunger, the predatory essence she'd envisioned.

She frowned and dropped her bag, walked over and yanked the painting off the easel. She hated it. Laurel smashed it down on her knee, over and over again.

It's shit. It's shit. It's shit.

The tears fell down her cheeks, and she fell to her knees. *Damn it, Luke, why did you have to be so stubborn?*

She cried until she was all cried out. He'd maintained his position even to the end, not even attempting a compromise.

Stop dabbling in your silly little paintings, Laurel, come be my freaking secretary. Like hell, she'd stop painting.

He drummed his fingers as he held the phone to his ear and waited for Laurel to pick up. Finally …

"Laurel? It's Gregor. I had to call you as soon as I saw your email." He knew he was talking too fast, but he couldn't help it. "This painting, the one of the wolves? You completely redid it."

"Yeah, the first one was crap. I tore it up. I had … a situation. Nothing you need to hear about."

She sounded down, but he had news to cheer her up. "Well, this one isn't crap, far from it." No, he'd examined it on his computer screen and marveled at the strokes, the fire in her presentation. It was far beyond what he'd seen her do to date. "Could I add it to my showing in Madrid next month?"

"What?" She sounded dumbstruck.

He repeated the offer. "I add a student's works to my exhibitions sometimes." Oh, gosh, she probably thought he was going to take advantage of her art, claim it as his own. "It'll have its own placard, giving you credit."

"You're serious? I never expected this. Oh, my gosh, I've got to sit down or I swear I'll faint. Oh, Gregor, I'd be honored to be part of your exhibition."

"Good. Ship it over." He hung up. Once he saw it for himself, he'd determine if she was as good as he suspected. If she was, he had another surprise, one she'd be a fool to turn down.

Marcus watched downtown Las Vegas come into view as his brother drove. They were in his maroon Jaguar, nice. He eyed the leather in the high-end luxury sedan. Yeah, he had a vehicle with leather seats, too, but his conniving wife had it now. "I feel like a damn fool," he muttered.

Winslow looked over. "Why's that?"

"It's pretty bad when a law enforcement officer has no clue his wife is cheating on him, wouldn't you say? And then trust her to move out when she's actually changing the locks." He wouldn't be surprised if she'd had her lover move in.

"Peter will get the ball rolling. He knows his stuff, handles all the firm's divorce cases."

Yeah, shove it off to someone else. He'd been hoping his brother could do it, but Winslow only handled corporate law, mergers and takeovers and high-powered shit like that. He was proud of his brother, sure, but did some stranger have to delve into his finances and decide how things would be divvied up? "I should have known she was a liar. Said she liked football then asked me what an 'inning' it was."

Winslow cracked a smile. "Love is blind, my brother."

"I get a cut rate for being family, right?"

"Consider it my gift to you. Peter Willoughby is a top notch divorce lawyer. I want you to have the best."

"The sooner I get rid of Suzie, the better off I'll be."

Luke looked up. Shit. What was *he* doing here?

"Thought I'd look up my buddy while I was out here on business," Anthony said, pulling up a chair. "Of course, you realize this isn't merely a social visit."

His stomach clutched. He wanted to be anywhere but here.

Anthony leaned in. "Your loan's coming due soon, dude. My uncle don't like it when people ain't paying him back."

"You uncle? I though *you* loaned me the money." This was bad, this was really, really bad. Rumors had circulated about Anthony's family back when they were in junior high, sure, but who really listened to such things?

"It's family money, Luke. First I sent you two grand, so that's due –"

"You never said when I had to pay it back."

"– then I sent you three more, then five more after that."

Ten grand. It was an enormous sum when you barely had two hundred dollars in the bank. "Listen, I can pay you as soon as the device sells."

"It'd better sell fast."

"These things take time."

"Shut up, you little wimp. If you don't have the money, all the money, by Friday, then I'm going to have to come visit you again." He frowned. "I'd hate to see anything happen to our friendship, but family comes first." He reached out.

Luke flinched.

"You're shaking like a rabbit." He patted his hand, then his voice turned hard. "Pay back my money, and it'll all be good between us, Luke. Just honor your end of the bargain."

CHAPTER TEN

Marcus shook hands with Peter Willoughby, his divorce attorney. "We're going to make this as painless as possible, right?" Listen to him, he sounded like he was talking to a doctor. Get out your lawyer's scalpel and slice my share to Suzie as thin as possible.

Peter Willoughby opened a file and made a couple of "uh huh" sounds as he flipped through the papers. "In looking over her filing, she's asking for the house, the Lexus and annual support for her and your three kids in the amount of -"

"They're not my kids."

"I see." He scribbled something. "Did you adopt them?"

He might as well tell the attorney everything. "I didn't even know she *had* any. They were living with her mother in Texas until this whole marriage blew up." He squirmed in his chair. "I caught her messing around on me, in my house, my *bed*, no less." He would have tossed out the mattress if Suzie hadn't changed the damn locks. "She's out to soak me."

Peter Willoughby smiled at his frustration. "Look, I know it's rough. I handle cases like this all the time. We'll see that she doesn't soak you. Now, let's talk about what *you* want to see happen."

Laurel plopped into her easy chair and shuffled through her mail. Bill, bill, advertisement, junk mail ... what was this?

It was from overseas.

She opened the envelope. What the heck? It had to be Gregor who sent it.

She found the note and opened it.

"Dear Laurel;

As you can see, I've enclosed a ticket for you to come to Madrid. I want you to be here for the art exhibit, to be present so I can introduce you.

Your Raging Wolves picture is too vibrant, too mesmerizing for you not to get first-hand exposure from this event. You are a fine artist and this is your chance to shine on the international stage.

Your friend, Gregor."

There was a plane ticket inside.

Laurel jumped up and shrieked for joy. She was going to Spain!

Luke waited at the airfield, biting his lip. Where were they?

Finally, a small plane appeared on the horizon. He watched it come in, land and taxi over to park.

Floyd Charestimi and Andrew Stanton got out.

"So, Luke," Andrew called over, "what have you got for us to test today?"

He took a deep breath. "I want to propose something new."

"Another invention? We're all ears."

"Actually, this is an opportunity." He had to convince them. They were his last hope. "You know how the Close Call detector works. You've both seen it in action."

"Should have been in planes years ago," Floyd agreed.

Oh, heck, just blurt it out. "I need investors. There's no moving forward without more capital. I've tapped out my bank for loans, maxed out my credit cards, used all my scholarship money – I'm broke." He gestured to where he'd parked. "I'm about to sell my car. It should bring in five or six grand."

"And then you're without wheels," Floyd said, "Which would really leave you stuck."

Andrew spoke up. "What's the cash going toward?"

Asking questions, that was a good sign. It meant the pilot was considering it. "I need to apply for the final patents – there are three. I need to set up the manufacturing location and get this thing off the ground, so to speak."

The two pilots shared a look.

Floyd set a hand on his shoulder. "Let's sit down and talk about this, son."

Laurel tossed in her bed and realized why she wasn't sleeping. There was a light coming in her window.

She got up to shut the blinds. There was movement just outside the window.

"Luke? What are you doing out there?"

"Come back to me, Laurel."

Her heart ached, but she couldn't go through that emotional rollercoaster again. "It's not that easy. We show our true selves by what we do. You already showed me that I'm not important to you."

"But you are," he insisted, his voice muffled by the window pane. "You *are* important to me."

Sure, now he said that. But where had his priorities been before their break up?

He looked at her with puppy dog eyes. "Can I come in?"

Through the window? Funny that he could cross the void between the waking world and the unconscious one, but he needed her permission to enter the window. "I don't think so, Luke. It's tough enough, just seeing you this way."

"When I have money, I can take care of you."

"Luke, don't you see? How am I going to know my talent is good enough to stand on its own if I don't make my own way? I can't rely on you and your accomplishments to see my art gets out there. It's got to be recognized for its own worth."

He hung his head. "I miss you, Laurel. I miss you more than anything."

I miss you, too. Or maybe she missed what she'd *thought* he was like. But that had been what she'd wanted him to be. It wasn't reality. No, his actions had shown her a different Luke. "The school art show is tomorrow, I need to get some sleep," she said. "Goodbye, Luke."

Laurel eyed the clock as she sat at her easel. It was eight in the morning. Since Luke's window visit, she hadn't been able to sleep. The sense of melancholy was too overwhelming.

"Oh, Luke, we could have been so good together," she whispered, dabbing more paint on the canvas. She sat back, studying it. Where the idea for it had come from, she didn't know. Usually, she sketched out the figures before taking paint to board. But last night had been different.

She'd dived right in, pulling the brush down in sad, sorrowful-looking lines as she created two lovers desperately trying to reach for one another across a dark, wide chasm. Lost in the Abyss, she would name it. Yes, it was a good name for the painting, the one that would expose her feelings to the world and show how her heart had been broken.

The school art show reception was black tie. Laurel recognized the mayor and a local politician whose name she didn't recall. There was Teddy Swan, the guy who owned five car dealerships and did his own commercials, urging viewers to "Come on down," like that game show did.

Elan came over, towing a man with a diamond stud in his nose. "Laurel, I want you to meet Marcel Blount, art critic."

She shook his hand. "Of course, thank you for coming."

Marcel nodded, but looked bored.

Elan forced a smile. "Laurel is one of our up and coming artists. Gregor Andrysiak is sponsoring her to go to Madrid and be in his exhibit later this month."

That got his attention. Marcel looked at her with new appreciation. "That's quite impressive. Gregor only mentors those he feels are qualified."

Really? She thought he was just being nice to a student who needed direction. "He's not mentoring me, per se," she felt compelled to explain. "It's one exhibit, and only one of my paintings will be in it."

Marcel smiled patiently. "Don't be so sure. Gregor doesn't extent invitations like that on a whim."

"I thought he helped out art students all the time."

"He does, my dear, but only a select few."

"So, he truly sees something in my work," she muttered, amazed.

"Which painting is yours?"

"This one." Laurel gestured. "I call it, 'Missing Home.'" It was a childish name, but as soon as it had popped into her head, it had stuck.

Marcel nodded as he studied it. "Raw emotion artfully revealed, fascinating."

"Gregor considered it for his exhibition, but it wasn't completed in time. Anyway, I was flattered that he even invited me."

"I'd say he's testing the waters to see if your talent is truly worthy. Just being invited to join his exhibit is high praise indeed, but don't be surprised if he offers you more." He moved off.

More? What did he mean by that?

The night continued. Teddy Swan, the car dealer, wandered over her way. His breath broadcasted that he'd hit the hard booze.

"You're the prettiest lady here. How come you're not on the arm of some dude?"

A pang hit her heart and suddenly it was like she was back in front of Lost in the Abyss, painting her heart out for all to see. She shook it off and composed herself. Two could play this game. "How come you're not on the arm of some fabulous fashion model?"

"That was wife number three," he said and chuckled at his joke. "No, wait, she was number two. The pharmacy heiress was number three." He leered down at her, trying to see down her dress.

Not much to see there, pal. Both she and Theresa had grown up to be flat chested. Maybe she should opt for a boob job like her sister had.

"How old are you?"

Twenty one. "Sixteen," she lied. That ought to make him move along.

Instead, he edged closer until he was practically leaning on her. "Really, now?"

Dumb move, Trenton. She pushed him off of her. "I think wife number four is looking for you," she said and extracted herself.

Peter Sabastian maneuvered over to her. "Congratulations."

On being invited to Spain, he meant. "Yes, I'm looking forward to seeing Madrid."

"No, no, I mean your painting." He pointed.

There was a card attached to the easel for "Missing Home." It was in bold letters: SOLD.

Theresa drummed her fingers on the table as she took the call.

"Baby," her husband slurred on the phone. "I'm going to stay here in Seattle a while longer."

She pulled the phone away to stare at it. He couldn't be serious. They'd been apart for ten months already and now he wanted to stay even longer? Honestly? It was his druggie friends who were at the root of this. They got high together and that was their world. "Have you found more work?"

"It'll come," he assured her.

Yes, but when would the money come? Setting up stages and running lines for sound equipment had seemed like fun. That's how they'd met years ago, when she was dancing in a traveling show and he'd been the audio tech. She'd found him funny, easy going. They'd smoked a joint together, but it was his thing more than hers.

But over the past two years, things had escalated. Dirk wasn't just doing marijuana. He'd discovered harder drugs, higher highs. He'd changed.

Now, getting high was all he did, all the time. Every phone call, his words were run together, his thoughts disjointed.

How many times had she broken up with him, only to give in to his charisma? She had to get through to him, had to lay down the law and mean it this time.

"Dirk, if you won't agree to go to rehab, then I don't see a future for us," Theresa said on the phone.

"You're over reacting, Theresa. I'm fine, babe." He paused and there was the sound of him inhaling something. "It's cool. See you in a couple of months."

"Damn it, Dirk. Get clean." Or we're through.

The line went dead.

Great, just hang up on her. That was the last straw. She'd had enough. It was time to call it quits and get a divorce.

There was movement in the doorway. Arielle was home from school. "Come here, honey," she said and gathered Arielle in her arms.

What was going to happen to them if she had to support her daughter all by herself? Maybe she should hire a detective first, to document how Dirk wasn't fit to be a parent.

Luke punched in his account information and felt a thrill serge through him. Floyd Charestimi and Andrew Stanton, his two test pilots, had each invested one hundred thousand dollars. After they earned back that money, they'd be getting a percentage of the business, of course, but now he had capital to get things moving. First up, paying for the final patents, a lawyer, his business license and setting up the supply line he'd investigated and seeing that was in place.

It would take up most of the two hundred thousand, but the two pilots had mentioned they knew a couple other guys who might be interested in investing, too.

He'd get this venture going, then fly out to Philadelphia and camp out on Laurel's door and wait for her to come home from art school. He could see it now. She'd round the corner, spot him and drop everything to run into his arms.

They'd make up and the ring would go back on her finger. Maybe he should insist that they get married right away. Yeah, that's what he'd do. There was no way he was going to let her slip away from him.

The 747 touched down and the flight attendant's voice came over the PA system.

"Ladies and gentleman, welcome to Madrid. When we get to the gate, we'll be deplaning through the forward left and mid section's left doors. Thank you for flying Century Airlines."

Laurel peered out the window of the 747. She was here, for real. This was amazing. She gathered her belongings from the overhead bin and headed into the terminal.

Gregor was waiting for her as soon as she cleared customs. He'd flown in from Malaga just an hour earlier. He looked tanned, happy.

They air kissed.

"This place is amazing," she said. "The countryside as we flew in, I saw flocks of sheep, then the city appeared, sprawling in the distance. I wanted to paint it all."

"I warn you, once Spain gets under your skin, you may not want to leave," he said.

"I can see why. It's gorgeous here," she said.

"Not as gorgeous as where I live on Costa del Sol," He took her suitcase from her. "This way."

The rental car was tiny, like a toy version of an American car. He pulled out of the parking garage and into the maze of traffic. Good thing he was driving, because she would have caused an accident, staring at everything. "Where are we going?"

"We're staying with a friend of mine." He shot her a wink. "He's a count."

Her jaw dropped. She was going to meet royalty, honest to goodness royalty. This was like being in a fairytale. She'd have to call Grams and let her know.

Suddenly, she felt totally out of her element. She knew nothing of continental protocol. "Wait. What do I do when I meet him? Do I curtsy? Do I call him 'Your Highness'?"

Gregor laughed. "No, silly. You shake his hand and say, 'How do you do?' and then," he shrugged, "then you just be yourself."

OK, she could do that. Gregor sure moved in different circles than she did.

The Count's home was a mansion on a tree-lined street. An electronic gate opened for them once Gregor spoke into the intercom. A two story home with vines climbing up the sides and arched architectural features was before them.

"Nice place," Laurel said.

"That's the groundskeeper's quarters."

They kept going, and Gregor pulled up to a massive building like something out of a movie.

Laurel stared. It was a palace. At least, that's how she would have described it. "Wow."

"There's our host," Gregor said, pointing. "Shall we?"

The Count stepped off the front veranda. He was tall and thin and not a very handsome man.

Laurel watched as he and Gregor greeted one another with a hug and kisses. That's right, guys did that kind of thing in Europe. She stepped up, hand extended. "I'm Laurel Rebecca Trenton. How do you do?"

"We must be related, we're tall, and we both have a crook in our noses," he joked. He leaned closer. "Only, you wear it better than me. Welcome to my little abode, Laurel. Call me Bernard."

He pronounced it funny, like Bare Nard. She'd have to be alert to how she said it.

He took her arm. "Let me show you around. Do you like horses?"

He had a couple of horses? She'd ridden a pony once when she was six, that and in her seaside meditation.

"Next to dogs," Bernard said, "they're my favorite animals."

Hers, too. She smiled. He wasn't stuck up at all. She was going to like it here, she could just tell.

CHAPTER ELEVEN

"Here's your room, Madame," the maid said, opening the door for her.

Room? It was more like a suite. A huge poster bed had oodles of pillows. At the windows, long silky drapes fluttered in the light breeze. No, not windows, but garden doors to a private balcony. She stepped out and let the sun play on her face.

Bernard had already whisked her away and shown her his stables. The man had ten horses – ten. And when he'd confided how much the stallion had cost, she'd nearly choked. So much for telling him how she'd once ridden a pony at the fair.

She stepped back indoors just as Gregor knocked on her open door. "Find everything OK?" he asked.

"I wanted to show you something," she said, gesturing him in. She opened her suitcase, pulled out her latest painting and freed it from its bubble wrap.

"What's this?" he said, taking it.

"It's called 'Lost in the Abyss,' "she said and watched his face intently. Did he like it?

"My God, Laurel," he said. "Every time I see your work, you utterly amaze me." He looked from her to the painting and back again. "Let's show the Count."

"He's a patron of the arts?"

"Of course. How do you think we got to be friends?" He gestured her out of the room ahead of him. "Come on, this way."

They found the Count in his study. He looked up from a massive desk, surrounded by floor to ceiling bookcases. "What have you got there?"

"Laurel brought this painting with her. She carried it in her suitcase. I want you to see it."

"All righty." Bernard took the painting in both hands and held it out before him. His eyes shot from one area of "Lost in the Abyss" to another as he took it all in. "My God, it's like it's crying out to me."

Gregor took it from his friend. "You felt it, too? It causes an instantaneous, visceral reaction. I can't explain it." He turned to her. "Do you mind if I keep it in my room this weekend, Laurel? I want to study it some more."

He was certainly making a fuss over it. "Of course," she said. She had her own request. "Do you mind if I check out your art collection, Bernard? I spotted a Matisse in the hallway that I've only seen in books."

He waved her away. "Enjoy yourself, my dear. We'll call you when it's time for dinner. And we'll see you that get a good night's sleep so you're not jet lagged. After all, tomorrow's a big day."

The art exhibit was held at the home of Lady Alejandra. Gregor pulled up and parked alongside the catering trucks. "We of the working poor," he joked.

Laurel looked up at the turrets of the castle-like residence. Lady Alejandra's estate was even larger than Bernard's. Gregor sure had friends in high places.

They went inside. It could have been Buckingham Palace. There were gilded mirrors, lavish furnishings, thick rugs, chandeliers, candelabras, statues that belonged in museums.

A woman in her sixties with too many facelifts was walking toward them.

"Gregor, darling," she greeted him, taking both his hands.

They air kissed.

Lady Alejandra pulled back and passed an eye over her. "And this is –?"

"Lady Alejandra of the House of Cantebria," Gregor said, "may I present Laurel Rebecca Trenton of Philadelphia, art student."

Laurel put on her brightest smile. Bernard may have been casual, but this woman obviously took her station in life serious. "I'm honored to meet you, Lady Alejandra. Thank you for having me." This time, she *did* curtsy.

The next two hours were spent setting up Gregor's paintings and ensuring that they were spaced at specific intervals with sufficient lighting. It wasn't so much setting things up as commanding where they be put. Lady Alejandra's houseman relayed their needs, pointed here and there and the other servants scurried to do his bidding.

"No, no, facing more in this direction I think," Gregor said.

Laurel nodded. He was right. The man knew his staging.

The houseman gestured. The servants jumped to see it done.

She wandered off to peek at Lady Alejandra's private gallery. Gregor had said she was a fan of Spanish painters, carried over from her heritage, no doubt.

"You like them?"

The voice had come from behind her. Laurel blushed. "Lady Alejandra, forgive me. I didn't mean to intrude without permission."

She waved away the concern. "You're an artist. Artists don't abide by the same rules as most people."

"I suppose so." She gestured, arms sweeping wide. "Your collection is simply amazing – El Greco, Velazquez. I think I saw a Goya over there."

"Oh, that old thing. I only keep it to impress people." She waved it off. "I like new artists. They see things with such vibrancy and a zest for life."

Did her art have vibrancy and zest? Other people would decide that. She could only paint the way her heart told her to paint.

Lady Alejandra ran a finger down a statue of a nymph frolicking in the flowers. "I'll be interested to see your painting, my dear. Gregor seldom disappoints me when he introduces new talent. You see, I'm known as the ultimate voice of new artists in Europe."

Which meant that one wrong word from this woman, and her future in art was on the line.

"I hope you like it," Laurel said. If Lady Alejandra didn't, then she'd better find a new career path.

Laurel emerged from the room and snagged an appetizer off a food tray. She hadn't eaten since breakfast.

Gregor crooked his finger at her and called her over. "You need to verify your work is presented correctly, too."

She gulped down the food and looked about. She hadn't even seen "Raging Wolves" since they'd arrived. "Where is it?"

He took her by the elbow.

They were in an alcove near the bar. Two paintings were on easels. "Raging Wolves" was figured prominently, even more so than the one of Gregor's with which it had been paired. It felt so good to see it there. She shot him a look, eyes shining. "Thank you, it looks great there."

"And the other one?"

Oh dear, her manners had deserted her. She should compliment him on his work and tell him how nice their two pictures played off each other. She glanced over to see which one he'd chosen to display alongside hers. It was …

She gasped. "You put up 'Lost in the Abyss' as well?" Her hand flew to her heart. "But, but, you said you only chose one artist, and only one painting, any time you featured a student artist."

He took both her hands in his. "Rules are meant to be broken." He looked deep into her eyes, holding her gaze. "Remember that."

Luke pulled out his check book. He had twelve thousand left in the account. Next up, was giving Anthony Amalfitano back his ten grand. It would only leave him with two thousand dollars available for unseen expenses, but he couldn't leave his old friend waiting any longer.

He dialed Anthony's number in New York.

"Yeah, talk to me."

"It's Luke, in L.A. I have your money."

"Yeah? Well, you're two days late."

Late? "We never set a time frame for when I had to-"

"My Uncle Sal don't like it when people don't pay him back."

Great, he was bringing his uncle come into the picture again? "I borrowed the money from you, not him."

"You borrowing from me means you're automatically borrowing from my family, you understand?"

All right, fine. He had the money, so the loan would be paid in full, no matter who got it. "I'll send you a check for the ten thousand dollars."

"News flash, Luke. You're late paying it back, so you owe more."

"Hold on a minute, you never specified a time or said anything about -"

"Interest has been added."

"Interest? What interest?" It was no fair that Anthony was suddenly changing the rules. "This was a loan between friends."

Anthony chuckled. "You now owe me twenty-five grand."

He couldn't be serious.

"Twenty-five grand, Luke. Don't make me mad. I may be on the East Coast, but I have associates and I know where you live." He hung up.

Luke's heart pounded. This couldn't be happening.

Gregor found Laurel and guided her to the foyer. "The art exhibit guests are arriving," he said.

He watched as she ran to a mirror and began checking her makeup. Like she had anything to worry about.

There was movement on the spiral entry stairs. It was Lady Alejandra of the House Cantebria, now wearing a stunning gown for the evening's event.

He straightened his spine. She needed to know how much they both appreciated her patronage. "My dear Lady Alejandra," he said. "I had to do a double take when you walked up; you're such a vision in that dress."

"Stop trying to flatter me, Gregor," she said and jutted her chin at someone outside. "That man getting out of the Bentley? Have you met him?"

"I don't believe so."

"That's Prince Igon. Don't get on his bad side, but do keep him away from dear Laurel. He'll devour her as his latest conquest."

"Thanks for the information."

Lady Alejandra whispered, "He'll maneuver her to a corner, cover her with compliments while he gets her drunk, then tell her that his name means 'rising' before going in for the kill."

Now back at his elbow, Laurel emitted a little whimper. Apparently she'd heard.

Lady Alejandra's voice became louder. "Prince Igon, welcome to my little soiree. It's been too long." She pulled him over. "This is our artist for tonight's event."

Gregor gave a slight bow. "Nice to make your acquaintance. I'm Gregor Andrysiak."

"Ah, the painter."

No one light a match. The man's breath was pure fumes.

More people trickled in. There were more introductions. Some of them he knew and greeted warmly. They paid little attention to Laurel, but then, why would they? She was a mere student in their eyes. They didn't realize how special, how innately talented she was.

"Gregor, darling," said a woman in a tight gown, breaking into his thoughts, "It's about time you finished more paintings to show us."

Who was she, again? Then he had it – Lucille, married to an industrialist in his eighties. She'd undergone more plastic surgery. Her skin was so tight he'd barely recognized her. He took her hands and kissed them. "Lucille Buchanan, you look lovely. Have you lost weight?" That line had sold more paintings than he could count.

The evening continued. About seventy-five guests were there, he estimated. He made an effort to speak with everyone. One-on-one contact was a better sales tool than most people realized. He'd lost sight of Laurel. How was she holding up? She was probably charming the pants off all of them.

Lady Alejandra, drew him aside. "I'll introduce you now." She led him to the far end of the hall where there was a raised floor set off by pillars, a perfect stage for an event like this.

She took the microphone. "Attention, everyone." She paused as the room went quiet. "Thank you for coming to my little evening soiree. As you know, I am a patron of the arts and have the pleasure of hosting one of Europe's greatest painters. Without further ado, I wish to present Gregor Andrysiak."

He nodded and pretended to be flattered. Social events like this were not his cup of tea, but necessary if one wanted to sell their paintings. Gregor gave a self-conscious little wave and stepped up to the microphone.

"Hello, every -" It squawked with feedback. Great. He'd wanted to appear suave and austere in front of these people, not like some jackass who'd never handled a mic before. "Let's try that again," he said.

He thanked Alejandra and said how he valued her patronage. "They say an artist is always evolving. Over the past year, my approach to art has taken a turn. I think you'll see that if you compare my past work to these new pieces. I've entered a more nature-driven phase." He gave a short explanation. The guests were shuffling their feet. It was time to wrap it up. "You'll also see two paintings by a young lady I discovered in America and insisted she join me for this exhibit, Laurel Rebecca Trenton." He gestured for her to come on stage.

She blushed and stepped up, nodding hello to the crowd. She was the only woman in a short, cocktail length dress, but, to her credit, she carried it off as though she were a fashion model. It felt so right to have her here with him.

Gregor bowed. "We both thank you for sharing this evening with us."

It was time to work the crowd some more. He left the stage and took a post by his latest painting. Even if he only sold one, it would support him for a full year. *Stop thinking that way, like you're looking at this as merely a business. Selling art should not be like selling appliances.* Art was to be bought by the wealthy, yes, but appreciated by the masses.

The guests peppered him with questions. What was the inspiration? Why had he chosen those particular colors? What was he thinking about when he was at his easel? How did he know when a painting was finished?

He groaned internally, but kept a smile on his face. Couldn't these people come up with more original questions?

Lucille approached. "I bought two of your pieces, darling," she said, her words slightly slurred. She sipped her wine and played with his jacket buttons. "I wonder. Do you ever paint in the nude? Hmmm? It might be fun."

She ran her hand down his suit jacket in a pretense of straightening it. Her hand went way lower.

Whoa. His face heated up, and he stepped back. "Now, now, you're getting naughty," he cautioned her.

"My dear Gregor, you haven't seen how naughty I can be."

Lady Alejandra appeared magically beside him and caught Lucille's hand, leading her away. "Why, Lucille, I don't think you saw my prize winning roses."

He sighed. Thank goodness for a hostess like Lady Alejandra. She might be wearing a gown, but in his eyes, she'd just arrived in a suit of armor atop a white stallion.

Gregor looked around. His feet hurt. His stomach growled.

Where was Laurel? He scanned the room. There she was. She was talking to some man whose back was to him. Maybe the guy was about to buy her work. At least, he hoped so. Student artists needed that kind of ego boost.

He across the room and stepped up to them. Shit, it was Igon, and he was looking Laurel up and down like she was for sale.

Igon grinned. "Tall, svelte, you're a vision to behold. You know, a name is an indicator of the person. Mine means –"

This was not good. He got the prince's attention. "Please come with me, Igon, I have a painting that needs a manly assessment. Would you do me the honor?"

Two hours later, Gregor waved goodbye to the last of the guests. He'd sold all but two of his paintings, the last one to that warped little Igon.

Laurel approached with a plate of food.

She shrugged. "It's cold, but it's all that was left."

They found a spot outside on the empty patio. He gazed across the grounds of the estate.

Laurel looked as though she'd withstood the evening relatively unscathed. Still, she must have been overwhelmed. He patted her hand. "The evening was quite a circus, eh?"

She sighed. "At first, I was so in awe of all these people. I mean, I'd never met a prince or a marquis before. What would we talk about? How should I address them? But behind the money, they're just people."

"People who buy our paintings."

"They buy *your* paintings," she pointed out.

Lady Alejandra joined them. "Yours, too," she said, taking a seat.

Laurel looked shocked. "I sold one? Really? Oh, my gosh. It was 'Raging Wolves,' wasn't it? It fit with Gregor's theme."

Their hostess shook her head. "They both sold. In fact, 'Lost in the Abyss' created a bidding war. The buyer ended up paying triple your asking price."

Laurel blinked in amazement. "Triple?" She reached out and gripped his hand. "Oh, my gosh, Gregor. I sold both paintings. For more than I thought."

Gregor smiled. The look on Laurel's face was priceless. This was why he'd brought her here, to realize the impact her art could have on others.

He drank in her eyes, her legs, that tight butt. If only she realized the impact she was having on him.

CHAPTER TWELVE

Laurel found their host, Bernard, was already at the breakfast table the next morning when she came downstairs. "Good morning."

"How did it go?" he asked, folding his newspaper and setting it aside.

"Can you believe? Gregor sold almost all his paintings and both of mine sold." She took a seat as a server poured her coffee. "Thank you."

"Yours sold, very nice." Bernard stopped. "Wait. Both?" He sounded just as shocked as she'd been.

"Yes. There were, apparently, two people interested in 'Lost in the Abyss,' and that jacked up the price." She would never have believed that one picture would bring in nearly ten thousand dollars.

"So, who bought it?"

Gregor appeared. "One of the Dukagjini family members. Lady Alejandra said he was quite taken by it."

Bernard gave a snort. "It's too good for the Albanian bastard if you ask me." He checked his watch and got up. "I have a conference call. If you'll excuse me."

Gregor helped himself to the spread before them. "Eat up. We have a lot to do today."

They did? "But my flight is this afternoon."

"The paintings have to be packed up and shipped off." He made a gesture like it couldn't be helped. "That's part of being an artist, the not-so-fun part."

Laurel watched as Lady Alejandra joined them. She was dressed simply, in slacks and a floral print top, but the air of elegance still wafted about her.

"My dear," the older woman said, taking her hands. "You look so fresh after that long night. But then, you're so young."

Next to her, Gregor shot her a look. "How old are you, anyway, Laurel?"

"Twenty-two in two months." It made her wonder how old *he* was, but it would be rude to ask.

Lady Alejandra sighed. "Twenty-two. Just a baby." She led them to the great hall. "I had the staff put your paintings in here, your boxes and bubble wrap, too." She pointed to the materials in the corner. "I'm off to my women's group. Have fun, you two." She bade them goodbye and left.

Gregor handed her a box. "Pack them securely just like you did the one that you mailed to me. A note is attached to each painting and will tell you who bought it and where to send it."

Hmmm, shouldn't she include a note saying, "Thanks for buying my work?" Apparently such things weren't done in the snobby art world. "I'll write out the mailing label first and then pack it up."

"Smart girl."

She went to work, grabbing packing materials and sitting on the cool marble floor.

Two hours later, a staffer came into the room. "You have a visitor," he announced.

Bernard stepped inside. What was he doing here?

Gregor stopped wrapping up a painting and greeted his friend. "Couldn't make it last night so you're joining the party late, eh?"

"I'm here to claim my painting."

"There are only two that didn't sell," Gregor said, gesturing to the un-sold paintings. "Which one did you want?"

"Actually, I want Laurel's," Bernard said. "The one she brought on the plane with her."

What was he talking about? He knew it was already sold. She went up to him. "But I told you at breakfast, 'Lost in the Abyss' was sold."

"Sold to the wrong person," Bernard said. "I convinced Dukagjini that he was 'ripping you off,' as you Americans say."

So, what was he saying? That he'd convinced this Dukagjini fellow to pay more for her painting? This was crazy. Once a painting was sold, it was sold ... wasn't it? That's the way it worked in America.

Bernard pulled out a check ledger and began scribbling in it. "I've out bid him." He tore out the check and handed it to her.

Gregor came closer, peered over her shoulder at the amount and did a visible double take.

Laurel accepted the check. What? Thirty thousand dollars? Her hands shook. "This is too much."

Bernard shook his head. "No, it's not. It's a stunning piece. Besides, it's an investment."

Gregor raised his eyebrows. "You never offered that much for one of *my* early works." He turned his attention to Laurel and nudged her. "What will you do with it, Laurel?"

"Are you kidding? What any recent grad would do, pay off my students loans as soon as I get back to Philly," she said.

It was time to leave Madrid. Gregor took her suitcase from her and set it in the rental car before getting behind the wheel.

There was a tug at her heart. Laurel paused in the driveway and cast a final look at Bernard's magnificent home. She'd felt like she was in a fairytale for the weekend she'd been in Spain. The trip was over already, way too soon, but she had to get back to reality.

"Your flight to Marbella leaves about two hours after mine, right?" she asked, getting in the car. Her arm bumped him, and he sent her a strange look. She must have hit his funny bone. "I'm sorry."

Gregor hesitated.

Oh, God, she must have really knocked into him. "Are you all right?"

Gregor turned to her. "I don't want you to go," he blurted.

What? She hadn't expected this. "Believe me, I'd love to extend my stay, but –"

"No, Laurel. I don't want you to go back to states. Not today, not any day. I want you to stay here, to study under my tutelage."

Was he serious?

"I support young artists, let them live at my compound for as long as two years while they perfect their craft. I oversee their work, encourage them and introduce them to the people who can make a difference in their art. Now, I want *you* to be my protégé."

She couldn't believe what she was hearing. Gregor wanted to take her on as his guest student, have her live on his estate in Marbella. Her heart pounded in her chest.

Part of her wanted to throw her arms around him in glee and accept, no questions asked. Part of her said to take a step back, to think this through.

Wait. She had to be smart about this. "But, but, I have school to finish," she reminded him.

"You graduate in two weeks. I already spoke to Marion's CEO. You've fulfilled your requirements; all your assignments have been turned in. They can send you your diploma."

"What about my apartment? I've got projects in the works that I need to complete."

"They can be packed up and sent to my place on the coast."

She thought of all that needed to be done. It was an apartment, not a home. Most everything she cared about inside of it had to do with art.

He looked at her in earnest. "This is doable, Laurel. All you have to say is, 'Yes' and we'll make it happen." He looked at her long and hard. "I see real talent in you, Laurel. I want to help bring that talent out."

She couldn't hold it in any longer. She squealed and threw her arms around his neck, hugging him like there was no tomorrow. "Yes!" she exclaimed. "I'll be your protégé."

She opened her apartment door in Philadelphia and looked about. There were her art materials – paints, brushes, canvases. They would all have to be packed up, shipped to Spain.

What else? Her clothes, of course, but everything else, was all just "stuff." Pots and pans, they were nothing to her. Her coffee maker, OK, that would be going with her. A girl had to have her morning coffee, after all. The furniture had come with the apartment, so that stayed.

Yeah, this would be a breeze to pack up.

As for her car, she could put a "for sale" card up on the bulletin board at Marion, and one of the students would snatch it up in a heartbeat.

She could be back in Spain within the week, easy. Then she'd paint alongside Gregor, learn from him, try his techniques, and let her art flow unobstructed. She couldn't wait.

Her cell rang. "Laurel? It's Theresa."

Something was wrong, she could feel it. "What is it?"

"It's Grams," Theresa said, and started to cry. "She collapsed. She's in a coma."

"Oh, my God."

"They think she had a heart attack, but no one is sure. I'm about to get on the road now with Arielle to drive to San Diego. You've got to fly out to California."

"On my way."

Theresa met up with her at LAX. Laurel hugged her and then crouched down to greet Arielle. "You OK, honey? You are? That's a trooper." She stood back up and adjusted her shoulder bag. "How's Grams? Has she come out of the coma yet?"

Theresa shook her head. "The doctors aren't optimistic."

That wasn't good. "Let's get to the hospital. I want to see her."

The hospital smelled of antiseptic and pine scented cleanser. They went up to the eighth floor. Arielle took a seat near the nurses' station. Her sister had said she hadn't made a peep the whole drive there. What a good kid.

Theresa pointed at one of the rooms, and Laurel stepped inside.

Grams was hooked up to a breathing apparatus with sensors and wires everywhere. She looked so frail.

Laurel turned and stared at Theresa. "You didn't tell me she wasn't breathing on her own. You deliberately kept that from me. How dare you?"

Her older sister passed a hand over her face. "I thought it'd be best to go over everything once we met up in person."

Laurel went to retort, but bit her tongue. Poor Theresa, she looked miserable. She'd raced here from Vegas, and tried to keep Arielle shielded from the worst, all while dealing with the doctors, with the insurance company and making the decisions. "I'm sorry, Theresa, I shouldn't have lashed out at you like that."

A doctor came in. He had a robust build with gray at his temples. "Ladies," he said, with a nod. "I'm Dr. Johnson. I assume this is the entire family?"

"Yes," they said unanimously.

"We just got the scans back," he said. "I'm sorry but there's no brain activity."

No brain activity, how could there be no brain activity if she was lying right there in front of them, alive? Laurel found her voice. "What are you saying?"

Dr. Johnson looked grim. "You have a decision to make, ladies. All that's left to do is to decide when to shut of the life support machines."

Pull the plug, he meant. Why didn't he just say it? He marked a chart and turned away. "Just let the nurses know when you're ready to let her go."

Laurel felt the tears threaten and she flung herself across the hospital bed. "Oh, Grams, Grams," she sobbed. "I love you."

Laurel opened the front door. Gram's house was silent. She walked through it alone, expecting to see her grandmother step around the corner any minute, hear her laughter.

But there was nothing.

She had to face the truth.

Grams was gone.

She recalled that moment when she and Theresa had nodded at the nurses to unplug the life support systems.

She'd slipped away just seconds after everything had been switched off. The only indication that Grams had been aware of them was a slight smile that had crept onto her lips.

Then … nothing. She was gone.

Now, the house seemed so lonely without her.

There was a knock. Had Theresa forgotten her key?

Laurel stepped up to the front door. "Yes?"

"Laurel?"

"Oh, my God." She flung the door open. "Luke? What are you doing here?"

"I heard about your grandmother. I'm sorry. Is there anything I can do?"

That was so sweet of him. She slipped into his arms. The tears trickled down her cheeks. "I never thought this would happen," she hiccupped. "I thought when I left for art school, I could come back, and everything would be the same. That she'd be here, baking me goodies, cheering on my latest painting."

"I know," he said, burying his chin in her neck. "I know."

"I miss her so." All the things she'd meant to say – thank you for taking me in when my parents died, thank you for not getting angry when I lashed out at you when all I really wanted to do was cry, thank you for just being there, for being a rock who I could depend on, no matter what - she'd never said any of that to Grams. Even though she'd meant to.

She'd moved into this house as a knock-kneed kid who didn't even acknowledge that Grams had been hurting over her parents' deaths, too. But Grams had never complained, had never pointed out her shortcomings and had never once withheld her love.

And now she was gone.

Luke slipped his arm around Laurel as they sat on the couch. He kept the pressure light. Would she reject the intimacy, tell him to knock it off?

But, no, she eased into him as though longing for his touch and set her head on his shoulder.

He relaxed. Maybe they could be a couple again, the way they were supposed to be.

"Tell me about your invention and what stage you're at," she said. "What's the latest?"

"I, uh, have two investors. You met them, the two pilots who tested the device."

"That's good."

"And I set up the corporation in Nevada." Wait until she found out he'd named her as partner, along with his investors, Floyd Charestimi and Andrew Stanton.

"Nevada? Why Nevada?"

"Tax purposes," he said. "California would have been a nightmare for a start up like mine. Plus, I've got the patents."

She smiled. "Wow. It sounds like it's really coming along, Luke. Good for you."

He sat a little taller. Laurel sounded really impressed. "There are a few things to be worked out, of course. Like, I have to repay this one loan."

"Oh? What loan is that?"

"A loan from a friend, or at least I *thought* he was a friend."

She lifted her head and looked over at him. "I don't like the sound of this. What's going on, Luke?"

He took a shaky breath. "I asked Anthony for money."

"Anthony, Anthony," she said, trying to place the name. Her face registered recognition. "That *weasel* you introduced me to? The guy from your boyhood street in New York? He gave me the creeps."

Yeah, so he'd gathered. She'd left rather than be around him. "He, uh, sent me ten grand altogether."

"And now he wants it back." She looked him in the eyes. "He's pressuring you for it, isn't he?"

More than she knew. "He now claims there was a time element involved and that I owe him interest." He regretted ever making that phone call – stupid, stupid, stupid.

"So, what does he want, an extra couple hundred in interest?"

If only. He swallowed, hard. "Twenty-five thousand."

CHAPTER THIRTEEN

Laurel was staring at him. "Twenty-five thousand?" she echoed.

It may have well been twenty-five million. "And I'm afraid he's going to send some goons after me." He turned away, couldn't face her. "I don't know what to do."

"How much money do you have?"

His face burned. "There's just a few grand left."

"Let's go to the bank."

It wouldn't do any good. "I already went through my bank for loans. They won't give me any more money."

"I can help you."

Sure, she could. She was an art student, she didn't have that kind of dough. "Look, Laurel, I appreciate –"

She held up a hand, stopping him. "My turn to cut you off midsentence," she said. She pulled a check out of her purse and held it up for him to see.

Luke peered at it. Banco de Espana? What the heck?

"I just sold a painting. It'll pay off this weasel and get him off your back." She hesitated. "I'm afraid for you, if you don't."

No, no, this was all wrong. *He* was the one who was supposed to make sure *she* was all right. "I can't take your money, Laurel."

"You don't have a choice," she said. "Besides, when your Close Call device is sold, you'll pay me back. And *I*," she said, looking him straight in the eye, "don't charge interest."

Two days later, Luke drove her to LAX. God, he wanted to hold her so badly, but they weren't back to being a couple, not yet anyway.

They stood inside the terminal near security. Couldn't she feel how much he wanted to take her in his arms, hold her close?

"It was good to see you again, Luke," she said, touching his sleeve gently. "Thanks for being there when Grams died, for listening to me blubber on and on."

"I told you, I'll always be there for you." He went to reach for her, but that barrier was between them, besides, she was all set to go to Spain for this protégé opportunity. He was too late, and he knew it. He let his arms fall.

"Keep working on the Close Call," she said. "I know you'll get it out there, and it'll be a success." She gave him a peck on the cheek, turned and trotted off.

No, don't go. His heart ached as she entered the security check point and disappeared.

Luke's heart winced. He'd win her back one day, he just had to.

Laurel stood on the balcony, hands on the railing, and looked out over Marbella. The Costa del Sol certainly lived up to its name. It was sunny, the countryside was green and the ocean blue, blue, blue. She breathed the salt air deep into her lungs.

Gregor came up behind her. "All settled in? Did you forget to pack anything?"

"I'm ready to start painting, so you can teach me everything."

He grinned. "An eager student, that's what I like. How about we celebrate your first night here with dinner? I know a little café that will make you wish you'd lived here forever."

She glanced back at the sea. She already wished that. "Actually, I'm really feeling the urge to put paint to canvas right now."

"You're in the middle of one, didn't you say?"

Yes, but that wasn't the one she was drawn to work on just now. "A new inspiration has hit me," she said. Ever since she and

Theresa had given the OK to have Grams' equipment disconnected, the urge to paint had been overwhelming. "It's something I need to do."

He nodded. "All right, El Morocco can wait for another night. Let me show you where things are in the studio."

Anthony Amalfitano watched the strippers on stage at Succulent Peaches as the morning crew mopped the floors and cleaned the place. Cheri was dancing slowly to a different beat, obviously high, but with those tits of hers, who cared? Vixen was looking good, very good. He liked the way she bent over and wiggled her butt at him, very nice. Maybe he'd have a little one-on-one time with them both after his uncle's visit.

There he was now. He stood up.

Uncle Sal hustled over, moving his bulk as fast as he could between the empty tables. He plopped into a chair next to him, wheezing.

"Uncle Sal, good to see you. What's the rush?"

"Damn federal agents are out to bust my chops," he said, trying to catch his breath. "Anyway, that's my problem, not yours."

Right, because he wasn't part of his uncle's upper tier. He knew his place in the lower ranks, much as it grated on him.

His uncle looked around and stared at the dancers. "Mercy, would you look at those watermelons," Uncle Sal said under his breath. He shook his head to break the spell and tore his eyes away from Cheri's incredible breasts. "I only have five minutes. What you got for me?"

The money, it was always about the money. "Right." Anthony pulled two fat envelopes out of his inner jacket pocket. He'd had a tailor create over-sized pockets because he only dealt in cash. "Count it if you want. Twenty grand even." He sat back. It had been a sweet deal, easy as cake to shake down his childhood friend. Uncle Sal didn't need to know that he'd pocketed Luke's extra five grand for himself.

His uncle smiled, reached over and patted his cheek. He slipped the envelopes into his own deep pockets. "Now, Anthony, you're my nephew and I love you, but deals like this are small potatoes. Come up with something that *really* brings in the bucks and you'll impress me." He shot him a look that said, "Pay attention." "Understand what I'm saying?"

Yeah, he understood. Bring in the big money and he'd get to move up the ranks, not have to deal with small potato operations like Succulent Peaches, his little strip joint.

Anthony watched Uncle Sal leave. Come up with a big deal, he'd said.

Wait a minute.

Maybe there was a way to make Luke his cash cow.

Laurel turned over in bed and stared out the window. The blue light of the moon was splashed across the balcony outside her room. In the corner, leaning against the wall, was her latest painting, "*Ignorance,*" nearly finished with Gregor encouraging her, it was really taking shape.

Gregor, she was drawn to him. Those eyes, that mouth. Sometimes she couldn't stop watching him. Did he feel it, too?

She got up, opened the French doors and stepped outside on the balcony. The ocean was glimmering silver in the night below Gregor's compound.

His home wasn't a mansion, but it was impressive on its own. Across the courtyard was his house with its Mediterranean architecture and red tiled roof. She was in a separate building comprised of three bedrooms, each with an en suite, and a tiny living room bordered by an efficiency kitchen.

Student quarters, Gregor had called it.

She was the only one in the student quarters for now. He was so generous. No rent, free meals, and all the art supplies she needed, what more could she ask for?

There was a shadow.

Laurel gasped.

"It's just me."

"Luke?" If he was here, visiting her in Spain, then she was in a dream state, like when she was meditating. "What are you doing here?"

"I didn't mean to disturb you. I just," he sighed, "I just miss you. It was hard to see you when you flew back to California for Grams."

Yes, Grams. Her guilt was driving her to paint "*Ignorance*" for Grams' sake. "It was hard to see you, too." Going back to California had brought up those feelings that she still harbored for him, but they were tempered with sad feelings, sad that he'd thrown away their shared path.

He shot her a dark look. "You should have stayed. We'd be together if you'd only listened to me."

If *she'd* listened? "Luke, I –"

"You didn't take to heart what I had to say."

The nerve of him. Had he listened to her when they were together? "Luke, you have to stop thinking of us as a couple. We're not anymore."

"We should be."

"But we're not." She turned and stepped inside, shutting the French doors behind her as he watched. He couldn't come in unless invited, she knew. Well, she wasn't inviting him.

Gregor dabbed more paint onto his canvas and pulled back, judging the effect. He was painting beside Laurel in the studio. They'd been at it all morning and much of the afternoon. It was time for a break.

He stood up and came up behind her leaning in to study her work. God, her hair smelled so good. Laurel was a statue, staring at her painting with her brush poised midair, but not moving.

He chuckled. "Mesmerized, are you?"

She shook off her trance. "What?"

"You're not painting, just staring. What's wrong?"

"I'm lost." She sighed, putting down the brush. "It's like I'm trying to pack everything into it – childish stupidity, realization, guilt."

"Your strokes are strong." He placed a hand on her shoulder. "Get up, stretch your muscles. We'll step back and look at it from that perspective."

She rose and followed him to a spot about ten feet away to study her work in progress, "Ignorance."

He knew what it needed, but this was her creation. She would have to come up with the solution.

"I don't know," she said, tipping her head one way then the other.

He hid a smile. She was like a puppy dog, turning its head to figure out a puzzle. Only, she was much more stunning to look at than a puppy dog. He set the thought aside. He had to help her, that's why she was here as his protégé. "Look at it. What does it say to you? What words pop into your head, first impression?"

She nodded. "OK, yeah, I get it. It says, 'Stupid child, caught up in pain and wanting others to feel that pain, too.' Then this part –," she gestured, "– says 'Now I realized how terribly I treated you when all you gave me was love.'" There was pain in her voice.

"Laurel?"

Suddenly, she turned into him, pulling him in and pressed her cheek to his shirtfront.

His arms encircled her. She felt so soft, so warm, so … right. Holding her in his arms was just as he'd imagined. "Laurel," he whispered, reaching to cup her face in his hand. He'd wanted to kiss her so badly, and here was that moment.

"Oh, Gregor, all she gave me was love," she whimpered, crying on his shoulder.

He froze, then let his hands drop. All he wanted was to give her love, too, but she was hurting. She'd only pulled him to her because she was grieving and needed to be held. Now was not the time to admit to his feelings.

Besides, there were nearly fourteen years between them. Maybe she wouldn't want him.

Luke put on the Boeing badge.

"This way," the young man said, leading him to a locked door.

There was a buzzing sound, and his escort opened the door.

He was here, in the inner sanctum of one of the biggest aircraft manufacturers in the world. That he'd been granted an interview with the head engineer was nothing less than a miracle. Thank God that Floyd Charestimi and Andrew Stanton had tapped into their vast network of airline contacts and managed to get him a face-to-face with Arthur Lathem.

The elevator took them to the top floor, where the doors opened. Before him was a huge reception area with a massive counter.

A woman stepped up and smiled at him. "You must be Luke Sullivan. This way, please. Mr. Lathem is expecting you. He has a busy schedule but has five minutes for you."

Five minutes? All he got was five minutes? How could he possibly make a presentation in five minutes? His charts, his diagrams, he'd have to forego all of them. "Five minutes is fine."

She came to a pair of wooden doors and opened them. "Mr. Lathem, this is Luke Sullivan, your ten fifteen appointment." She let him step past, then closed the doors.

It was just the two of them. Luke hurried forward, hand out. "Mr. Lathem, thank you for seeing me."

"Sit down, son. What's this invention of yours all about?"

"Well, I don't know if you know anything about avoidance systems –"

"Hell, I'm head of Boeing's engineering operations. I didn't get here by sitting on my ass all day." He gestured to the wall behind him.

Luke's face got warm. Damn, the man had degrees from the highest schools in the country. "Yes sir, I'm sure you didn't. My device, I nicknamed it the Close Call, will ensure there is never a mid-air crash again."

"That so?"

He had Mr. Lathem's attention. So far, so good. He opened his brand new briefcase, pulled out his business card and handed it over. It was time to do his big spiel. "Here is how it works."

He launched into an abbreviated explanation, hitting all the major points.

Mr. Lathem chewed on a pencil as he listened. "Hold on a second. So this Close Call of yours, how close can planes get before it sounds?"

"That's the beauty of it. You can set it to any range you want within twenty miles." He was going to make it only ten, but had rethought that decision and extended the range.

"What if you think it's set for twenty, but it's really set for five?"

"Good question. The Close Call requires you to verify the distance with a double check system, so both pilot and co-pilot are on the same page."

Lathem nodded. "What if you're flying in a high traffic area, like New York? You got Newark, LaGuardia, JFK, all those flights stacked on top of one another. The pilot doesn't want the controls jerked out of his hands just because there's another plane stacked below him."

"It can be switched off in an instant at any point, such as should you know you'll be flying into a congested area."

"Show me those diagrams you've got there."

An hour later, Luke stepped out of the Boeing building and into the Seattle sunshine. Clouds threatened in the distance, but where he was, all was sunny. He couldn't wait to tell Laurel about the meeting and how great it went.

Mr. Lathem said he'd present the idea to the board and see where they wanted to go with the information. "Expect a call within two weeks, son," he'd said.

Luke did a fist pump. All his dreams were coming true.

CHAPTER FOURTEEN

Gregor finished his coffee on the patio. Funny that Laurel hadn't joined him. It had become their daily ritual. Maybe she was still asleep. Maybe it was something else, some *one* else.

He thought back to the day two weeks ago, before when she'd reached for him and cried on his shoulder. Maybe she'd been playing with his emotions.

He looked up at the balcony for her room and scowled. He'd given her the best room in the student section, the one that looked out over the ocean, just like his room in the big house did. How had she rewarded his generosity?

She'd invited some guy into her bed.

Maybe that was why she was late this morning. Maybe she'd snuck the guy in again and they'd spent the whole night in each other's arms, kissing and –

He shook off the visual. He'd confront her when he saw her next. She wasn't here to mess around with young guys, she was here to bring her art to the next level. He'd have to set her straight, put his foot down, and then put aside his silly notions that she could ever find room in her heart for him.

He'd have the maid wake Laurel. He scoffed. If there was a guy in there with her, he didn't want to see him.

He opened the studio door. There was a bundle on the floor in the dark corner. What was that? It moved. It was …

Laurel, asleep in the studio, a blanket pulled up to her chin.

It wasn't a guy who had kept her from their morning coffee. It had been her art. Gregor suddenly felt better. He walked over and gazed down at her. She looked so peaceful, he knelt, reaching out to move a strand of hair off of her face.

Her painting caught his attention. He stepped over and let his eyes take in her work. Amazing. She'd gone over the strokes on

"Ignorance"' and made the childish part bolder, sharper, as if she was slashing out at the world.

She roused from her sleep. "Gregor?" She sat up. "Sorry, I fell asleep."

He swallowed hard. "Laurel, there's something I have to bring up, a 'rules of the house' kind of thing."

"Did I do something wrong?"

He might as well blurt it out and confront her with it. "I don't know." He hesitated. "Who was the guy you took up your room the other night?" he searched her eyes. Would she deny it?

"What guy?"

So, she *was* denying it. How dare she? "Don't play games with me. I know what I saw."

"Gregor, I never took a guy to my room. I don't know any guys here, only you."

She wasn't going to get off that easy. "You're here to advance your art, not add another notch to your bedpost."

She pulled back, blinked hard. "Whoa. That was totally uncalled for." She sent him a look of confusion, edged with anger. "I told you – I never took a guy up to my room."

"I saw him."

"Then you saw an intruder."

"The two of you were standing on your patio together, looking out to sea." And she hadn't exactly been dressed in anything modest, what with that sheer short nightie barely covering her rear end.

"Look, I don't bring guys to –" She stopped. "Wait. You saw that?"

Oh, so, now she was confessing. He ought to toss her out on her tight little ass, and send her packing right now. "Yeah, I saw."

"And did you see me go back inside and shut the door on him?"

Well, yeah, he'd seen that, thought it was odd, the way she'd stopped him from following her and closed him out. "I thought you two had an argument." Or something like that.

"Did you see what happened to him?"

"He, um, kind of disappeared." Her visitor must have jumped off the balcony, but that didn't make sense. Who in their right mind jumped off a two-story balcony?

She sent him a solemn look. "He disappeared, because he really wasn't there."

"Oh, come on, now."

"Do you meditate, Gregor?"

No. "Sometimes."

"Then you know how you can enter an altered sense of reality and connect with others, especially at night when our brains are more receptive. My old boyfriend from high school, Luke, he'd always talk woo-woo stuff. Now, I believe him. That's who you saw. He's in L.A., but he reached out to me that night."

She kept talking, but his mind barely followed. The guy had not been real. He hadn't really been there. He was on the opposite side of the world. Better yet, she'd called him her "old" boyfriend, meaning they were no longer a couple.

His mood lifted.

Laurel hadn't rejected him. She was still free to pursue.

The El Morocco was busy. They were lucky to get a table.

Laurel slid into the chair opposite him. She looked ravishing, even in a simple tank top and jeans.

Her eyes were sparkling, taking it all in. "It's a busy place."

"I know the chef. He never steers me wrong."

"Sorry it took so long to visit this place, but I just had to finish 'Ignorance' before it escaped me."

Like he didn't understand the compelling feeling to get inspiration down on canvas? "You did a beautiful job with it."

Three weeks after he'd found her sleeping in the studio, she'd finished it. This was their celebration dinner. He wanted it to be a special night. He hoped she liked his plans for later.

Before that, though, they needed to eat. He pulled two menus from the holder. "Fair warming. Save room for dessert."

The waitress came with a bottle of wine and two glasses. It was Rosa, the owner's daughter, who he'd mentioned to Laurel earlier. Mentioned? He'd gone out of his way to leave no doubt that she held no appeal to him. "Rosa," he said. "Is your father ever going to let me hang a painting in here?"

Rosa waggled a finger at him. "Don't expect me to stick up for you, Gregor. You know how my papa is." She pulled out her order pad, pen poised.

Laurel blushed. "The menu, I, um, can't read it."

He'd have to teach her Spanish. "Do you like crab?" At her nod, he spoke to the waitress in Spanish.

"What did you order?" she asked when Rosa departed.

"It doesn't matter," he said, and threw up his hands in a gesture of surrender. "Rosa's father never listens to me. But he'll come up with something spectacular, he always does."

Laurel giggled. "I'd love to paint this place."

It was good to hear her laugh again. Her painting had taken her to a somber place, had sapped the energy out of her.

"I like it here in Marbella, Gregor. It's so vibrant, so alive."

He sipped his wine, watching her. "Most people come for the beach, but there's so much more to see." And he wanted to show all of it to her.

Gregor pulled into his driveway, parked the car and jumped out, rounding it to open Laurel's door. He felt like he could do the hundred yard dash. Their dinner at El Morocco had been that much fun, that special. "Tell me about your sister."

"Theresa? She left the house at seventeen to be a dancer."

"Is she as tall as you?" Few women were at his eye level.

Laurel made a funny face. "Two inches taller. She's gorgeous, could have had any guy she wanted."

Like Laurel could? He led her around the side of his house, back where the trees encroached. "But she ended up with, what was his name again?"

"Dirk. She calls him Dirk the Jerk, not in front of their daughter, of course."

He had to ask, to find out where Laurel's head was focused. He was years older and wasn't looking to start a family, not at his age. "Do you want kids?"

"Me? Kids?"

"Seriously."

Laurel shook her head. "It's never even entered my mind. No, I don't think so. I'm too stuck on my art to have room for a baby. She smiled. "What about you, Gregor?"

"No kids."

"Anyone special in your life?"

"Not anymore."

"But there has been, hasn't there? A good looking fellow like you?"

She thought he was good looking, did she? He stood a little taller. "Maybe at one time."

"So, what happened?"

He shrugged. "It ended. Badly."

"And?"

"And she left me for another guy."

"Ouch. That would hurt." She gave a snort.

Was Laurel passing judgment with that reaction? Telling him that his former lover had been a fool? He hoped so. He led her to the back side of his house. "The experience made me a fortune, though. All my paintings after that were dark, sinister, sold like crazy." He chuckled. "Guess something good came of it, after all. Sort of like your paintings."

"Mine? They're not dark and sinister."

"No, but you paint with more passion when something happens in your life, something that touches your emotions."

They were at the bottom of the outside staircase.

"Watch your step." He led her up the stairs on the outside of his house. He couldn't wait for her to see the sight.

They gained the rooftop.

"I never knew this was here." She was drawn to the view and tugged him over to the half wall. "Wow, look at that."

Below them, in the harbor, hundreds of yachts were lit up with strung lights, the twinkling duplicated by the water.

"This is why I bought this place," he said. "It has a completely different view from what you and I see out our bedroom windows."

She lost her balance, and his arms shot out, catching her. "You OK?"

She giggled. "A little tipsy."

He slipped his hand around her waist, pulled her close. "This is nice," he said, fighting the urge to nuzzle her hair.

"Nice," she agreed.

He looked into her eyes. God, he wanted to kiss her so badly. "I want to –"

"I know," she said. "Me, too. But ... I can't."

He pulled back, nodded. It was their age difference, she meant. That many years between them, what had he expected her to say? She'd been gentle, kind even. "I can't," she'd said.

OK, he'd respect that. It would take a long, cold shower, but he'd respect that.

Luke turned the key in his door and heard the phone ringing. Most of his friends called his cell, not his landline. He ran over and snatched it up. "Hello."

"Luke? It's Arthur Lathem."

Holy crap, Boeing was calling him. This could be it. "Mr. Lathem, yes sir, how are you, sir?"

"Boeing has decided not to move forward with negotiations on your invention."

What? No, no, no, this couldn't be happening. His knees gave way and he dropped into a chair. "But sir –"

"We've decided not to purchase it because this is something Boeing doesn't install in its planes. We sell airplanes as shells, without seats, without engines, without landing gear."

He didn't know that.

"That's left up to the airline to buy, their expense. We install them, but they buy that stuff from other manufacturers."

"I wasn't aware."

"Son, that's what you need to do, take your invention to each and every airline and convince them to buy your invention for each and every plane they have in their fleet. With the international regulations about to be put in place, your timing couldn't be better."

"Yes, sir."

"You sell to every airline, you hear me?"

Sell to every airline, not manufacturers, not Boeing, not Airbus. OK he could do that. "I see."

"Now, I like you son, so I'm going to hook you up with the people who are in the position to make these decisions at every airline in the world. I'll be sending you a list of who we deal with so you don't waste your time. You call these people, tell them that I said to get these damn Close Calls purchased so we can install them here at our factory. Then you get those units built and delivered up here to Seattle as fast as you can, son."

"Yes sir."

"Between retrofitting and new plane orders, by this time next year, you'll be pulling in more cash in one week than, hell, I don't know, than someone like me makes all year long."

Luke ended the call.

Holy shit, it was all coming together. It was all finally happening and he was going to be rich.

Theresa pressed her hand to her forehead. This damn headache was back.

Below the stage by the front seats, Raphael clapped his hands for attention. "OK, everyone, take your places. Cue the music from the top. Let's go people."

Theresa hurried back up the stairs, holding her headpiece in place with one hand. For some reason, they'd been ordered to do a full dress rehearsal, totally unnecessary, if you asked her.

She got into place and set her feet, did the tra-la-la pose, that's what Arielle had called it, and waited for Raphael's cue.

"And one, two, three, here we go," he called out.

The music began. The dancers on the tiers below did their thing. "And one and two," Theresa counted in her head. "And step and step."

She listed left, caught herself and picked up the count.

"Stop, stop, stop," Raphael yelled. He glared at her.

Theresa gave him a faint smile. "Sorry."

Marissa, the dancer beside her, shot her a look. "You OK?" she whispered.

They got back to their marks.

"Here we go again," Raphael called out.

The dancers stepped forward in unison. "And one and two," Theresa counted down in her head. "And step and step."

Forty minutes later, Raphael dismissed them. Phew, she'd made it.

A costumer helped her lift the forty pound headdress off her head. She stretched her neck, leaning her head side to side.

Marissa came up to her. "I saw you taking Tylenol. Is it that time of the month?"

"This headache just won't quit." She'd had it three days now, totally out of character for her.

"They're working us too hard," Marissa said. "All these freaking promotional appearances at the airport, at the convention center, down on Fremont Street – whose brilliant idea was that? Like tourists don't already know Vegas has showgirls?"

Theresa smiled. Marissa liked to complain, but you couldn't argue with her logic.

"Hey, if that headache continues, I have a little 'something' that could make you feel better."

Theresa knew what Marissa was getting at – that little vial in her coworker's makeup drawer where she kept a hit of cocaine. She shook her head. "No thanks." She was probably the only cast member in a Vegas strip show who didn't do drugs, not after what she'd seen it do to Dirk.

She walked backstage to her dressing station, pulled off her dancing shoes, stripped off her G-string and joined the other girls in the showers.

She soaped up, letting the warm water flow over her body. Marissa was probably right, the extra hours out in the community to help establish the show, that's what had brought on the migraine. It had better ease up soon or she'd go certifiably nuts.

Laurel lugged her art supplies to the top of Gregor's house. The morning sun was just coming up and she wanted to experience this before the feeling faded.

The light to the east was brilliant red, almost unnaturally so. Maybe the light was different here in Spain, because she'd never seen anything like it.

She pulled out her camera and, framing carefully, snapped off some shots. They could be uploaded to her laptop later and opened in full screen view, a great reference for finishing what she would start painting up here.

She checked them on the camera's tiny screen. There, that ought to do.

Now, time for the actual painting. She got out her brush and paints, pulled a new canvas from her satchel. Funny how it seemed a part of her now.

Her easel was too bulky to drag up here, so she threw one leg over the fat perimeter wall and rode it like a pony with the blank canvas balanced before her.

Two hours later, Gregor emerged from the house below her. He was carrying two coffee cups and looking in the direction of the student portion of the compound, no idea she was up here.

She smiled. He was trying to determine if she was awake.

It felt a little naughty to spy on him this way.

From up here, she could see the broadness of his shoulders, the slim hips. Good looking men like him were usually snatched up right away. But he'd remained unattached, on his own all this time.

He turned back and disappeared from view but he was still on her mind.

She'd been so in awe of him when he'd come to the Marion school, she'd barely gotten up the courage to speak. Now, here she was, living in his compound half a world away. He was talented, accomplished, knowledgeable, admired around the globe and, OK, she had to admit it, handsome as heck.

Yeah, he was older than her, but the physical attraction was undeniable. What would it be like to be held by him, to have his lips swoop down to capture hers and –?

Maybe she shouldn't have stopped things that night that he'd shown her the rooftop.

"Laurel? Oh, there you are."

She threw a hand to her chest. "Oh, crap, you startled me."

"I saw your leg dangling off the roof. Thought I'd better hurry up here and see what was up." He handed her the extra cup of coffee. "You weren't about to jump off, were you? Leave me without even a kiss to remember you?" he teased.

Laurel caught her breath. If she ever did kiss him, he'd remember it, she'd make sure of it. "Actually, I was inspired." She hopped down and showed him the photos. "This is what you missed by sleeping in."

He leaned over her shoulder to peer at the small screen. He smelled of soap and men's cologne.

She could get used to that cologne.

"So, this is your latest inspiration," Gregor said. "Good thing you took shots of it for reference."

"Don't you?"

"When I see something that moves me? Sure, I do." He took a sip of his coffee. "It's just that you photographed the morning of a storm. The sky usually isn't like that."

He was right. It had looked more like a sunset than a sunrise.

"See down there? Boats are already getting prepared in the harbor. 'Red sky in morning, sailors take warning.' We'll have to batten down the hatches, so to speak, before it hits here tonight."

He was serious. "Just how bad do you think it'll be?"

"We'd better make sure we have candles."

CHAPTER FIFTEEN

The wind whipped about in the darkness outside, rattling the windows and scraping tree branches against Gregor's main house. When it gusted, it moaned, just like in the movies.

She peered out a crack in one of his living room shutters. Newspapers and other debris flew by. When he'd said it might storm, she hadn't quite believed him.

She believed him now.

"Laurel, come fill up these jugs with water," he called from the other room.

"Coming." She entered the kitchen and took the empty jugs from him. Their hands brushed lightly against one another and she nearly flinched, it was so intimate, so sultry. Had he felt it, too?

Gregor hesitated. "Yes, well," he said, then stepped back and into a small ante room.

The spell was broken.

He returned with his arms full of fire wood.

He couldn't possibly be serious. "Will it get that cold?"

"No, but the stove is electric," he said, dumped them near the fireplace. "It'll be kind of hard to make coffee in the morning without a source of heat." He crossed the room, opened a cupboard and pulled out a bag of marshmallows. "Dessert."

"Yum." She smiled. It would be like camping, only indoors, their private adventure. She finished filling the jugs and found him in the living room, piling a few blankets on the sofa for her sleeping spot. He'd insisted the student's quarters might flood. He would know, she supposed.

She watched him, liking the way his muscles strained against his shirt as he moved. Gregor had no idea how difficult it was getting to concentrate when painting alongside him.

The lights flickered.

She pushed aside the curtains and peered outside again. It was unbelievably dark. Rain hit the window like a slap in the face, then the wind whipped up and the rain slapped at the pane. She jumped back at the sudden onslaught. *Wow.* "I take it you've lived through one of these before and come out relatively unscathed."

"Well, it's not like we'll be in here for weeks and turn stark raving mad." He patted the couch cushion beside him. "Come here. Want to watch a movie?" He turned on the TV and flipped to the on-demand channel, scrolling through the titles. He highlighted one. "Ever seen this, Laurel?"

"A cop movie? No, not tonight. Scroll down and see what else they have."

Gregor flicked down the choices.

The TV died.

The house went dark.

"Shit," Gregor said. "There goes the electricity."

Laurel looked about, trying to see. It was pitch black. It must be how the pioneers lived. She raised one hand and couldn't see it in front of her face.

There was a shuffling sound. Something was in the house. Oh, God, did Spain have a problem with rats? She hated rats.

"Gregor, is that you?" She reached over for him but he was gone. "Where are you?"

Nothing. Just the wind, the rain.

"Gregor?" Shit, was she here all alone? She rose to her feet, hands in front of her, taking tentative steps. Her knee hit something. "Ah!" she winced.

His hands caught her. "It's OK. It's just me."

She hugged him back. "I've always been afraid of the dark."

"It's all right. I'm right here."

Yes, he was, he certainly was. His back was broad, she could feel his muscles. His breath wafted over her, Colgate fresh. His arms encircled her, strong and hard. There was a tug of longing between her legs. "Gregor, I want you." There, after tossing and turning at night from wanting him, she'd finally said it.

"Shhh." His lips found hers, brushing lightly against them, like a whisper.

She didn't want a whisper. She wanted a man.

Laurel kissed him back, pressing her lips hard into his, falling into it as though it was meant to be. Oh, God, how she'd hoped for this moment. She let the kiss linger, melted into him, pressed against his body and reached up to hold his face.

"Oh, Laurel," he breathed, breaking the lip lock. "I know you're not over Luke, but we have something special, too."

It was true, they did. She felt it in her core. From the moment she'd laid eyes on him at Marion, to coming here where every moment was like magic. Her heart beat faster, her senses came alive. "Gregor. I want this, but I can't promise you my heart," she said.

"Stay with me tonight."

Stay with him? She wanted to do a lot more than that. He was more man than she'd ever encountered before and there was no holding back. She ripped open his shirt buttons, kissed him hard and moved her hands to his fly.

His hands bushed hers aside. "Let me undo it."

"Hurry. I can't wait," she panted.

"Neither can I," he said. He picked her up in his arms and headed to his bedroom.

Luke dialed Laurel's number. It had been months since she'd moved to Spain. Everything was falling into place for the Close Call and he needed to share the news. It rang two, three times. Come on, come on, answer the phone.

"Hello? Luke?"

"Yeah, it's me." It felt so good to hear her voice again. "How have you been, Laurel? I read about your latest success."

"Only because you Google-ed my name. Yeah, my art is selling. It feels good."

There was a heavy silence.

He couldn't hold it in any longer. "I've got news of my own, Laurel. Close Call is really taking off."

"That's wonderful."

"Lufthansa, Columbian Air and United are in talks with me and my lawyer. We're going to sign any day now."

"Luke, that's great!" She sounded really happy for him. "I knew you could do it."

"Pretty soon every airline in the world will be jumping on board. Do you know what that means?"

"That you're set for life."

"It means that I can take care of you now, now and forever. Come back to me, Laurel. I miss you so much."

"Things are ... complicated."

So, she'd found someone. It stung but it was probably a summer romance. Yeah, that's what it was. He'd ride it out. They were too connected to ignore their eventual life together. "Let's reconnect when you come back to the states. I'm always here for you."

Theresa sat on the paper-covered exam table. Why were physician offices always green?

The door opened and the doctor came in, peering down at some paperwork. He looked up. "Miss Trenton?"

"Yes."

"Nice to meet you," he said as he tapped a pen on her chart. "You're experiencing migraines, huh? Your vitals look good. Let me check your eyes."

He shined a light in her eyes, had her open her mouth. He snapped off the light. "So far, so good."

He went through a litany of questions – eating habits, sleeping disruptions, sleeping positions, digestion and excretion. He stood up and used one hand to feel the back of her neck. "You're quite tall. What's your occupation?"

"I'm a dancer."

"On the Strip?"

"Hot Stuff at the Potenza."

"Are you one of those girls who wear the headdresses?"

"That's me. Six nights a week, two shows a week." Plus all those extra appearances and dress rehearsals.

"The headdresses, they're heavy aren't they?"

"It's like lifting weights."

"That's your problem. The migraine is brought on by muscle spasms in your neck and upper back. You just need some physical therapy."

"Are you sure?"

"Trust me. Physical therapy will do you wonders." He scribbled on a pad and tore it off. "Here you go. Your insurance will need to approve this."

"How long I have to be in physical therapy?"

"If it took six months to get to this point, it'll take maybe a year to correct it. It's physical therapy, not a miracle cure." He kept writing and tore off two more sheets. "This is a script for muscle spasms. And this one is for the pain."

Theresa thanked him. She was going straight to the pharmacy. She'd had enough of this migraine shit.

At the El Morocco, Gregor and Laurel stabbed their forks at the single slice of key lime pie in the middle of their table.

He took a bite and savored the flash of flavor. Across from him, Laurel was practically swooning.

"Have you ever tasted anything so good?" she breathed, closing her eyes momentarily as she gave in to the pleasure. She gestured with her fork. "You'd better cut it in half or I'll devour your share before you know it." She scooped up another bite.

It was refreshing to see a young woman demolish a dessert instead of pretend she "just wanted a nibble." But then, Laurel was like that – real, unpretentious, someone who enjoyed living life. "I have someone, a young woman, I want you to meet this weekend."

She shot him a quick look. "Oh, God. Not your former lover, I hope."

"Hardly. No, this is someone else. She's about your age, kind of a free spirit. I think you'll like her." He took a second bite and moved the plate in front of her. "Yours."

"You're killing me," she said and proceeded to polished it off, every crumb. "Delicious." Laurel pushed away from the table. "Now, we pay for it."

What was she talking about? She knew the ground rules – as his protégé, she didn't have to foot the bill for lodging or dining, silly girl. And now that they were lovers, he would have insisted, anyway. He signaled for the bill.

Outside, as they approached his Porsche, Laurel slid into his arms and locked her wrists around his neck. "We make a good pair, I think," she declared and kissed him. She pulled back, danced to her side of the car and got in his two-seater sports car. "So, shall we start with a one miler?"

He had no idea what she was talking about. "One miler?"

"To get you started."

Oh, that's right, she liked to run in the evenings. "I never said anything about running."

"If we're going to eat rich food like that, you'd better start."

His heart gave a lurch. He looked down at his stomach. He wasn't out of shape, was he? But he was closing in on thirty-seven, had heard of how much harder it was to fend off the pounds as one got older. Shit. "Sure," he said. "Let's start with a one miler."

Heck, she'd gotten him into meditating, why not running, too?

Theresa squeezed her eyes shut. This headache. Would it ever go away? Some days it eased but it was still there, striking at the most inconvenient times. She opened her eyes and looked in the dressing room mirror.

She was losing weight. She could see it in her cheekbones. Heck, who could eat with this monster headache stalking her.

"You OK, sweetie?" one of the other girls asked.

Theresa nodded. "I'll be fine." She cast a glance at Marissa's dresser drawer. She knew what was in there. She knew one hit of that white powder could make all this pain go away.

One hit.

It wouldn't be so bad to just do it this once.

Shit, she couldn't. Not after seeing what it had done to Dirk.

He'd been so fun, so loving and so attentive. She was sure she'd found her soul mate.

And then the cocaine use had gotten out of hand. Dirk had gone out partying and forgotten to come home. He'd eventually shown up, apologized and acted sheepish.

But it happened again. And again. Then he'd forgotten to put his paycheck in the bank. But he hadn't forgotten to cash it. Where was the money? He couldn't say. But she knew where it had gone, up his nose.

He lived for that next hit, that next line.

One time, he'd come home so boozed up and stoned he had trouble remembering her name. He'd seen Arielle, who was just learning to walk, and looked shocked that a little person was in their home.

"Who's that?" he'd gushed. "Where'd you find her?"

Theresa looked away from Marissa's drawer with its little vial. No, she'd forego the white powder.

She popped more Tylenol in her mouth instead.

"Just get me through tonight's shows," she groaned.

Gregor put his Porsche through her paces, zipping through the streets of Marbella with Laurel. He turned off and soon they were winding their way up a hill. It was good to get away from the tourist-heavy area with Laurel beside him.

Half an hour later, he pulled up to a massive gate.

The intercom squawked. "Are you expected?"

"Yes. Gregor Andrysiak and Laurel Trenton," he said.

She shook her head at him. "Laurel *Rebecca* Trenton."

"Too long," he said as the gate opened. "Your name takes up half your freaking paintings."

She scoffed. "Does not," she said.

They pulled through and were soon under a canopy of trees. Laurel was obviously in awe. Wait until the grove ended and the estate came into view. He hoped she wouldn't be overwhelmed by Josephine's immense wealth.

He parked. When Laurel got out, she stared up at the eight-story estate looming above them, an even bigger castle than the one Lady Alejandra had.

He came around the car and took her hand. "Shall we?"

A doorman greeted them with a bow. Josephine and Nikolai appeared at the top of the staircase almost before they could be formally announced.

Josephine bounded down the steps. "You must be Laurel," she squealed. "I've heard so much about you, I feel like I already know you. Isn't that silly?" The two hugged and acted like long-lost friends.

Gregor watched, amused. Guess he didn't have to worry about Laurel and Josephine getting along.

Josephine tugged on Laurel's hand. "I want to show you pictures from our orphanage program. We're doing such great work."

Nikolai stepped up and greeted him. "Let me show you where we hung your latest masterpiece. We couldn't be more pleased with it."

And he couldn't be more pleased with the check they'd sent. He only sold a few million-dollar pieces a year, but when he did, it was a thrill like no other to see the money in his bank account. He glanced at Laurel, scooting off with Josephine. He wanted to get her art to that price point one day. She had the talent, she just had to find her niche, the thing that set her apart.

Theresa entered the attorney's building. Time to get rid of Dirk the Jerk. In Nevada, divorces took a mere week. She found the proper floor and took the elevator.

A receptionist looked up. "Miss Trenton, yes?"

These people sure were efficient. Maybe divorcing Dirk would be relatively painless. She was shown to her attorney's office.

Peter Willoughby came around his desk and shook her hand. "Have a seat. Tell me about your situation." He took his chair and opened a file.

"I don't have many assets, just my house which we bought together, so I'm willing to split that," she said.

He scribbled.

Theresa took a deep breath. Here came the sticky part. "I *do* want custody of my child, sole custody, with no visiting rights."

His face tightened. "I see. It's his child?"

Unfortunately. "Yes."

"That could prove to be a little," he hesitated, "challenging."

"My husband's a druggie. I can prove it."

"I see you have papers, may I?"

She handed over the manila file. She'd looked at the pictures a dozen times. "I hired a private detective. He found a police arrest from five years ago." It had been while Dirk was on the road as the crew for that rock band. The record company must have smoothed things over because she'd never known about it. He'd also taken numerous photos of Dirk snorting up and documenting suspected drug buys. The P.I. she'd hired had been nothing if not thorough.

Peter Willoughby flipped through the file. "I think we can work with this, Miss Trenton."

Good. The sooner she got rid of Dirk, the better.

CHAPTER SIXTEEN

Laurel turned over in bed beside Gregor. It was the middle of the night, something was trying to get her attention. It was outside.

She slipped out of bed and felt night air envelop her as she moved to the French doors and opened them to the balcony. She stepped out and the moonlight showed silver blue on everything.

In the courtyard below was Josephine. Laurel could think of no reason why she'd be here in the middle of the night. She was lounging on the grass, wearing a billowing dress like something out of Marie Antoinette's wardrobe. She was playing with something small, a puppy, maybe?

"Josephine," she called out. "What are you doing here?"

Her new friend looked up and gestured quickly. "Come down and see what I have."

Laurel was suddenly at Josephine's side. It wasn't a puppy at all, but an infant. "How precious."

"I just found him," Josephine said, sounding bewildered. "Want to hold him?" She held out the child.

Laurel took him in her arms and looked down into his tiny face. He smiled up at her and cooed. He couldn't be more than a week old.

Josephine disappeared.

The baby grew until it was a five-year-old child with curled wisps of hair and a beguiling dimple.

Laurel gasped. This was amazing. "Who are you?"

"My name is Cristol." He stared at her with eyes much older than any child she'd ever encountered. "Don't be afraid. You're the only way I could reach her."

"Reach who?"

"My mother. I have a message for her."

"Well, OK." This had to be pretty important for a newborn to morph into a child.

"Tell her she'll have a life-threatening blood disorder, caused by her iron levels, and that if she doesn't deal with it by her fourth month of pregnancy, we'll both die. And that can't happen. Can you get that message to her?"

She nodded. *Iron disorder, get it checked out by the fourth month of pregnancy or you'll die.* "Who's your mother?"

"I thought you knew - Josephine." He smiled and disappeared.

Her eyes opened. She was still lying beside Gregor.

What an encounter, so real, so detailed. Laurel jumped out of bed and hurried to the studio. She placed a new canvas on her easel and picked up a brush. She had to do this while the sensation was still fresh, the emotions still raw.

This was what Gregor had been trying to convey to her – create art with your whole self.

She selected a clean brush, dabbed it in pigment and began to paint.

Theresa rolled her head down, pressing her chin to her chest. "Like this?" she asked the physical therapist.

"Yes, and hold it. That's it." He pressed his hand to the back of her skull. "Feel it?"

"Yeah." It felt tight.

"If you can, really stretch it. Pull your shoulders back, like you're squeezing a ball between them."

It had taken almost a month for her health insurance to approve this, but now that she was here, it was worth the wait. It seemed to make a difference.

The prescriptions had helped, too.

Too bad the co-payments were so high.

The only obstacle was that she had to come here after dropping Arielle off at school, instead of going home to get some much needed sleep. But if this strengthened her neck muscles, and got rid of her headaches, then this was what she would do.

"Anthony, I *said* you're dismissed."

"Huh?" He pulled his eyes from the dancer on stage who was massaging her tits at him.

Uncle Sal gave him a "get your ass moving" look.

All right, already. He knew when he wasn't wanted.

Anthony pushed away from the table, grabbed his jacket and strutted out of the meeting. He let the door slam behind him.

His stupid uncle had no idea how valuable he could be to the family. His sole responsibility was overseeing this strip club. Where was the challenge in that? When booze and nude dancers were your big draw, the money came flying in the door to you.

The club had reported profits every month. Uncle Sal didn't need to know he'd pocketed a nice chunk of change for himself each week.

He grabbed Frankie, his buddy, on the way out. "I need your help, Frankie."

"Anything you got, I'm in."

That was Frankie, always willing to participate, no questions asked. But then, he'd always had a thing for steel bats and batons.

"Nah, it's not a muscle job, Frankie. It's just divvying up the dough."

They went into a small back room.

"Grab some newspaper, Frankie," Anthony said as he spun the dial on the safe. "We got to wrap this stuff."

"Right, boss."

Anthony pulled out a sack and dumped it onto the table. Good, there had to be eighty or ninety grand there, easy.

He divided the money into eleven piles. The eleventh was smaller than the rest, less than half as tall.

Frankie noticed. "Hey, who's that for?"

None of your damn business. "No one. It's operating capital, that's all. Got to have money to pay the suppliers when they deliver goods."

"Yeah, yeah, I knew that," Frankie said.

Sure he did, the dumb schmuck. Actually, the small pile was going in his pocket, with Uncle Sal none the wiser. Heck, if no one else was looking out for him, then he had to look out for himself. That's how he saw it.

Frankie handed him a portion of the newspaper. It was the financial pages. Wrapping money in the financial pages, now there was a joke.

Hold on. That headline, what did it say?

He snapped open the paper.

The headline was in smaller lettering than most, but it seemed to scream out at him.

Young Inventor Signs First Deal, Becomes Millionaire Overnight.

He scanned it.

"Airlines eager to buy … new invention … aircraft avoidance detector … Close Call … quit school … Luke Sullivan."

Shit. His old boyhood friend had done it. He jabbed the article with one finger. "Hey, Frankie. Look at this."

"What?" Frankie hurried over and peered over his shoulder. "Close Call, huh?" He jabbed an elbow and grinned. "You need one of those in your car, Anthony, the way you drive."

"Shut your trap. I'm thinking."

Frankie returned to wrapping the money. "I sure wouldn't want to be there when my plane collided with another one," he muttered. "No sir. I mean, it's not like those airlines give you a parachute." He looked over. "So, Anthony, you thinking of flying somewhere?"

Yeah, California, to go see an old friend.

Laurel bit her lip as Gregor pulled his van up to the front of the mansion and killed the engine. "I'm so nervous. I just hope Josephine likes it." She'd used a photo that her friend had given her. If Josephine liked the photograph, then she had to like the painting.

"It's well executed." He patted her hand. "Every artist questions themselves over their first commissioned portrait. It absolutely looks like her."

It was the other element in the painting that had her worried. "I don't want her thinking that I'm butting into her business."

"Well, there's only one way to find out." He got out, opened the van's rear doors and pulled out her painting, wrapped in padding. "Let's present it to the princess."

Gregor had insisted her full name was too long, too self-indulgent. "You need a shorter name, one everyone will remember." He'd come up with a variation of her middle name, Becca. It felt right. "You can take a dramatic French last name for legal stuff," he'd said, "like you thought of, Becca de la Croix, but paint as just 'Becca'."

Ten minutes later, Gregor, Josephine and Nikolai were seated in front of her and her draped painting.

Laurel took a deep breath. Her hands were shaking. "This is my first piece under the name Becca. Before I unveil this, I want to thank you for commissioning a piece by me. If you have issues with any part of it, any at all, I can redo it."

Josephine waved away her concerns. "Silly, just show it to us, would you?"

Laurel pulled off the cover. Did they like it?

Josephine jumped to her feet, clapping furiously. "It's beautiful. Oh, Laurel, you've exceeded my expectations. Thank you." She ran up and gave Laurel a big hug.

"Wait," Nikolai said. "What's that part, there?" He approached and pointed.

Everyone stared.

Oh, no. Laurel glanced from one to the other.

Nikolai looked puzzled.

Josephine looked like she'd been struck.

Her new friend threw her hands to her face. "Oh, my God. Whatever possessed you to put *that* in the picture?" She turned and stared at Laurel.

How was she going to explain the little boy strolling up in the background? "It's your child," she said quietly.

"What?"

She'd better explain this and tactfully, too. "He came to me one night in a dream."

Josephine stared at her, looking puzzled. "A boy?"

"At first he was an infant then he aged so that he could talk to me." She pointed. "That's what he grew to look like." Oh, God, they were going to call her a nut case, label her a crazy artist.

Josephine turned to Nikolai, started to say something, leaned sideways and then wilted to the floor.

Nikolai caught her in a flash.

Servants rushed up.

Josephine's eyes fluttered open.

Laurel stared in horror. She'd insulted her new friend with the painting and now the poor thing had fainted.

Nikolai smoothed the hair from his wife's face. "I'll carry you up to bed."

"No." She clutched his shirt and drew herself up until she was standing. "It was the shock of seeing the painting, that's all."

Laurel found her voice. "Perhaps you should sit down." She took her friend's arm and sat on the sofa beside her.

Josephine gestured to her husband. "Show Gregor," she urged him.

"I will," he said, but he stayed right beside her.

"Now," she said, giving him a playful shove. "Go on, I'm fine."

Nikolai gestured to Gregor and the two of them went down the hall.

Josephine turned to Laurel. "I'm pregnant. We just found out." She touched her stomach and smiled. "We couldn't be happier."

Laurel took both her hands. "That's wonderful." There was something she was supposed to convey to the princess. She recalled it now. "Your iron levels, you have to get them checked out. Promise me you will."

"OK, but why?"

"That's what the little boy, Cristol, said he came to me, to warn you."

Josephine gasped. "His name was Cristol? We were considering that name just last night. If he came to you in a dream, then you have a real gift."

"He just said he was your child, yet to be born. But that both of you would die if you didn't get these iron levels straightened out by the fourth month of your pregnancy."

"I will, believe me. But his name was Cristol?"

"Josephine, it was only a dream. We don't have any proof he really was there last night."

"Oh, but we do."

Whatever that meant.

Gregor strode into the room. "Laurel, you've got to see this." He took her hand and hurried her down the hall to where Nikolai stood before a huge portrait.

Gregor pointed. "Look."

The painting, he meant. It showed three little children, two of them were girls, and their mother. The little girls were frolicking, but the little boy stood still and stared out at her. Laurel peered closed. It couldn't be. But it was.

Those were the same eyes she'd seen late at night. He had the same golden hair and the same wisps of curls. He even had the same dimple. "That's him," she whispered.

Nikolai nodded. "That's my ancestor, Cristol. He died in the sixteen hundreds. But now, with this pregnancy, Josephine and I will bring him back to life."

Laurel pushed away from her easel and eased the stiffness from her shoulders. How had she and Gregor ever been convinced to have another art show so soon? But Josephine had insisted. She'd declared herself their patron, and any artist with brains knew that you didn't insult your patron.

Gregor looked over. "Taking a break?"

"It's lunch time. Let me see what you're working on." She wandered over and trailed her fingers along his shoulder.

Gregor's painting was half finished, a landscape with dramatic lighting. His work always amazed her. "You haven't lost your touch."

"If only I worked as quickly as you, Becca."

Becca, it was still taking some getting used to the name, even though she'd been using it for nearly a year.

Still, she knew what he meant about working quickly. Since Josephine's commissioned piece, she'd turned to more abstract work, letting feelings and notions feed her art. She'd created "Passion," "Fusion," "Gratefulness," "Synergy." It didn't hurt that her meditations had taken her places where emotions ran strong. "They just come to me," she said.

"Yes, well, they come out of you in artistically striking ways."

"What are you saying?"

"I think you can command a higher price tag."

Really? Certainly not as high as what Josephine had paid, six figures, all for a painting that had taken her a week to complete. "How much were you thinking?"

He made a wishy-washy gesture with his hand. "Twenty-five or thirty thousand."

That much? For one piece of art? He had to be kidding.

They went to the kitchen and turned on the TV as they prepared lunch. Good, they could catch the news as they worked side by side.

A shot of a castle came on. Wait, she knew that place.

The announcer came on. "Now for some royal news. Princess Josephine has had the baby, a little boy who she and Nikolai have named Cristol."

Laurel stopped chopping the fruit and hurried over.

The newscaster continued. "Here is the new mother now, at home with her first child."

"Oh, my gosh," Laurel said. "Gregor, look at this. She's got my painting there, right beside her."

The rest of the segment was a blur. Josephine presented the baby to the cameras, explained how the painting was commissioned before she even knew she was pregnant, and how it resembled her husband's ancestor.

"And the artist who did this painting, Becca, created this without references, without knowing any of our history," Josephine explained. "It's all from intuition. The woman is so in tune with people, it's like she knows your inner thoughts. That's why she's called 'The Painter of Emotions'."

Gregor came over to watch. "She just announced you to the world on CNN."

"She did, didn't she?"

"You're suddenly a bigger name than me. I'm jealous," he teased. He set his hands on her shoulders.

"I could never be bigger than you."

He grew serious. "Forget what I said earlier. Charge fifty thousand, no, seventy-five thousand a painting. We've got to start making giclees so you can mass produce them."

Anthony checked that no one was around, walked up Luke's door and rapped on it. His two buddies were right behind him. This was going to be fun.

The door opened.

Luke stood there in jeans and a button down shirt, bare foot. He stared at Anthony and his mouth dropped open.

"What? You're not going to invite me in?" Anthony pushed past him, followed by his men. He looked around. Cheap furniture and an efficiency kitchen. What a dump.

Luke looked dazed, following behind. "Wh, wh, what are you doing here?"

"Can't I pay a visit to an old friend?" He gestured. "So where's this big invention thing?"

"The Close Call? It's not like I'd keep it in my apartment." He looked from one guy to the other. "Why do you want to see it, anyway?"

Anthony narrowed his eyes. This little twerp still didn't understand the game. *He'd* be the one asking questions. "So where is it?"

"Um, on the assembly line."

"Oh, hey everybody," he announced to the room, "listen up. Mr. Big Shot here has an assembly line."

His two goons chuckled.

Yeah, laugh it up. He'd be the one laughing after Luke realized how the game was played. Anthony motioned for his two buddies to wait outside. "I got personal business here with my friend. Make sure we're not disturbed."

CHAPTER SEVENTEEN

The goons nodded in tandem and stepped out.

Anthony shut the door behind them. Now, for his old friend, following him like a puppy dog. Anthony spun on one foot and slammed his fist into Luke's jaw.

Luke stumbled and fell to the floor, dazed.

Anthony grabbed the front of his shirt and yanked him up to a sitting position. *Don't pass out, it's more fun when my targets stay conscious.*

Luke swayed, still trying to focus.

Yeah, that's what happened when you messed with an Amalfitano. Was he getting the message loud and clear?

Luke spat out blood and found his voice. "Anthony? Why are you –?"

"So, you come into money and you don't share?" He slapped Anthony. It was so hard that his head was flung to the left. *Don't pass out, you wimp. Lesson's not over yet.* "You think maybe you'll keep it all to yourself, huh?" He slapped him on the other cheek and watched Luke's face swing in the other direction. "You wouldn't have finished that invention if I hadn't bankrolled you."

"But, but, I paid you back."

"Like shit you did. I haven't even started collecting on your debt, my friend."

"What?"

"I read where you're ready to sign contracts worth millions. *Millions,* for some dumb ass machine that anyone could have come up with. You'll share all those millions with me."

"Why?"

"Why? Because I'm your best friend." He slammed him with an uppercut.

Luke wilted to the floor, out cold.

Anthony finished off the lesson with a few kicks to the ribs. There, that ought to get his message across.

Becca sat beside Gregor as their hostess introduced them. She squeezed his hand nervously.

He leaned closer. "You'll be fine, sweetie," he whispered.

Easy for him to say. He wasn't the one who was expected to get up in front of this soiree crowd and paint in the moment. Since Josephine had gone on CNN, she'd been swamped with commission work.

First, they'd gone to Monaco. Now, they were in Japan, where their hostess, the wife of an electronics mogul, was paying her a million dollars to appear at her dinner party. That much, just to paint at her home, it was a ridiculous amount. But her artistic persona, Becca, wasn't about to turn down a million bucks.

"I've got five minutes. I just want to check my makeup." She slipped away. Her phone rang. Damn, she'd forgotten to set it to silent mode. She checked the caller ID. "Luke? Hi, you caught me at a bad time."

"We need to talk."

"Now?"

"It's serious."

She felt the urgency in his voice creep into her body and her heart rate ramped up. "I'm about to be introduced at an event."

"Call me as soon as you can, Laurel."

"I go by Becca now. What's wrong? You sound like you're upset." She felt his tension. It was like he was afraid, panicking.

"Just call me back, promise?"

"OK, OK, I promise."

Gregor was peering her way, gesturing for her to come back.

She switched off her phone and hurried back to the main room.

The announcer said, "So, without further ado, I give you, Becca."

This was it. She took the stage to the applause. An easel had been set up, twig-thin models standing on either side.

Becca picked up a brush, but her hands were shaking. The call from Luke had rattled her. She'd felt his desperate state and had taken it on, internally absorbed it. She stared at the canvas.

Run. Flee. Hide.

She tapped the bristles into the paint and took a deep breath.

Run. Flee. Hide.

Now!

She slashed out with her brush, throwing the paint on the canvas, pelting it with colors, slashing it with streaks, this way and that.

There were gasps from the audience.

Becca kept painting, blindly adding paint strokes as oohs and ahhs broke out.

The model to her left shifted position.

Run. Flee. Hide.

Becca ran her brush off the canvas and onto the model's white dress, adding more color and more slashes.

The second model, where was she? There, there she was, to her right side. Becca threw paint on this sterile white dress, too.

Run. Flee. Hide.

Safe!

She executed the final stroke and stepped back, catching her breath. What had just happened? What had she just done? She'd ruined two beautiful dresses and hadn't painted anything even *close* what her hostess had requested.

Oh, no, she was in a big mess.

Where was the hostess? She turned around. Everyone was staring at her with shocked faces.

She had to explain. "My emotions took over and -"

The dinner party guests erupted in applause. "Painter of emotions," someone called out.

She swayed on her feet.

Gregor appeared at her side and caught her around the waist. "My dear, I didn't know you were going to do that. Well done. Well done, indeed."

"I'm not sure what happened, Gregor."

Her hostess came up and took her hands. She looked radiant. "What a fine performance. I couldn't have asked for anything better. Congratulations, Becca. You've been dubbed 'The Painter of Emotions.'"

Luke found the FBI office. The receptionist greeted him in a no nonsense way. "Name?"

"Luke Sullivan."

"Who are you here to see?"

"Um, Agent Pratt."

"Sign in."

Another efficient-type agent appeared. He was a guy about his own age. "Mr. Sullivan, come this way please."

A door buzzed and his escort opened it. "We'll go down the hall and to the right then two lefts."

Many workers passed them in the halls. Maybe he should make small talk. "It sure is a big building."

"Keeping the country safe requires a big staff." After a while, he stopped at a door, rapped on it, and poked his head in. "Agent Pratt? Your ten o'clock is here."

Luke was shown in. Agent Pratt was a big man in his fifties, the kind who played linebacker in high school. His handshake was solid. "That's quite a shiner you've got. Hope the other guy took some hits, too."

Hardly.

Agent Pratt gestured. "Sit down, young man. What can I do for you?"

Luke eased himself into the chair, careful not to shift his sore ribs. Where to begin? "I'm an inventor," he said. "I've come up with a device all the airlines want to buy."

"American ingenuity, good for you."

"When it was in its prototype stages I borrowed money from a friend, Anthony. We grew up on the same block but I went on to college, and he, uh, went into the family business."

"And?"

"And when I borrowed ten thousand from him, Anthony suddenly up the repayment to twenty five grand."

"I get the drift."

"Now, I paid him off, happy to get rid of the debt, but last week, he flew out here and visited me." He pointed to his eye, now purple and green as it healed. "He kicked me around, cracked a couple of my ribs, told me that he would be back to collect 'his' money."

"I see." He picked up a pen. "What's this friend's last name?"

"Amalfitano."

Agent Pratt stared at him. "Dang, son. The Amalfitano family is connected, if you get what I mean." He shook his head. "You're in some really deep shit."

Becca paced with her phone to her ear.

"Hello?"

Finally. "Luke? Are you all right? I've been trying to reach you."

"Laurel –"

"Call me Becca. That's what I go by now."

"From your middle name. That's smart. You've got to change your looks, too," he said in a rush.

"What? You're not making sense."

"Get that nose job the kids used to tease you about. Change your hair color. He knows what you look like."

"He? Who is this "he"? Luke, slow down. What are you talking about?"

"It's Anthony. You remember meeting him, right?"

Oh, *that* guy. Yeah, she remembered.

"He knows the Close Call is worth millions and he wants a share."

He told her about Anthony's newest demands.

Her heart sank deeper with every word. She had to sit down. "And he beat you up? Are you all right?"

"I'm fine. But he'll come after you, too because I filed for the patents."

He wasn't making sense. "What do the patents have to do with anything?"

"The owners of the company would not normally be public knowledge. But when you file for a patent, the names of the investors are made known."

So, what did that have to do with her being in danger from this New York goon? "I still don't follow you, Luke."

"I made you a partner."

He'd done what? "Luke, you didn't have to do that."

"I knew we'd get married, one day. Even if we didn't, I wanted you to share in my success."

What a sweet gesture. Her heart melted, hearing how miserable he sounded. "I'm already a success," she said gently. "I paint for royalty. I've painted before audiences in Brazil, India and the United Emirates. You don't have to take care of me."

"But I do. I named you as a partner, so Anthony will come after you, I'm sorry that I involved you in this. I thought, at the time, that I was doing the right thing. Now, you're not safe. You have to buy a place with alarms and high walls and guard dogs."

"I need to share my paintings with others."

"If you won't give up this dream of yours, then, then hide in plain sight," he insisted. "I'm warning you, hide in plain sight, or they'll hunt you down, beat you until they force you to sign over everything and then –"

"Then?"

"Then they'll kill you."

CHAPTER EIGHTEEN

Gregor flipped through the pages of the magazine, trying to focus. Sure, like he could digest information at a time like this.

The surgery center's waiting room doors whisk open and he jumped up, magazine forgotten. "How is she?"

The nurse smiled. "She'd just coming out of anesthesia. Do you want to see her?"

"Yes, of course."

"This way."

He followed her into the post-op recovery room.

Becca was in a hospital bed, her face bandaged, hair tousled, her chest wrapped. She had two black eyes. She reached for his arm. "Gregor?" she said weakly.

"I'm here. Everything's fine."

"How do I look?"

Like shit. "You look great, baby."

"Is there a mirror?"

There was one on the cart right beside him. Better to wait. He pushed the cart away. "No, there's not. How do you feel?"

"Like I've been in a train wreck."

He eyed the bandages around her chest. In the doctor's office, she'd opted for three hundred cc implants. Maybe this was what three hundred cc's of saline looked like, all wrapped up, maybe not. He couldn't tell.

"They have some paperwork to go over with me." He kissed her forehead. "I'll have you out of here in no time."

He found the reception desk.

The surgeon appeared, still in his scrubs. "Ah, Mr. Andrysiak, there you are. She came through like a trooper."

"You got my message?" It had been a last-minute instruction, something Becca had no idea he'd done.

The surgeon nodded. "I did indeed."

"And?" He held his breath.

The surgeon's eyes sparkled. "Six hundred cc's fit her just beautifully."

Gregor peeled off ten large bills. "Appreciate the artistic change of enhancement, doc."

Theresa was shown into Peter Willoughby's office.

He gestured for her to take a seat. "Well, I have good news for you, Theresa. You sign this paper and you're free."

Her divorce, he meant. She'd be free of Dirk the Jerk. She broke into a big grin. "Got a pen?"

She signed the paper with a flourish. "Is that it?"

Peter Willoughby nodded, collecting the papers from her and tamping them together on his desk. "I go to the court house and file the papers and the moment they're in the court's possession, you are a free woman."

Fabulous. "If I still wore my ring, I'd take it off. I guess I should go celebrate."

"I know of a quiet place not too far from here," her lawyer said. "We could get a drink, talk about what you're free to do now."

Men were hitting on her already, go figure. She let him down easy. "I'll think about that and get back to you if it feels right." She left his office.

Now that Dirk was out of her life, these headaches would most likely go away. Stress, had to be. What else could possibly be causing them?

Luke was shown into Agent Pratt's office.

The FBI man extended his hand and they shook. "Good, I see you brought the paperwork."

"There's not much. Anthony insisted on dealing in cash."

"But you have bank receipts?"

"Of when the money was deposited and when I used it to pay for things? Sure." He'd been meticulous in keeping his personal banking separate from his company dealings.

"Were there any witnesses to you opening this package of money that you say was from Anthony Amalfitano?"

Luke shook his head.

"Did anyone see the package, and by that I mean someone who could confirm Amalfitano's name or address was on it?"

"Um, I had to sign for it, so I think my dorm kept a record of packages coming in and out. But this happened a few years ago." This was hopeless. "I don't know if they'd keep the paperwork this long."

"It's a long shot, but sometimes long shots pay off. You'd be surprised how willing institutions become when they know it's the FBI who wants answers." He asked for specifics – dorm hall, probably date, if he remembered the name of the person on duty that day.

There was a knock on the door.

Agent Pratt looked up. "Oh, good you're here, just in time." He gestured. "Luke, I want you to meet my associate who'll be working this case with me. You won't find a better man."

They were putting more than one agent on his case? That was reassuring. He turned in his chair to say hello.

What the hell?

It was one of the Amalfitano family goons that Anthony had brought with him when he came to beat him up. The goon extended his hand and watched him with steely eyes. An oily smile crept onto his face.

Luke shivered involuntarily. This guy was on the Amalfitano payroll and would see him dead, no question. He grabbed his things and dashed out the door.

Marcus left the mom and pop café in downtown Las Vegas and stepped out into the night. It didn't offer the same ambiance as his favorite eatery, but Suzie worked there, so it was off limits. Great, another thing she'd managed to swipe away from him, her and her divorce demands.

He threw one leg over the saddle of his motorcycle, called in and let dispatch know he was back on the job. Then he switched on his motorcycle and set off.

Charleston had too many traffic lights. He knew a quick way to get there. He powered down the side streets and a woman ran out in front of him.

Shit. He swerved, barely missing her. He stopped and looked back to where she was making a scene in the middle of the street. *Crazy woman, waking up the neighborhood.* He got on the radio. "Dispatch, I have a woman acting nuts in the street. Near Nelson and fifth."

She was waving her arms at him, screaming, stomping around.

He circled back to her.

Something was wrong.

Smoke. He smelled smoke.

Shit, a house was on fire. "Dispatch, get the fire trucks here, pronto," he yelled. He dropped his bike and tore off his helmet.

"My child's still in there," the crazy woman screamed, pointing.

"Who's still in there?"

"My baby," she wailed, falling to her knees.

Shit, shit, shit. He ran to the house.

Black smoke poured out of the front door. She must have left it open in her haste to get help.

It was the middle of the night. The kid would probably still be in his bed. These were old homes, from when the town was just starting to grow. That meant two bedrooms, both in the back, probably separated by a bathroom. He took a deep breath and ducked inside.

Total blackness enveloped him. The smoke stung his eyes. *Get low, get low.* He dropped to get out of the smoke. He could see down here, but there was only about a foot of air.

He crawled like a madman to the back of the house.

A child was crying.

He followed the sound. His lungs were out of air, the urge to breathe unbearable. His eyes were stinging.

Bulbs in a light fixture overhead burst, showering him with glass.

The child was shrieking louder. *Hold on, hold on. I'm coming.*

He took a breath. Damn, it burned his throat.

There was a doorway. He reached up, found the handle and turned it. The flames flared with the new source of oxygen. The child screamed in sheer terror.

Shit, he'd brought the fire to the child.

Forget crawling. There wasn't time. Marcus flung himself at the bed. His arms felt a body.

It was the child, he was coughing with the smoke that now filled the room. "I've got you, I've got you," he wheezed.

A window. There had to be a window. He grabbed the child with one arm and, squeezing his eyes shut at the sting of the smoke, felt the wall.

Where was the window?

Where the hell was it?

There!

Marcus yanked the collapsible Billy club from his utility belt and snapped it open. He wailed blindly against the wall.

There was a smash of breaking glass. *Please don't have security bars.*

He had to protect the screaming child. Marcus shifted the boy, holding his head close, and launched himself through the window.

They hit the ground.

Fresh air, at last.

He rolled onto his back, gasping for breath. A flash went off. Neighbors came running up. One of them pulled the screaming child from his arms.

His lungs refused the toxic black smoke, and he coughed and coughed.

"Are you OK, officer?" a man said. He helped Marcus to his feet and walked him away from the burning building. "It's safe here."

Marcus looked about, wheezing. "Where's the mother?"

She came running up. "I'm here, I'm here." She gathered her little boy – now that he could see him, Marcus put his age at about six – to her and sobbed. "My baby," she wailed.

He'd just saved her baby. "He'll be fine. The paramedics are on their way. They'll –" he hacked out more black smoke "– check him out."

"No, my *other* baby," she wailed. "She's in the same room."

Shit, there was another child in there?

"She's in her crib. She's only three months old."

Marcus ran back to the house and hefted himself through the window he'd just broken. Glass cut into his leg, his hip. He ignored it.

He dropped down to the floor, took a stab at where the crib might be and felt the legs of some kind of furniture. He raised up and, closing his eyes, felt the bars of a crib. He reached in and felt around. There, he'd found her.

Why wasn't she crying? Maybe he'd found a doll. No, couldn't be. Who would put a doll in a three-month-old's crib? It had to be her.

He picked up the "maybe child" and dropped back to the floor, risked opening his eyes. Shit, they burned like crazy in this smoke. But he forced them open.

It was the baby girl.

Marcus shot upright and raced back to the window, throwing himself out of it. Another flash. Maybe the fire was causing the electrical wires to do that.

The baby girl wasn't moving. She wasn't doing anything. He put his ear to her chest. Oh, God, she wasn't breathing.

Shit, shit, shit.

He set her on the ground, face up, and immediately began CPR, using two fingers to press on her tiny sternum. *Not too hard. Not too hard.*

The mother ran over, "My baby, my baby." She reached out and began tugging on the child.

"Get her away from here," Marcus ordered, taking another breath. Oh shit, what if he was breathing toxic smoke into her lungs?

There was a crowd around him.

"You, there," he said, pointing to a young man nearby. "Come here and take over breathing while I do compressions."

"Well, OK, yeah, sure." He hesitated, held back. "What, what do I do?"

"Never mind." Marcus looked up and grabbed the shirt of a different young man, the one who had led him away from the burning building after he'd smashed through the window. This one sported a military haircut, a good sign. "Listen. I'm afraid I'm putting bad air in her lungs. Can you take over that part?"

"Yes sir."

"Let's do this," he wheezed. "Ready? On three. One, two, three, blow."

There was the fire truck siren. They were close.

Thank God. He kept up the rhythm.

The baby girl stirred. Marcus stopped pushing. "Hold up. I think we got her back."

The mother wailed anew as someone held her back, the first child clutching her leg.

The EMT fire fighters ran up with their gear. "We've got it from here, officer."

Somewhere off to the side, someone said, "I caught it all on camera."

Becca sat in the makeup artist's chair, watching herself in the mirror. This guy, Angelo, knew what he was doing, but then, Gregor said he was the best movie makeup artist in Spain.

"You gave me cheek bones," she said, turning her face side to side. "I've never had cheekbones before." They looked great with the cornflower blue contact lenses she wore.

Angelo smiled. "Now, some women add a little drama with a beauty mark." He pulled out a sheet with dozens of stick-on ones attached and showed it to her. He peeled one off and added it near her jawline. "Just adhere it before you add your makeup."

"It won't fall into my lap?"

"You could sleep with it on, but I wouldn't recommend it for your skin."

She stared in the mirror.

Was this even her? Even *she* would have to look twice to be sure.

The beauty mark helped pull the eye away from her features that couldn't be changed. Angelo was a genius.

"My nose job, the cheekbones, the beauty mark. I feel look like a whole different person."

"That's the idea, right?"

Hide in plain sight. "Right."

Theresa slid Arielle's dinner plate on the table. "Your favorite – macaroni and cheese." She turned to scoop out her own portion as the local news came on the TV.

"Don't be surprised if I only eat half."

Aliens must have abducted her child and replaced her with a look-alike. "You feel OK?"

"I'm watching my figure," Arielle announced matter-of-factly. "Evan Janowitz said if I gain extra weight at this age, I'll be fat all my life."

"Is that so?" All she knew was that it was nice to have dinner with her daughter before the she left for work.

"Mommy, look!" Arielle pointed at the TV screen. "It's that police officer who used his lights to bring you home."

She turned to the TV.

There he was, the same NHP officer who had told off their stupid babysitter. He was bleeding from his side and handing over a young child to someone in the crowd that surrounded him.

"Oh, my God," Theresa said. "He just pulled that poor child from the flames." Her hands flew to her face as she waited to see the outcome. She couldn't take her eyes off the video.

Behind him, the fire was raging as black smoke billowed out of the house. If she hadn't seen it with her own eyes, she would have sworn no one could survive such a fire.

The screen blipped and suddenly the same officer was crashing through the remaining shards of glass, staggering as he got up off the ground, bleeding from his new injuries. He produced an infant that he'd clutched to his body, placed her on the ground and began giving CPR.

Arielle tugged on her sleeve. "Mommy, he's a hero."

"He certainly is."

"And he was right here in our house. I'm going to tell everyone at school."

The newscaster came on screen. "Officials have not yet determined the cause of the fire, which started in the living room, but neighbors say the home was a known crack house."

Shit, drugs again. People thought all that happened was a drug overdose, go to the hospital, get your stomach pumped and you're fine and dandy. They didn't know how drugs ruined the life of everyone around you.

She slipped her arms around Arielle and hugged her. She'd never let any harm come to *her* child.

Marcus entered his superior's office. "You wanted to see me, Captain?"

Captain Schiff closed the file he'd been working on. "You run into a burning building, save not just one child from the flames, but two, and then you bring an infant back to life by giving her CPR. Am I supposed to be impressed by that?"

Marcus had to admit, it sounded like a scene from a movie. "No, sir."

"And now, I hear that you expect me to give you a day shift, the *prime* shift, that guys who've work thirty years for the NHP wish they had."

Oh, quit ragging on my ass. You know you're going to give it to me. "No better time to ask, sir."

"Yeah, no better time than when your face is all over the news and the governor is flying in to give you a hero's award and even the President of the United States cites you as a damn hero in a televised speech."

"So, do I get it?"

"The day shift? Hell, yes. You're a freaking hero." He grinned. "And that means I get to sign you up as the face of the NHP for every special event in town. And don't think I won't."

Anthony finished his beer as his uncle entered the bar. He stood up, had to show deference to the old coot. "Uncle Sal, good to see you," he said.

The old eyes peered at him. "You spend too much time in this tittie bar, playing with your dick all day. You're not watching the books, Anthony. Someone's stealing from this joint."

Yeah, me. "I'll find out who it is and cut his nuts off."

Uncle Sal nodded. "OK, so what have you got? And I warn you, this had better be good."

It was good, all right. "I can get us a cut on a contract that's about to be signed."

His uncle drew back in horror. "Not on paper. You *never* do a deal like that on paper."

"Nah, nah, it's all under the table. You see, I have this friend who came up with an invention."

He laid out the deal, how he would squeeze Luke into handing over cash.

"By the time he's done, we'll be sitting pretty."

"Let me get this straight. Your friend is going to sign a *ten* million dollar contract, right?"

Damn, didn't his uncle read the financial pages? Didn't he know Luke actually stood to eventually earn one hundred million, maybe more?

Anthony smiled. "Yeah, yeah, ten million is what he told me."

There, blame it on Luke. If his uncle got wise, he could say that it was Luke who had low-balled the number.

He sat a little straighter. "So, I figure we muscle him for half – why be greedy, right? –we'll have five million, no sweat off our backs." He threw a fake punch, just to show he was sure of the deal. "It'll be a piece of cake."

Uncle Sal gestured. "Five million. You pull this off, and you can keep a million of it for yourself."

"You're all heart, Uncle Sal." He watched his uncle leave.

One shitty million, for finding this gold mine of a deal and doing all the dirty work, taking all the risk? It served the old man right to get his dick twisted this way.

He was going to squeeze Luke for the whole hundred million and spend the rest of his days sipping champagne on some island and fucking every woman on it, all day long.

Fuck you, Uncle Sal, you and your measly one mil payday.

CHAPTER NINETEEN

Theresa stood in her tra-la-la pose and listened for the music to cue. Her neck was stronger, thanks to the physical therapy, but she'd dropped twelve pounds, causing Raphael to send her a box of donuts with instructions to eat every one of them.

Now, she wish she had. She had no energy, felt unsteady on her feet. Damn this headdress, it was like a pillar of rock on her head. A semi truck weighed less.

Just let me get through this show.

She remembered to smile, but it was that fake, plastic smile that didn't reach her eyes. Too bad, it would have to do for this show.

OK, time to pose – arms wide, chest out so the audience could get a good look at her spectacular breasts. Lord knew she'd paid enough for them.

The curtain opened.

There was a collective "Ah" from the audience. It happened every night.

Take a good long look, folks. That's what you came here to see.

The music started.

Here we go. One, two, three.

She started down the tiered steps, felt her balance start to falter and caught herself. Raphael had seen it, she just knew he had. She'd probably get an earful about it after this segment. He'd probably dock her pay.

She kept the smile plastered on her face and looked straight forward.

The lights seemed to dim. Maybe the hotel was having a power outage.

The stage seemed to tip.

No power outage, but rather, an earthquake, it had to be.

The stage spun and she couldn't make sense of it.

Something was happening, something bad.

A lightning bolt struck her in the head, she stumbled forward.

Everything went black.

Theresa opened her eyes. The lights were so damn bright. Marissa's face, still in full makeup, came into view, peering down at her. "Where am I?"

"The emergency room, sweetie," Marissa said. "Everything's going to be all right."

The emergency room, what the hell? She grabbed her friend's hand. "What happened?"

"You collapsed on stage."

She remembered now, the dizziness, the fading eyesight. Holy shit, she might have been out for hours. "What time is it? Is Arielle –?"

"Calm down. She's fine. The babysitter said she'd stay until we got someone to take over." She smiled. "I volunteered. She's a cute kid."

"This isn't good, is it?"

A young doctor came in, reading a chart. He was good looking, with a runner's build. "I'm Doctor Diego Juarez," he said, absent mindedly, "and you're –" He looked down at her. "Ah, a showgirl. Five ten, I should have guessed."

Marissa smiled, striking a seductive pose. "We're both showgirls. I'm five ten and a half."

"I see. Tell me what's going on, Miss …," he checked the chart again, "… Trenton."

"She collapsed on stage during the first number," Marissa said. "Boom, just like that, took out two whole rows of dancers."

Theresa cringed. She hoped no one had gotten hurt.

Doctor Juarez smiled. "OK, thanks. I'll need to speak to the patient alone now."

Marissa waved goodbye cutesy style and ducked out.

Theresa sighed. Her friend really needed to act less desperate if she wanted to get a man.

The doctor turned to her.

Those eyes, wow.

"So, what's going on?"

Theresa gathered her thoughts. "I've been having migraines. My doctor said it was the weight of the headdresses we wear." She gave him the names of the prescriptions she was taking and told him about the physical therapy. "But it really hasn't helped that much."

He pulled the stethoscope from his neck, listened to her heart, her lungs, had her breathe in, breathe out and did the pen light thing in her eyes.

Dr. Juarez checked something on her chart. "OK. I'm going to run a series of blood tests. The nurse will come in for all that." He patted her arm. "You take it easy 'til I get back, OK?"

"Wait. Will I be here all night? I have a little girl at home and _"

He gestured helplessly. "At this point, I can't promise you anything. We have to see what the tests say." He smiled. "Whatever it is, we'll get you through this, Miss Trenton."

"Theresa."

He nodded. "Theresa."

An hour after the nurse drew five vials of blood, he was back.

She sat up. Maybe there was news. "What did you find?"

"Nothing," he said. "I'm ordering more tests – a CAT scan and X-rays. You'll stay tonight for observation and can be released in the morning if you feel all right."

"But I feel all right now. Can't I just go home?"

Dr. Juarez shook his head. "Absolutely not. I'd be remiss if I sent you on your way –"

Remiss? Who used a word like that?

"–and something more happened."

He was right. She could walk out of here, get her car and have another blackout, cause an accident, maybe get herself killed.

She looked down at the ugly hospital gown she wore. All she'd been wearing when she arrived was a G-string and heels. It would be hard to waltz out of the hospital in that attire.

"I see." At least Marissa was with Arielle. She'd have to call her again with an update.

"Get some rest, Theresa."

Gregor got out of bed and eyed Becca's long leg, exposed as she slept. He should paint her this way, keep this moment forever.

Her two-year tutelage under him was about up. He'd watched as her art had been elevated and then taken off in her own direction.

She was in demand now, Becca, Painter of Emotions, pulling in gobs of money. She no longer needed him, not for her art, probably not for his physical companionship.

"I can't promise you my heart," she'd said.

He looked down at his own body. Yes, the daily runs with Becca had melted off a few pounds, kept him toned. But the difference in age would catch up with him and one day she'd look elsewhere for her physical pleasure.

"You deserve better," he whispered.

They were so alike in some ways, so different in others. Losing her would hurt him, but keeping her here would hurt her.

He'd have to find the right time to have a talk with her, tell her she was ready to conquer the world on her own terms, set her free and let her fly away. As much as that would hurt.

The hospital room door swung open. Theresa looked up from her magazine expectantly. "Arielle?"

But no, it was her doctor. She'd had another blackout during the evening, and she was running out of hope that anyone could help her.

Dr. Juarez smiled at her. As handsome as he was, the smile did not reach his eyes. He pulled up a chair and sat in front of her.

What? No stethoscope to listen to her lungs? No shining a light in her eyes? Something was up. "What did you find?"

"Your test results came back," he said.

There was a pit in her stomach. She steeled herself. "What do I have?"

"There's no way to sugarcoat this, Theresa. It's cancer."

She reeled as if someone had slugged her in the gut and sucked all the air from the room. Cancer. This was not good.

All this time, she'd wasted on a doctor who insisted it was her headdress. She ran her hand down her face. "How bad is it?"

"We need to operate, like, now."

Now? But what about Arielle? Who'd take care of Arielle?

"We might have to follow it up with chemotherapy. We can't say at this point. I can tell you that this is not going to be a picnic."

At least he was giving it to her straight. "My only family is my sister and she lives in Europe. She'll need to come and watch over my little girl."

"Have her hop on a plane. This can't wait."

Cancer, surgery, it was all coming at her too fast. She searched his eyes. "This is Vegas, doc. What are my odds?"

Dr. Juarez started to speak, caught himself and looked away.

That bad, huh?

He filled out a new prescription and tore it off the pad. He hesitated and wrote some more. "This is my cell number. As soon as arrangements for your daughter are made, let me know so we can schedule your surgery. All that matters is getting you well."

No, all that mattered was that someone to step in and look after Arielle because it didn't sound like she'd be around much longer.

Laurel checked her cell phone. She'd missed a call from her sister while she and Gregor had been out running. She took a swig of water, wiped the sweat from her brow and hit the "dial" button. "Hey, Theresa, what's going on?"

"Thank God you called. I need you." She began sobbing.

Something bad, real bad must have happened. Theresa was usually the Rock of Gibraltar. "Oh, my God, Theresa, What's going on? Where you in an accident? Is Arielle all right?"

"Can you come here?"

To Las Vegas? "Of course, but tell me what's wrong."

"Promise me you'll take care of my little girl."

"Theresa, what's going on?"

"Promise me!"

"Yes, yes. I promise you. You have my word. Now, calm down and tell me what the matter is. What's happened?"

"I've been diagnosed with cancer."

No, it couldn't be. Not her sister, not Theresa. Her head was spinning. She didn't even know her sister had been feeling poorly. "Are they sure?"

"Sis, promise me you'll come and take care of Arielle."

"I'll be on the first flight out of here."

Luke tore a fifty dollar bill in half and handed it to the taxi driver. "You get the other half when I return. I'll only be ten minutes."

He got out and eyed the building, a three-story brick rectangle on the fringes of the seedy part of town. He went inside. The staircase was concrete and smelled of urine. He climbed to the third floor, muscles burning, and found the apartment.

Good, no one was around to see him. He rapped on the door. "Victor?" he said quietly.

The door opened a crack and two eyes checked him out.

"I'm Lu – uh, Danny."

Victor eyed the hallway. "Come on in, man."

The apartment was dark. A chemical smell hit his nose. Luke followed Victor to a work desk. "Did everything come out all right?"

"Sure, man. Thanks for sending the photos." He pulled out a manila envelope and handed it over. "Check it out."

Inside were three passports in different names, three drivers' licenses from different states and birth certificates to match. He held them up to the light and inspected them.

Victor made a consolatory gesture. "Sorry man, but the social security cards were a hassle in such a short time. You'll probably never need them anyway."

Yeah, who needed social security benefits when you were a multi-millionaire? "Here's the money." He handed over an envelope and peeled off five one-hundred dollar bills. "For making this a priority."

"A bonus?" Victor smiled. "Wow, man, cool."

"Not a word about this to anyone, right?"

Victor pocketed the money. "Not in my line of business, Danny."

Luke let himself out and hurried down to his waiting taxi. He jumped in and handed the driver the other half of the fifty. "Thanks for waiting."

"In this neighborhood?" the driver said. "I should have insisted on a C-note."

A what? Oh, a hundred dollar bill, he meant. But if he paid that much, the driver would pay more attention to what he looked like, and where he was dropped off. It was information he couldn't risk having get out there. "Sorry, dude. Times are tough."

But they wouldn't be for long. He'd be leaving Los Angeles as soon as the last contract was signed.

And then Anthony could kiss his ass.

Gregor held her tight and inhaled Becca's perfume one final time. "I'm going to miss you," he wanted to say, but he stopped himself. No sense in making this any harder than it already was. "Have you got everything?"

Becca nodded and eased out of his arms.

"Don't go -" But she had to, he knew. Her sister could be dying, and she needed Becca in Vegas. He started again. "Don't go wasting your talents on fads."

"I'm already locked into bookings in New York and San Francisco. They'll each take me away from Theresa for just one night, so it should be doable."

"Take care of your sister, your little niece, too."

Becca reached out and smoothed his cheek with her hand. "I'll always value this time with you, Gregor. You helped bring my art up to a level I never thought possible. And you made it hard for any man to live up to my standards."

But she couldn't promise him her heart. She'd made that clear from the beginning.

She kissed him goodbye with teary eyes and a sad little smile and turned away.

He watched her walked away, until the airport crowd swallowed her up.

His heart winced. He'd just let go of the best thing that had ever happen to him. "I love you, Becca," he whispered.

Luke scribbled his name once again on the legal paper with the United Airlines logo and handed it back.

Charles Shellenberger, pushed another sheet at him. This one had American Airlines. "Sign here and here," he said, pointing.

Korean Air was next, then British Airways and Canadian Air. The papers kept coming.

Luke signaled to stop. "Hold on. I'm getting a cramp," he said, shaking out his hand.

His lawyer smiled. "Yes, it's a tough task, signing all these lucrative licensing contracts."

All the major airlines had negotiated for the Close Call, the regional ones, too. Only a few little feeder lines in obscure lands had held off until their respective governments forced it on them. They were only postponing the inevitable, Shellenberger had said. That was OK. He didn't need them. The top five airlines had sent the balance of his brand new Swiss bank account soaring.

Soaring. An apropos word. Luke would have smiled … if he wasn't afraid for his life.

"Last one, son." Shellenberger pushed another one across his desk.

Two seconds later, Luke returned it. "So that's it?"

His attorney nodded. "That's it." He gathered the papers, tamped them into place and slid them all in a file. "You're leaving today?"

"Soon." He couldn't risk even his lawyer knowing his plans. "I can't say what destination."

"Well, wherever you're going, I wish you well." Shellenberger hesitated. "How will I reach you? Your phone?"

"No, I'll be destroying it. I'll be in touch when I feel it's safe."

"Understood." Shellenberger stood up and straightened his designer pinstripe suit. "It's been a pleasure, son. I hope you and your lady love, well, work things out."

"They will." Once Laurel, no, she was Becca now, Becca the Painter of Emotions, saw how well he was taking care of her with the Swiss bank account he'd set up for her, she could focus on her art to her heart's content and realize that he'd always been supportive of her, that they should always be together.

Luke got up and clasped his attorney in a quick embrace. "Thank you for everything."

"Are you ready?"

He nodded.

Shellenberger gestured. "This way."

Luke hurried through the secret door in the paneled wall and found the private elevator. He had a rental car in the parking garage and would be leaving his old car behind, just in case he'd been followed here.

All he had to do now was get out of the country alive.

CHAPTER TWENTY

The man in black crept up the stairs in the darkness. He pulled on gloves, picked the lock and slipped inside. The odor of chemicals hit his nostrils.

Victor, the forger, was snoring lightly in the next room. Hopefully, he would be sleeping alone, no girlfriend. He always hated encountering the girlfriend. They woke up screaming.

The man stepped carefully. Silence was his friend. The bedroom was small. He pulled the switchblade, his other friend, from his back pocket, and crept up to the bed. Good, no girlfriend.

His knee was on Victor's chest in a flash. "Not a sound," he warned. "I've got a knife at your throat."

The forger quivered. "Who are you? What do you want?"

"Luke Sullivan. What name is he using?"

"Who? N–never heard of him."

What a dumb ass. This would get his attention.

The man nicked Victor's throat.

Victor squealed.

"Tell me his new ID or I start cutting off body parts."

Ten minutes later, the man stepped away from the body, now bound and gagged and sporting a gaping slice to the throat. He grabbed a beer from the refrigerator and made the call.

"Hello?"

"Yeah. It's me. I've got three names. Here they are …"

Marcus stood before Judge Crawford. Divorce court, he couldn't wait for this to be over.

"Mr. Meddevia," the judge said, "did you buy this house together? You and the claimant?"

"No. I was nineteen when I bought it, sir."

"Rather far sighted for a nineteen-year-old." The judge peered at his paperwork. "And after you were married, did you ever add your wife's name to the deed?"

"No, sir."

Suzie jumped up. "But he said he would, he *promised* me."

Marcus shook his head. He kept his voice controlled like his attorney had advised. "There was no conversation about that, your honor." He glanced at his wife. "Ever."

Suzie sat back down and pouted.

The judge adjusted his reading glasses. "I see. Let's move on to child support. It says here that Ms. Caminski came into this marriage with three children."

"I didn't know she had kids, your honor." Beside him, Peter Willoughby nodded as if to bolster the claim. Willoughby had coached him in what to say and what not to say in front of this judge. Keep the answers short and sweet and to the point.

Judge Crawford cleared his throat. "How could you not know that?"

"I've only recently learned they were living with her parents in Texas. She never mentioned having children. I only found out she had kids after she changed the locks on my house and moved them in." *Short and sweet enough, judge?*

Suzie grumbled. "Any decent man would take them on. They're good kids."

The judge shot her a look. "No more outbursts in my court, understood?"

Suzie scowled and nodded, arms crossed.

Marcus tried not to smile. She didn't look happy, but she'd agreed. Maybe Judge Crawford was getting a taste of her true self.

The judge peered down at him. "Trooper Meddevia. Why does your face seem familiar to me? Meddevia, Meddevia, I seem to recall that name in the news recently."

Marcus shot a look at Suzie. This would cook her goose, but good. "There was some TV coverage about a house fire –"

"With two children inside," the judge finished for him. "Yes, yes, I remember now. Very commendable." He turned to Suzie. "You asked for the SUV, so granted. But from now on, the monthly car payments that go with it, those are yours. No alimony. No child support. In all the other contested matters, the court finds in favor of the defendant, Trooper Meddevia." He hit his gavel. "Court is adjourned."

Twenty minutes later, Marcus raised his beer mug in a salute to Peter Willoughby. "Here's to divorce lawyers." He'd kept his house and Suzie's claim of child support had been laughed out of court.

His brother, Winslow, came into the bar and joined them. "I heard the good news. Let's hope you make wiser choices in the future."

"No, don't," Willoughby joked. "Bad choices mean more business for me." He excused himself to go and say hi to someone.

Winslow eyed his brother for a long moment. "You could come and work for my firm doing detective work."

"Follow wayward spouses cheating on one another? No thanks."

"It wouldn't all be cases like that."

Sure it wouldn't. "I don't think so."

"Don't be so fast to say 'No.' Hell, you'd make enough money to buy that six-bedroom place down the street from me, the one I told you about."

"Not going to happen."

"You make shit for a salary. And yet you put your life on the line every day."

Didn't he understand? "I'm a protector. It's in my DNA."

Winslow shook his head. "Yeah, well, your DNA is crap when it comes to choosing marriage material."

Seated in Josephine's private jet, she turned the business card over in her hand. "Becca, Painter of Emotions," it read. It was a new name for a new person. She would add her studio information as soon as she was settled in Las Vegas.

She stared out the window, not really seeing the sky but rather the life she was leaving behind. "Ah, Luke," she sighed, "what did you get me into?"

"Hide in plain sight," he'd insisted. "Hide in plain sight or they'll hunt you down."

So that was what she was doing, restarting her life – new face, new body, new name - hoping no one would learn her secret and come to abduct her, torture her. For the rest of her days, until her dying breath, she would have to hide in plain sight, all while living a very public life.

But right now, Theresa needed her in Nevada. Of all the people to get cancer, it was hard to believe it had struck her sister. Theresa, the dancer, the one who drank weird concoctions like spinach juice and blueberries, who practiced yoga and could torque her body into unnatural positions, how could that be?

Becca shook free the thought. Her sister had cancer, period. It was time to deal with that fact and that fact alone.

"Get your sister through this surgery and back on her feet. She and Arielle are your focus now," she told herself.

Luke checked the rear view mirror as he drove the 405 freeway toward LAX. That same black car was behind him again, he was sure of it. He flipped on his directional and pretended to be exiting. The car mimicked him.

The exit was straight ahead. He jerked the wheel and made a last minute move, crossing the triangular lane paint so he was back onto the 405 freeway.

The black sedan did, too.

Shit. He hit the gas and his rented Ford surged ahead. He should have opted for the sportier model, but he didn't want to call attention to himself. Now, he was paying for that decision.

He eyed the rear view mirror. Was that Anthony in the passenger seat, or had he hired other guys, L.A. guys, to do his dirty business? They weren't close enough to tell. He crossed to the far left lane and stomped on it. *Let's see what this car can do.*

Eighty, ninety, he was nearing a hundred. "Get out of the way, move over, damn it," he shouted at the drivers ahead. Shit, the black sedan was coming up on his ass. Anthony was in the passenger seat, he was sure of it.

There were too many cars. He braked hard and slid over into a slot in the lane next to him He checked his mirror. *There, try that move, asshole.*

Luke braked again and shot over to the far right lane. There was another off ramp. He took the exit hard, the back end of the Ford fishtailing as he fought for control.

The exit light turned red. He hit the gas and roared through, barely missing a yellow sports car that had just started with the green light. Horns blared.

Shit, that was close. He took the next right, the next left and then right again. He had no idea where he was, but as long as the black car was far behind him, that was all that mattered.

He slowed down. This was a neighborhood. There were kids. Up ahead, a man was mowing his lawn. A moving van, taking up the whole right side of the street, told him that a family was moving out of their house.

Shit, the black car had just shot down the street behind him, streaking left to right. There was a screech of brakes.

They'd spotted him.

They were coming after him. He had to get out of here.

Luke pressed the accelerator. Maybe if he could swing the Ford right in front of the moving van, he could buy himself some time. He went to pass the moving van.

Oncoming traffic, shit!

He swung the wheel right and the Ford shot up the ramp into the van. He braked like mad and stopped into some mattresses.

The truck's door slammed down from the jolt, just as the black sedan came speeding around the corner.

Luke let out a deep breath. He was safe. "Becca, I hope you took my advice."

Becca awoke with a start to see clouds out the window. Luke! She'd seen him driving like a mad man on a freeway. He was in trouble and there was nothing she could do to help him.

She gestured the private flight attendant over. "Jenny, how soon before we land?" It was Josephine's jet. She'd insisted Becca use it, rather than hop three flights to get to Theresa.

"Less than three hours. Can I get you anything?"

"Two glasses of water, please."

"Of course. Perrier, Saratoga, Power –"

"Just plain water."

She rummaged in her bag and found her miniature watercolor kit and a five-by-seven sheet. The images had been striking, almost harrowing. Luke, gripping the wheel, fear plastered all over his face.

"Here you go." Jenny set down the waters.

"Thanks." She dipped the paint brush in one and let her feelings take over. The strokes were hard and bold. Fear, desperation, panic.

She finished in a stabbing flourish. There, done.

Becca looked up. Jenny was watching, transfixed. It was the same look she saw when she painted before an audience.

"Wow," the flight attendant said. "That's incredible."

"It's yours," Becca said. She signed it and handed over the painting.

"Thank you, oh my gosh, thank you." She hesitated. "I can't believe you're on my flight. Can I take a picture taken with you?"

Photo? Oh, that's right, she looked different now. *Hide in plain sight.* She nodded. "I'd be delighted."

Becca parked the rental car and raced into the hospital. "Theresa Trenton's room, please."

"Third floor, three oh two."

Third floor, three oh two. Third floor, three oh two.

Becca peeked into the room.

Her sister was sleeping, poor thing.

She hurried to the bed. "Theresa?" She took her sister's hand. "It's me, Laurel."

Her sister's eyes flew open. "Oh, my God, you're here. Thank you." She was slurring her words. "Love the red hair."

"How are you feeling?"

"They have me sedated."

Yeah, she could tell. "When is the operation scheduled?"

A doctor strode in. "Is this your sister, the one who lives in Spain?"

"I live here, as of now." Becca shook his hand. His grip was strong, and she couldn't help noticing the way he looked at her sister.

"I'm Dr. Juarez. Well, well, two tall ladies," he observed. "Amazon twins, well, except for the hair color."

Theresa gave them a sleepy smile. "He says stuff like that all the time."

After he was done checking her sister, Becca drew him aside and out in the hall. "Be straight with me. What's the deal? Will she make it?"

He hesitated. "We won't know until we go in. She's a strong woman, done everything right to stay healthy all her life. That puts her ahead of the curve. The trouble is, she was misdiagnosed, so things are a little more, er, advanced, than we'd like."

Advanced? Advanced was not good. She was going to die. Her sister was going to die. "She's young. She has her whole life ahead of her. Doc, you've got to do everything to save her."

He glanced through the open door at Theresa, lying in bed. "Believe me, we'll do everything we can to bring about a positive outcome."

"I don't care what it costs, see that she gets the very best treatment."

"We will. I've done dozens of these operations. She's in good hands. Now, if you'll excuse me, we're about to begin prepping your sister and getting her into surgery."

That fast?

He pulled out a recorder and spoke into it in Spanish as he flipped through pages of Theresa's chart.

Becca caught her breath. The medical terms she didn't understand, but she'd just spent years in Spain. She caught enough to know that this was bad.

She hurried over and gave Theresa a kiss and clutched her hand. "You're going to be fine."

"I wish I knew what he was saying."

No, you don't. "I'll be here when you wake up." *If* she woke up, that was.

Luke peered out the window of the cheap motel. Forget LAX, it was too obvious a choice. He should use a smaller airport.

He'd shaken Anthony yesterday, but who knew how close he was, whether he was ready to pounce and abduct him, torture him for his bank information.

What had ever possessed him to contact Anthony and ask for that loan? Stupid, stupid, stupid.

His phone rang.

Shit, it was Anthony's number.

He let it go to voice mail. "Luke, let's talk, man to man. You know what it's about. Listen up, pal," He growled. "Talk now or I'll find you. Make me go to all that trouble and it won't be pretty."

Luke grabbed his bag, made sure no one was around and left the room. There was a flight to Seattle. From there, he could head to the Orient and get lost.

Becca pulled her rental car, a baby blue Cadillac, up to the house on Crimson Canyon. It was smaller than she'd imagined, but then, she'd only seen a couple of photos. Two bedrooms, two baths, her sister had said, just right for a small family. Not so right for visiting family.

A young woman with big eyes and no makeup answered the door.

"Hi. It's Marissa, right?" she said. "I'm Becca."

A whoosh of movement caught her eye. "Aunt Laurel!"

She swept her niece up in a hug. "You've grow so big. I wouldn't have recognized you." She had her mother's legs and that same spark of impishness.

Arielle peered at her. "What did you do to your nose?"

Becca laughed. "I brought you something." She dug in her purse for the miniature pirate's chest. "Spanish gold."

She drew Marissa aside. "Thank you so much for stepping in until I could get here. Has Arielle had lunch yet? We should be at the hospital when Theresa comes out of surgery."

She nodded. "We were there to see Theresa earlier, but she's anxious to go back."

Yeah, so was she, but she had a couple of things to accomplish first.

The guard at the gate handed her a placard to hang from her rear view mirror.

"Thanks." Becca pulled away and made a left, then a right as she'd been instructed, then followed the snaking road as it rounded a bend. They passed high-end homes, each one surrounded by lush landscaping. She eyed the address numbers. They were getting closer.

"Where are we going?" Arielle asked, peering out the window.

"We're meeting a gentleman with whom I've been speaking lately." She pulled into a driveway. A Range Rover with a reality sign on the side was already parked there. "This should be him right here."

He stepped over and opened her door for her. "You're right on time, Ms. De la Croix."

"Mr. Stirling, thank you for meeting us on such short notice. We're in a bit of a hurry. You have the key?"

"I do, indeed." He gestured. "Follow me, please."

They strode up to the entry. It was a white stucco contemporary, twelve-foot tall double doors, just as she'd seen online. "Six thousand square feet, correct?"

"Six thousand four hundred and fifty to be exact," Mr. Stirling said. "It's been empty for a little more than a year, but the utilities have been on, so it should be move-in ready."

Arielle piped up. "You're moving in?"

He fit the key in and opened the doors. "Ladies, after you." He began rattling off the features, his voice echoing off the walls in the empty house as Arielle took the spiral stairs, but she couldn't care less how new the air conditioning units were or whether there was a butler's pantry.

She needed a large studio and it had to have sunlight. She hurried through the rooms.

No good, no good, maybe.

He tried to keep up.

Darn, this room was no good either.

She opened another set of double doors and stopped. Ah, this was it. The light was streaming in perfectly. There was plenty of room for her easel, her materials. Best of all, it opened onto the back patio, just like Gregor's had in Spain. She ignored the pang in her heart at the thought of him. "I'll take it."

"But you haven't seen the master or the –"

"Get the paperwork started, Mr. Stirling. I'll come by your office later." She peered up at the landing. "Arielle, honey, come on, we have to go."

She glanced at her watch. Theresa was still in surgery, but she didn't want to miss speaking to the doctor the instant he was through. "Come on, time to go see your mommy."

CHAPTER TWENTY-ONE

Marcus and Officer Keith Uberhoff finished up at the accident scene.

His fellow trooper shook his head. "Two car collision, all because one guy was talking on the cell phone. Guess we know whose insurance rate will be jacked up by the morning."

Yeah, it served them right. He saw it all the time on his new day shift. Officer Uberhoff saw it too, though, why the guy had switched from flying copters for the NHP to being on the ground, he'd never comprehend.

Marcus swung a leg over the saddle of his motorcycle and was about to fire it up when Uberhoff indicated a call coming in.

A baby blue Caddy with rental plates shot past them, going at least twenty miles over the speed limit. Shit, he would be on it if his colleague hadn't signaled for him to hold up. "What is it?"

"Captain Schiff wants to see you."

"Now?"

"Now." He paused. "I wouldn't keep him waiting."

Luke ducked into John Wayne Airport. No one would be looking for him here.

It was fairly empty, barely a line at the kiosk to pick up the ticket he'd bought online with one of his new aliases – Timothy Peters. Well, Timothy Peters was about to hop a flight to Seattle, then buy a one-way ticket far from Anthony and his slimy family.

The boarding pass popped out and he pocketed it. Good, no one was paying attention to him. He hightailed it to security and got in line. Come on, come on, move it along.

He got up to the matronly attendant who took his ID and checked his boarding card.

Shit, what if the forger had done a crappy job with the driver's license? What if they realized that he wasn't this Peters guy? He began to sweat. Then there was the possibility that Anthony had followed him here. He fought the urge to check behind him. He shifted his feet.

The attendant scanned his face. "Scared of flying?"

Huh? "I, um, I'd rather not be here," he admitted with a little laugh. There, that was true.

She stamped his boarding pass. "Have a good flight. Next."

Luke hurried off to find his gate.

There was a pretty gate attendant checking in a young couple ahead of him. They had their arms around one another, acting all lovey dovey. Probably honeymooners.

It was his turn. He stepped up and the pretty gate agent checked him in.

"We'll be boarding in fifteen minutes," she told him.

Good, he wanted to splash water on his face, and he had to pee. There was a men's room on the right. He swung into it and hefted his carryon to one shoulder as he stood before the urinal.

The newlywed guy stepped up to pee. He pulled a knife.

What the –?

The blade tore into his belly like white lightning.

"Nooooo."

A hand smothered his mouth.

He was flung back into one of the stalls.

The knife kept slashing into him, over and over.

"I'll teach you to mess with the Amalfitano family."

It hurt so bad, so bad.

The guy stood above him, still slashing as if in slow motion. Luke sighed. Things were growing dimmer. "Laurel," he whispered. Everything went black.

Becca looked up from her hospital seat. Dr. Juarez was coming through the post op doors. She hurried up to him. "Is Theresa OK? How's she doing?" She glanced down at Arielle, beside her.

He nodded. "We think we got it all. She's in recovery." He knelt down to Arielle's level and took her hands in his. "Your mom was very brave. You should be proud of her."

Arielle nodded. "Is she still pretty?"

Dr. Juarez grinned. "Yes, she's still pretty, very pretty." He got back up and turned to Becca. "She can be released in two days. You'll be staying with her?"

"I just bought a house. She'll be moving in with me." She'd need to hire round-the-clock nurses, a maid and a cook. She had to make sure Theresa had all the best care.

"Good. Just having her family around will keep her spirits up." He hesitated. "She's special, your sister."

Special enough to have stolen your heart? She could have painted the emotion emanating off him right now. "Will you let us know when we can see her?"

"Sure." His pager went off. "Duty calls," he said and left.

Becca tucked Arielle into bed.

"When will Mommy come home, Aunt Laurel?"

"Soon, honey. Now, go to sleep."

She went into Theresa's room and got ready for bed. She'd have to get Arielle into the habit of calling her "Aunt Becca."

She slipped into bed and felt the night lull her to sleep.

Someone was pacing on the patio outside. What the heck? She opened a sleepy eye and got up to check.

It was Luke.

Becca opened the window. "Luke? What are you doing?"

"They got me, Laurel. They caught me at the airport and killed me."

His shirt was covered in blood.

She stared in horror and threw her hand to her chest. "Oh, my God, Luke! Oh, my God. No!"

"I had to warn you."

"You came here to warn me?"

"Anthony will come after you, too. You're the main benefactor of my will."

"What?"

"You're worth *way* more than even before. He'll want it all."

"What am I supposed to do? Hide forever? Live in a cave? I'm an artist, Luke. I live to paint, to share my art with others."

"I can't protect you. Just remember what I told you."

"Hide in plain view," she said.

He nodded and disappeared.

Becca closed the window and got back in bed, shaking. Luke was dead. She'd always wondered if they'd get back together. Now, they never could.

There was suddenly an empty space in her world, a void deep inside. But he'd come to tell her, come to warn her,

He'd obviously been stabbed over and over. Had he screamed in pain, felt terrified and utterly defenseless? The tears streamed down her cheeks and her body was wracked with uncontrollable sobs.

Marcus stepped into the Captain's office. "Keith Uberhoff said that you wanted to see me?"

The Captain smiled. "Like being on day shift, do you?"

"Yes sir."

"You like having regular hours so you can sleep when it's night and get up for the day?"

He was going somewhere with this, but Marcus couldn't figure out where. "Yes."

"Good, because the annual Tip A Cop is coming up and you've signed up for it."

"I never signed up for –"

"I just said you did, and that means, you're signed up for it."

He'd heard about the event, hosted by some ladies' club where Metro and NHP officers worked as waiters to raise money for charity. But he never fathomed he'd be a part of it. "Now, hold on, I never agreed to that."

The Captain raised his eyebrows. "Don't you feel sorry for little orphans?"

"Well, of course I do."

"Don't you want to raise money so they can sleep in warm beds, have clean clothes to wear, food to eat?"

"Well, gee Captain."

"Then you'll do this." He slapped a flier across his desk. "Here're the details. It's in a month. Be sure you hit the gym."

What? That was all he did these days – work, sleep, hit the gym and stay away from women. They weren't good for anything but headaches.

Captain Schiff pointed a finger at him. "Be there."

Becca hovered as the hospital orderly helped Theresa into her car.

Theresa tried to smile. "You bought a Jaguar and a convertible one, too? Nice."

"Had to take you home in style, didn't I?" She tipped the orderly and hurried around to the driver's side of the white convertible. She got in and checked Arielle, already in the back seat. "All buckled in? Here we go."

She pulled out into traffic and they were soon on the freeway.

She hoped Theresa liked the new house and the way she'd furnished it. The house layout suited all of them with the bedrooms all on the second floor.

Theresa and Arielle had one side of the bridge, with three other extra bedrooms in that wing. There was a wet bar in the foyer off those bedrooms, so they had their own mini kitchen up there.

The nurse that she'd hired and the housekeeper she'd found had their own building with separate bedrooms and baths just off the pool. A cabana, the realtor had called it, but it was as large as Theresa's whole house.

Workers had swamped the entire place the past two days, running wires, installing intercoms. Her sister would have instant access to anyone, should she need something. She'd also had a crew put in place a new security system, with a dozen cameras to keep them safe.

Maybe she should get a guard dog. The gated community was home to lawyers and doctors and business owners and had a twelve-foot tall wall around it, but still, you couldn't be too careful.

Beside her, Theresa seemed so weak, so shrunken, a skeleton of her former self. "You OK, sis?"

Theresa smiled. "I am now. I hated that hospital. The only good thing about it was my doctor."

Becca nodded. Maybe not all the medicine that her sister needed to help her recover came in a bottle.

Two weeks later, Becca sped up the road to Mount Charleston.

"Where are we going, Aunt Laurel?"

"I'm planning a surprise for your mommy. She would always love coming up here when we visited family in Las Vegas." Her grandparents had built the cabin. Now that Grams was gone, it had been passed it down to her and Theresa.

The Jaguar ate up the grade until they were in a forest.

Arielle's eyes grew big as she looked out the window. "I saw a squirrel, wow. We should bring Mommy up here."

"That's the idea."

She parked by a little garage. It had seemed so much bigger when she'd been up here as a child. She unlocked the wooden doors and threw them open.

Dust flew everywhere.

Arielle waved it away and stared. "A Jeep?"

"That's right. You have to have four-wheel drive for where we're going." Becca slid behind the wheel, who cared that it was covered in a layer of filth? "Let's see if it starts."

It didn't. Too bad.

She shrugged at her niece. "Guess we get our exercise." She locked the garage back up and they headed up the dirt road.

Arielle struggled with some of the terrain. "Now I see why you need a Jeep, Aunt Laurel."

"You have to call me Becca, OK?"

Arielle pointed. "I see it!" She ran ahead.

There it was, the two bedroom cabin she'd loved to visit each summer as a child. They'd stuff logs into the fireplace, lit the fire and roasted marshmallows as they'd told scary stories. They didn't even have a TV set. There was no reception where they were located. Becca pulled out her cell and checked it. No phone reception, either.

She found the key and opened the cabin door. A musty smell hit them. It was dark inside. She felt for the switch and flipped on a light. At least the electricity worked.

Arielle crinkled her nose. "It smells old."

Dusty, was all. The kitchen was straight out of 1970. The walls had wood paneling. Did they even make paneling anymore?

Arielle raced up the stairs. "Hey, they wrap behind this big fireplace," she cried.

Becca joined her on the second level. "Wait until you see *this.*" She gestured for her niece to join her at the window. "Look out here. What do you see?"

"It's a water wheel!" Arielle shrieked. "Does it work?"

"It used to." She glanced around. Old, old, old. The place definitely needed a face lift. She'd have to contact her interior designer, the one who'd done miracles to get the house ready for Theresa's arrival, and have her oversee contractors to get this place back in shape. It would be a lot of work, up here in the woods, but the cabin was worth it.

"Come on, we'd better get back to town and see if your mom is awake."

"Why does she sleep so much?"

She tried to smile. "Your mommy's body is going through a lot, but she's being very brave. We have to help her as much as we can."

"I can draw her a picture. I'll draw the squirrel I saw. And the water wheel, too."

"She'd like that, sweetie."

Becca powered up her laptop as she sipped her morning coffee. She'd gotten up at four, had already run, already painted.

She clicked on her banking files. She'd paid for the house outright. Maybe that wasn't a smart move. She'd have to sell more paintings.

She entered her code and clicked her way through the maze of options. Savings. Withdrawals. Balance.

What? This number couldn't be right.

She found the phone number that Luke had given her before he died, grabbed her cell and dialed it.

"Shellenberger, Crenshaw and Martinelli. How may I help you?"

"Mr. Shellenberger, please. This is Becca de la Croix."

The line clicked. "Ms. de la Croix. Luke said you would be calling. I'm so sorry for your loss. Luke was a fine young man."

"Yes, he was. He died much too young."

"How can I help you?"

"I'm looking at my bank statements. I suddenly have twenty-two million in deposits."

"Yes, the first installments for licensing his invention are coming in. You'll see more over the coming months. We're monitoring them to make sure you get them on time."

"I appreciate that, but –"

"We're handling his will as well. You'll be notified when the reading will be." He paused. "Ms. de la Croix, you were already a millionaire in your own right, as I understand it, but now, you have joined the ranks of the super wealthy. We are here to serve your needs. Call us any time."

"Thank you."

She passed her hand over her forehead. Great. Now, Anthony Amalfitano suddenly had twenty-two million more reasons to hunt her down, with more on the way. She'd need a Swiss bank account ASAP.

The 9-1-1 operator hit a switch and spoke into her headset. It had been a long, crazy shift and all she wanted was to go home. But she kept her voice even toned. "Nine one one, what's your emergency?"

A female voice came on. "There's a woman driving in an open white convertible on the ninety-five freeway, and she has no top on."

"The convertible has no top?"

"No, the driver, some redhead. She's topless."

Only in Vegas. "As in, she has on no blouse?"

"Yeah. All these guys are going ga-ga and somebody almost hit me just now."

The 9-1-1 operator began typing away. "I see."

"I tell you, she's probably some damn stripper, and she's going to cause an accident."

The operator bit her tongue. "Is she driving erratically, ma'am?"

"No, but with all these guys straining to get a good look, she's a hazard, the hussy."

"I see. What's your position?"

"She's on south ninety-five coming up on Craig Road. You've got to do something about this."

"Don't worry, we've got someone on the way, ma'am."

Marcus hear the call come in as he cruised the ninety-five.

"All units, please see a woman in a convertible driving topless southbound 95."

Surely he hadn't heard that right. "Say again?"

"A woman is driving topless, southbound 95, passing Craig Road."

And he was the one who had to check things out? What a great job he had. "I'm one minute away."

CHAPTER TWENTY-TWO

He threw on his lights and hit the accelerator. Cars broke a path before him.

The suspect white convertible came into view just up ahead. Sure enough, a car that was passing it drifted into another lane before correcting itself. He caught a Nevada license on the convertible, a Jaguar. His brother-in-law had just leased the same make and model. It had been a dream to test drive.

Marcus watched the convertible. No weaving, no unsafe speed or other telltale signs of impaired driving. She was maintaining a constant speed, wasn't speeding, wasn't leaving her lane, so she likely wasn't on drugs or drunk.

He smiled. Maybe she just enjoyed the sunshine on her bare skin. Maybe he could enjoy it with her. He maneuvered behind her and hit the siren.

Her brake lights came on. She steered the car smoothly to the shoulder of the freeway.

There was long red hair beneath the scarf she wore, and, yup, from here, she sure looked topless. Marcus set the motorcycle on its stand and swung off it. He pulled his notepad out of its compartment and strode up behind the driver. "License and registration, please," he said.

Darn, she wasn't topless, just wearing a sleeveless shell that was flesh colored.

The driver pawed in her purse, found her license and handed it over.

He checked the name. "Becca de la Croix?"

She bit back a smile. "It's pronounced 'kwah,'" she told him. "I take it you don't speak French."

He scowled. She was laughing at him. And he didn't like being corrected. "No, miss, I don't. Do you know why I pulled you over?" He maneuvered so he was next to her side mirror, facing her head on.

"No. Why?" She reached into her glove compartment.

He paused. The sleeveless top was made from some fabric that had little swirls on it with dots of brown here and there. Two of those dots had caused motorists to do a double take. They were strategically placed, allowing her to go braless.

Her breasts pressed the fabric out and the breezy drive had resulted in stimulation of her nipples. Marcus cleared his throat. "Your outfit is, er, having an effect on other people."

"It's supposed to, Mr. Police Officer."

He was a state trooper not municipal police, but she'd showed respect so he let it go. "Excuse me?"

"It's called 'Enticement.' " She made a little movement that sent her breasts moving just enough to hint at how voluptuous she was underneath.

His face heat up. Yup, she'd been enticing people, all right. She was enticing him right now, he could feel it in his pants. Good thing he had his sunglasses on or she'd catch him staring.

She held out her insurance card. "What's the matter? You don't like enticement?"

Maybe she was a stripper. He ignored her insurance card. It was probably some pimp's name on it, anyway. "I, um, have to ask you to put the top up on your car."

She blinked in innocence. "Why?"

"Because you're creating a hazardous situation." He handed back her information.

She scoffed, which sent her breasts jiggling again. "I beg your pardon?"

Marcus squirmed, wishing he could adjust his package. "Other drivers assumed you were topless and nearly drove off the road, trying to get a better look."

"So I'm being penalized?" She shrugged. "That's their problem."

Jeez, every time she moved, he had to fight to keep his gaze off her chest. "Not if it's creating a public hazard."

Ms. Lah-de-dah Kwah or whatever her name was, gestured. "It's a beautiful day. This is the land of the free. I shouldn't have to raise the top."

"Well, you *do* have to."

"No, I don't."

"I told you. You have to."

She pointed at a passing car. "See? He has *his* convertible top down."

OK, she was being a pain now. "Miss, I'm telling you to put the top back up."

"Show me the law that says I have to."

He'd had enough of this shit. "Do you want me to take you in?"

"To jail? On what charge?"

She had him there, but damn, if she wasn't getting his dander up. He should pull her in just to show her he meant business. "Listen, miss, I'm not playing games here."

"Nether am I."

"You can't drive without your top on."

She cocked her head and raised a single eyebrow, letting his words hang in the air.

His face burned. Shit.

She acted amused. "It's called 'Enticement' for a reason, officer."

She set her elbow on the door and cradled her jaw, blinking her big, blue eyes at him. She smiled. "You don't know who I am, do you?"

Oh, so now, she was going to pull the old "I'm above the law because I'm rich" ploy. Now he knew just what type of woman she was. "I can guess who you are. You're some stripper slash hooker who thinks she's God's gift to man."

"What!" Ms. de la whatever pouted. She had those full, luscious lips of a lipstick model. "How *dare* you say that to me!"

He reached into her car and hit a switch on the dashboard. A motor whirred quietly as the top instantly raised itself. There, let her wonder how he knew exactly where the button was on an expensive car like this. "Have a good day, miss."

He strode back to his bike just as Keith Uberhoff rode up, lights flashing.

"I heard the call," he said, hurrying over to Miss Lah-de dah's Jaguar.

"Nothing to see," Marcus said, but he kept an ear out.

"Everything all right, Miss?" Uberhoff asked her, approaching.

"Apparently that other officer doesn't think so," she said, loud enough for him to hear as she got out of her car.

Marcus stared. She hadn't seemed that tall in the driver's seat but now, she unfolded her legs and matched the height of his fellow officer. And she was wearing flats.

Miss Lah-de dah flung a hand his way. "He honestly accused me of driving topless and forced my convertible top back up. Then, he called me a hooker."

"He's just having a tough day."

"If you ask me, he's frustrated," she said.

Uberoff shrugged. "He needs to get a life."

She twisted to look back at him straight on and those breasts jiggled some more. "Maybe he needs to get a woman."

They both chuckled.

Marcus' face burned. *Jeez, Uberhoff, stop thinking with your dick. Can't you see she's manipulating you?*

Half a dozen other officers raced up, some in cars, some on motorcycles, all of them swarmed her, eager to get a good look.

Ms. Lah-de dah began twirling around like this was a damn fashion show.

The damn woman would show up on his radar again one of these days, he was sure of it.

He started his motorcycle, revved the engine and pulled away. Ms. Lah-de dah was out of his hair and wasn't worth another thought.

Becca took the stage and greeted the ladies seated before her. More than a hundred were gathered at the MGM Grand banquet room. It was a Just For the Children event, raising money for those taken in by the county from indigent homes. They'd paid three hundred dollars to have lunch and now, a month after moving to town, she was the main attraction.

"How wonderful to see you all," she said. "I have to say, since moving to Las Vegas, I've met the most fabulous people. You're here to help out the children – did you see those incredible silent auction gifts? I was tempted to snatch up every one of them.

"But you're here to see how I work. As inspired as I feel today, being here with all of you, I know the results will be enticing. In fact, that's the name of my latest creative streak. I call it 'Enticement'." She gestured to her flesh-colored top and matching pants, letting the sheerness of the fabric float around her while the lining underneath allowed her to be discreet. "Wouldn't your man love to see you in this, huh?"

The women tittered.

"Twenty pounds ago," someone called out.

Everyone laughed. "Let me get my paint brush ready as my 'assistant' rolls out my specimen."

The assistant was one of the board members. The specimen was a department store dummy in a simple white shift.

She approached the dummy. "When I think, 'Enticement,' I see flowing lines like this," she told the audience, and let her paint brush scroll down the bodice of the dress. She added more lines; building off the first, then loaded her brush with more paint and created dots. "Gee, it reminds me the outfit I'm wearing." She gestured to her clothes. "Can you believe, a police officer stopped me on my way into town today and accused me of being topless? No, really, he did."

The audience cracked up.

She shrugged. "Well, I suppose that's *one* way to get a man's attention."

Of course, that man had been a certifiable jerk and he was the last man on earth whose attention she'd want.

A couple strokes and dots later, and the outfit was ready to be auctioned off to the highest bidder.

"Two thousand."

"Five thousand."

The assistant slash board member stood up. "Twenty-five thousand dollars."

Everyone burst into applause.

Not bad, for something she'd had a Philippine lady in Hicksville, Long Island sew up for two hundred bucks.

Becca retook the stage again and held up a white silk scarf. "If anyone wants their own, personalized scarf, with the design revolving around their name, I'll be happy to have you as a client. They're only a thousand dollars. All of it goes to the Just For the Children Foundation. My easel is set up right over there."

The ladies lined up as she took a seat. The first one was a heavyset woman who gushed as she approached. "I've got one of your paintings in my beach house in Miami. Everyone remarks on it."

A giclee, she meant. "You're so kind. What's your first name?"

"Henrietta."

"That makes me think of ocean waves and a romantic dinner on the beach." She dabbed her brush in a deep blue and made lazy strokes. "No one else will have a scarf just like this," she assured her client.

"Ooh," Henrietta cooed and clapped her hands.

A young lady dripping in jewels came up to her. "I'm Amelia."

Amelia Wutherbee been pointed out to her earlier. She was mistress to the biggest hotel mogul in Las Vegas. They reportedly liked to go on Safaris together. "Amelia, hmm, I'm getting a sense of African adventures with lines like gazelles and long legged giraffes." She painted the scarf and signed it in the corner.

Amelia burst into a huge smile. "You *are* the Painter of Emotions." She dropped ten large bills in the jar and then handed Becca ten more. "For you." She watched her closely.

It was a test.

Becca smiled, shook her head and dropped the tip in the jar. "Not for me, for the children," she said.

Amelia nodded and let the next lady have her turn.

Anthony clenched his fists. "You fucking idiot. I didn't say to kill him!"

The man stood still, eyes big. "I thought –"

"You thought nothing! I *told* you I wanted him to fork over information." He kicked over a trash can. "Can't you L.A. guys follow orders?"

"Had you agreed to meet with me, like I asked, your wishes would have been clear. But you went through three channels to relay them. I was told he had to be 'dealt with.' So, I dealt with him."

The man was right. They should have had a face to face. But there hadn't been time, damn it.

"Look," the man gestured, "I took his backpack, Anthony. Look in it. It's got the fake IDs, his laptop, his cell phone. You can get loads of information from that."

Anthony hesitated and stared at Luke's backpack. Well, at least the idiot had grabbed that. Luke's bank account information must be in there somewhere. All he needed was the account number and password. "You're a lucky man," he said. "Now, go."

Marcus pulled up to the elementary school, parked his motorcycle up front and swung one leg over the saddle. This was the fun part of the job, telling the kids why they should always obey the law and how to be a good citizen. The way they looked up to him, eyes wide when he handed out his junior trooper badges, there was nothing like it.

He glanced around. Graffiti. Crumbling sidewalks and patched asphalt. The school was in an older part of town and long neglected. These kids deserved better.

He went inside, removed his sunglasses and helmet. The office was up front, two clerks busy at computers. He caught the eye of one of them, an older woman with swept up hair and gave her an easy smile. "Hi, there. I'm Marcus, here for the assembly."

She jumped up. "Yes, you're our star speaker. I'm Miss Walker. Let me escort you to the multi-purpose room." She held open the swinging half door and gestured him to step behind the desk. "We'll take the back way."

Of course they would. The last time he'd done this, he'd been mobbed in the hallway, little children ringing around him, eyes alight with adoration. To them, he was a real live hero.

Miss Walker led him through the employee break room, past a storage area and down a hallway. He could already hear the children, chattering and laughing. Jeez, they must be really excited to hear a highway police officer was at their school today. "Big day for them, huh?"

"I'll say. Good thing we scheduled this for the last period of the day." Miss Walker threw open the door to the assembly hall.

The cacophony of noise hit his ears. What the heck was going on here? Little children were jumping up and down, talking, yelling, screaming and shrieking in joy. All of them clung to bicycles.

Up on the stage, adults were wheeling bikes over to children who were waiting anxiously in line. There had to be three hundred children, three hundred bicycles. He turned to Miss Walker. "What is this?"

She beamed and raised her voice so she could be heard. "We had a generous donor who decided to give new bicycles to every child in the school. Every single child, can you imagine?"

Money trumped public service, apparently. "Wonderful."

"The trucks pulled up half an hour ago." She gestured. "It's amazing, isn't it? We've never had a donation like this."

Great, but this was supposed to be *his* day. How was he supposed to speak? How was he supposed to get any safety messages across to little children who just been handed one heck of a gift?

It had been a waste of time, scheduling his talk for today, not when some big shot casino executive decided to jump in, steal the spotlight to play Santa. Boss-man probably just wanted to get thank you cards, printed in crayon and decorated with stick figures, to paper his office. "So, who's the big wig?"

"The what?"

"The donor?"

"Oh, she didn't want to be identified."

She. Elaine Wynn, had to be. She was known to be a champion for under privileged children, even had a school named after her. Now he felt ashamed for thinking badly about the person behind such a generous act of kindness.

"But I suppose I can tell *you* who it is," Miss Walker said. "It's an international artist who just moved here, Becca de la Croix."

Wait. The woman in the Jaguar? The one who'd unfolded her legs to get out of her car and twirled around for all the troopers gathered around? Shit, the woman wasn't even here and she still managed to be a thorn in his side.

Theresa heard the front door slam and the patter of feet running up the stairs. She smiled. Arielle was home from school.

Yup, her daughter charged into the room a few seconds later. "Look what we did today."

It was an art project, which her child plopped on her lap. "If I was sitting up, I could see it better."

"I'll do it." Arielle hit the switch and powered her bed to a sitting position.

One of the private nurses popped her head around the corner at the sound, a look of concern on her face.

Theresa waved her away. They both knew the automatic bed fascinated Arielle. "Why, what a good job."

"I did it just for you."

"I'm so lucky to have such a talented daughter."

"Can I have a cookie?"

"Sure. But just one."

"Oh, yeah, that doctor is here. He was pulling up when I came home."

Did she mean Dr. Juarez? He made house calls? "Quick, hand me my brush, my lipstick."

CHAPTER TWENTY-THREE

Two minutes later, Theresa watched as the doctor was escorted in. The guy sure was handsome. He'd brought flowers. "You shouldn't have."

"You mentioned that your sister was going out of town for some art event, so I thought I'd check up on you."

Becca had hired a private nurse, so he wasn't here for that. She smiled. "She's only gone for the day, not even twenty-four hours. So, tell me how you came to be a surgeon."

"Long story."

"Then you'll have to stay for dinner."

He smiled. "If you insist."

"I do, indeed."

Becca took the stage at the San Francisco museum. About two hundred people strolled among her giclees, exact copies of art she'd done in Spain. Thank goodness for the wonders of computer replication.

She switched on the mic set she wore over one ear. "Thank you all for coming tonight."

The place got quiet.

"When I flew in earlier, I was struck, once again, by your marvelous city. There's such great energy here in San Francisco, I'm feeling inspired. What do you say I throw a little paint on canvas?"

Everyone applauded.

The two models on other side, in the white shells and pants she'd had made up by her Long Island contact, placed a large canvas on the stage easel and stepped aside. The canvas already had her charcoal rendering on it, a subtle outline she'd done spur-of-the-moment as her private car had taken her into the city.

Becca poised her brush, took a deep breath and began to paint. "I'm feeling vibrancy, a real pulse to this city," she said into the mic. She slashed a wide streak of dark red paint near the bottom, changed colors and began painting the city – tall skyscrapers spiking into the sky, rushing vehicles streaking along the avenues, the hustle of people on the sidewalks.

The audience drew nearer to the stage, began murmuring.

"How can she do that so quickly?"

"Look, there's the bridge."

"That's how I see our city, too."

"George, we have to buy that. It would look great in our library."

Becca, stepped back, almost finished. "What do you say we add the final touch?"

The women tittered, as she'd hoped. Good, they knew what was coming. The two models stepped a little closer. The music came on, a throbbing beat.

Becca switched to a chromatic water color paint. She would be adding background color to the piece, the final touch.

"This is a city of power." She ran the brush off the canvas and onto the model on the right.

The crowd gasped.

"It's a city of industry." She took the brush to the model on the left. "It's the most exciting city in the world!" She added flourishes to the painting, to the clothes, letting the music drive her strokes. She ended with a flourish and a bow.

There was thundering applause. Her host took the stage. "What a dramatic demonstration – a Becca original created right before our eyes. Now, who wants to own this fabulous piece?"

"One hundred thousand," a man called out.

"Two hundred fifty," a woman yelled.

"Screw that, one million," yelled another man with a Texas accent. He looked about. "And I'll top anybody who wants to drive up the price."

Becca signed the piece. One million, all for a painting done on the fly. And they still had to auction off the outfits the two models wore. Whatever they brought in, she'd donate to charity, she decided.

A woman hurried up to her as she exited the stage. "That was quite a performance, Becca, very impressive."

"And you are?"

"I'm Afshama Lorrihami, the marketing manager for Xavier Fashions. We'd like to represent you, have you put out a line of Becca wear. Can we meet tomorrow?"

And leave Theresa for more than a day? Not going to happen. "Actually, I've got to catch a flight. But I'll have my rep contact you." She took the woman's card. She'd been meaning to expand the painted outfits to more than singular units. Now the opportunity was practically being handed to her. And to think she'd nearly cancelled this show out of concern for Theresa.

The art gallery was on the Strip in the Everest Hotel, a perfect location. Becca glanced at the art in the tasteful window. So far, so good. She stepped inside.

A hefty woman dripping in jewels came up to her. "Becca, Painter of Emotions," she sang out. "I've been simply *dying* to meet you."

"Are you the curator?"

"No, no, I'm Denise Schimmerwick. My husband owns this hotel." She gave Becca an air kiss. "I saw your work in a Paris gallery."

Paris? That's right. Gregor's influence had gotten a couple of her pieces in there. She owed her career to that man.

"I told him we simply *must* have your art on display here."

Becca smiled "Well, I was pleased to receive the invitation." The Schimmerwicks were worth more than six hundred million and were the sole owners of this mega operation, she'd been told. No way was she going to refuse an invitation from them. Still, an art gallery – in a casino setting?

"Let me show you." Denise led her to another area. "We've got a section right here that we want to devote just to you."

It was a corner, but a prominent one. The way the gallery was set up, everyone had to pass it on their way to view the other artwork. It truly was the perfect spot. "Wonderful. Let's look at the contract. I can have the paintings delivered tomorrow."

Denise Schimmerwick took her arm. "The office is this way. You know, Las Vegas has a reputation, a dark history."

The movie "Casino" jumped into her mind. Where was this lady going with this? "So I've heard."

"But we're much more refined now. We even have a philanthropic side."

"Really?"

"You should be at the Tip A Cop event."

"The what?"

"It's fun and it raises funds for disadvantaged children."

"How nice."

"We can count on you to donate a painting for the silent auction, yes?"

It looked like Denise Schimmerwick was a master manipulator. "Why, er, yes."

"And you'll come as my guest. Other women pay five hundred to attend."

Becca eyed the woman. Was that a challenge? "Look, I'll be happy to buy my own ticket."

"Wouldn't hear of it. Besides, you'll be passing out money right and left at the event, so bring a purse simply *stuffed* with money. I'll have Amelia Wutherbee get in touch with you about the details."

Becca came downstairs. Orange juice, then her run. She'd been up til midnight with Theresa, just talking about old times, Grams' cooking, little things they'd taken for granted as children. It had been like being college roommates reuniting, laughing and gabbing.

Arielle was eating breakfast. "Morning, Aunt Laurel."

"It's Saturday. Doing anything with your Mommy?"

"No, she'll be sleeping all day."

The medication, it wasn't chemo, but it still took its toll on Theresa. "I'm going running. How about you hop on your bike and go with me?"

Ten minutes later, they were on the meandering streets of their development. Arielle rode circles as she hustled along at a twelve minute pace.

"You're too slow," Arielle laughed. She stood on her peddles and pumped hard. "You'll never catch me."

"Honey, don't go too far ahead. I want to be able to see –" Shit, she was already around the corner.

A little red sports car zipped past her and rounded the corner. Too fast, he was going too fast.

There was a screech of tires.

Arielle, oh my God, Arielle. Was she all right? Becca threw her legs into overdrive and raced to the corner.

The old Mazda was parked at an odd angle, like it had fishtailed to a stop. A tall man in a ball cap and sunglasses was grabbing at Arielle, who was on the ground, her bike dropped on the road.

"You let go of her you brute!" Becca screamed, running up. She grabbed the man's arm and yanked it off her niece. "Oh, my God, you hit her." She knelt by Arielle, smoothed her hair. "Honey, are you all right? Are you hurt?"

Arielle looked up at her, dazed, but there was no blood.

The guy gestured. "I was just –"

Becca jumped up and turned on him. "You were just what? Trying to abduct a little girl? Huh? Is that how you get your kicks?"

"No, I –"

She got in his face, invading his space, forcing him back. *Yeah, I'm almost as tall as you. You can't push me around like you can my little niece.* "Looks to me like you intentionally hit her, tried to force her off the road. Is that what you did? Huh?"

He backed up, hands up in surrender. "No, I was –"

She shot a look over her shoulder at Arielle, who was just getting to her feet. "Are you OK? Did he hit you with his car?"

"No, he didn't hit me," she said.

Lucky for him. She stayed between the two of them, just in case he tried to get close to Arielle again.

Arielle brushed off some dirt. "My knee's a little scraped up."

Becca turned her full attention back to the jerk. OK, so maybe he hadn't hit her, but he must have come close. Now, Arielle was bruised. It wouldn't have happened if this stupid Neanderthal with his big muscles and his lead foot hadn't come careering around the corner. "What are you doing in this neighborhood, anyway? Huh? Who are you? The pool guy? The pizza delivery guy?"

"I'm –"

"You know what? Don't tell me, I don't want to hear it." She pressed into his personal space and backed him up all the way to his driver's side door. "Get in your little red jalopy and get out of my sight."

"Jalopy?" he sputtered. "You know what? Fine. I'm out of here." He got in his Mazda, slammed the door and threw it in gear. "You're crazy."

"I've memorized your license plate, pool boy," she warned. "I'd better not see you around here ever again."

He sped off.

"I think my bike is broken," Arielle pouted.

She hurried over and bent to inspect it. Sure enough, the front wheel was bent. It wasn't going anywhere.

Another car, a Jaguar like hers, only maroon, came around the bend. Becca stepped out and waved it down.

A nice looking man in a business suit pulled up and powered down the window. "Everything OK?"

Did she really want to get into a big explanation? Becca gestured to Arielle's bike. "We had a mishap. Could you possibly take us home? We live about five blocks that way."

"Sure." He got out. "Let me pop the bike in the trunk." He picked it up and wrestled the bike into his car. It just fit. He slammed down the trunk and held out his hand. "I'm Winslow Meddevia."

She introduced herself and Arielle.

He gestured for them to get in. "If you live five blocks that way, we're practically neighbors." He shot her a look. "Say, you didn't just move into the white contemporary?"

"That's us."

"Well then, we'll have to have a welcoming party soon. I'll have my wife get in touch with you."

She smiled. At least *some* people in this neighborhood were decent folks.

Anthony looked up from his breakfast. His uncle walked into the coffee shop and headed his way. What was he doing here? He stood up, had to act deferential. "Uncle Sal."

His uncle took a seat. "Your friend is dead."

"Those weren't my orders," Anthony said quickly.

"Calm down, I know that. The question is, what are you doing to get those millions that you owe me?"

That he *owed* him? How could he owe him if the deal hadn't gotten off the ground? "Excuse me?"

"Look, there's five million out there that should be in my pocket. It's your job to get it."

Anthony made sure no one was close enough to overhear him. "If he's dead, how am I supposed to shake him down for it?"

Uncle Sal leaned closer. "Think, Anthony. The man had a will, didn't he? Somebody stands to inherit that ten million."

He was right. There might still be a way to get the millions rolling in from every airline, worldwide. But ten million? He hid a smile. What his uncle didn't know, wouldn't hurt him.

"Find out who it is and, in that wonderful way you have, carefully explain to them that all we want is some of it."

CHAPTER TWENTY-FOUR

Becca inspected the bicycle Winslow had unloaded.

Arielle pouted. "Now I don't even have a bike. First, I move away from my friends and have to start at a new school. And now I can't even ride my bicycle."

"You sure you're not hurt? I still think that man swerved at you on purpose."

"No, I fell, is all." She hesitated. "He looked familiar, though."

Great, he was lurking around their new neighborhood, a stalker, a predator. She should report him to the police.

Theresa joined them in the garage. "What happened?" She knelt by her daughter and assessed her bruises.

Becca explained about the incident with the dark haired man. "I think he purposely swerved into Arielle and caused her to fall, though I admit, I didn't see exactly what happened."

Arielle brightened. "I know where I saw him before. He came to our old house, Mommy."

"He did? When?"

"You know, the night the babysitter was going to leave me all alone."

Theresa pulled back. "The officer who escorted me home with lights and sirens?"

Becca caught her breath. "You're telling me, this man's a cop?"

Theresa nodded.

Really? Becca folded her arms across her chest. "He didn't act like a cop today, trying to run Arielle off the road." In fact, he'd acted more like a hard-headed dick, just like that NHP trooper in the mirrored sunglasses who had given her a hard time, the jerk. She scoffed. "He was probably trying to impress you."

"No, he's a good man. He was the one we saw on TV when the house downtown caught fire. Remember, Arielle?"

"He looked different today in regular clothes," Arielle said.

"Yeah, he looked like a predator," Becca muttered.

Theresa shook her head. "Sis, you don't understand. He's a hero. He saved two children from that burning building. He didn't have to stop. He just happened to be driving by."

He'd stopped to save kids from a burning building? "Seriously?" Maybe she'd just assumed he'd tried to scare Arielle off the road.

Becca watched Afshama Lorrihami and Xavier Fashions' attorney enter her lawyer's office. The marketing manager was right on time, she liked that about her. She stood up. "Afshama, hello again. I appreciate you both flying all the way out here to Las Vegas."

"There are tougher assignments," Afshama said, smiling.

Tough to have to come to party town, she meant.

They shook hands all around.

The receptionist looked up. "Louis Valencia will see you now."

They were escorted down the hall and into a conference room. Her lawyer was already there, paperwork spread out on one side of the long table.

"Ladies, if you'll have a seat," Louis Valencia said. "Becca, you'll take this chair next to mine." He waited until they were seated. "We've had a lot of phone calls back and forth and just need to iron out the final details."

Becca spoke up. "I want a portion of the proceeds to go to a children's charity. I trust you've stipulated the same on your end?" She was putting them on the spot. How could they say "No" if it was for little children?

"Of course, we've already discussed it," Afshama said.

Becca smiled. "It seems we think alike then." She turned to her lawyer. "So, what little details still need ironing out?"

Forty five minutes later, Becca had negotiated a five-year contract for a guaranteed three million a year. She'd even made sure her Long Island seamstress had a secure part in the venture. She sat back. "I'm comfortable with the terms."

Louis Valencia clasped his hands together. "Then, congratulations. We have a deal. I'll have the changes drawn up and it'll ready to be signed tomorrow."

Marcus watched the little children crossed the stage in a long line, then stop and turn to face the audience, which consisted of him and a handful of adults.

A teacher at the front held up a baton. "One, two and three."

The children began singing a rock song.

Marcus shot a look at the teacher seated beside him, Allysa Something. Did the music teacher know what the real lyrics were to this song? Or were they trying to re-direct the lyrics to something much tamer?

He cleared his throat. "No 'Mary Had a Little Lamb' for these kids, huh?" he asked.

Allysa giggled. "Not these days. Not if you want to keep the children's attention." She touched his arm and left her hand there. "If you don't have children, then you probably don't realize things like that." She gazed into his eyes.

He shifted awkwardly in his seat. Did she really have to leave her hand there, or look at him like that? "Yeah," he said. "I, uh, never had kids."

Allysa batted her eyes. "There's still time, a strong, young man like you." She smiled, petting his arm. "It's nice to see a fine, upstanding man take an interest in children."

Shit. She was a shark and had him in her sights.

Why was he here again? Oh, yeah. Because he had a soft spot for disadvantaged kids. They deserved a chance in like, and that's what this foundation, Just For the Children, offered them. It had after-school art programs, bicycle rodeos, brought in puppeteers who talked about bullying and Mack King, a magician on the Strip, who did an abbreviated version of his show, then handed out free books.

Marcus shifted in his seat, easing his arm away from Allysa the Shark and wishing he'd declined the offer to see one of the programs in action.

A mature woman in a suit strode down the aisle, saw him and came over. "You must be Mr. Meddevia. Thank you for coming."

"Miss Vickins." He jumped up. "Nice to meet you. Let's talk over here."

He steered her to the far corner, far from the shark.

She glanced at the stage. "Tell me, how are you enjoying our little music rehearsal?"

With rock music sung by six- and seven-year olds? "It's an, uh, education in itself," he said. There, that was fairly diplomatic.

"I want to thank you for volunteering to be part of our career day later this week," she said. "The children will simply love watching you ride up on your motorcycle. It will be good for them to see that the police are really their friends."

He nodded. Yeah, where these kids lived, sirens usually meant Daddy was going to jail again. "I'm looking forward to it." He would hoist them up onto his bike, let them hit the light switch on it.

Miss Vickins shook her head in amazement. "You know, this foundation was barely keeping its legs under it, but we seem to have found a true benefactor, someone new to Las Vegas who really shares our vision."

"Is that right?"

"She's an artist, learned about us and said she has a real concern for disadvantaged children like those you see here. She wants to see they get a chance to make something of themselves."

Huh, it sounded like they shared the same goal. Maybe he should meet this artist, see if they couldn't come up with some inventive ways to draw in more community support for the kids. "I'd like to meet her."

"She doesn't just pump money into it, she's met with our board and wants to bring in new programming, field trips, hands on projects. She has all sorts of ideas."

"And who is this person?"

"Becca, the Painter of Emotions."

Wait, that name. Becca? Did she mean Ms. Lah-de dah? The woman in the Jaguar who he'd pulled over? "What's her last name?"

"De la Croix."

Yup, that was her. She cared about inner city kids? He would never have guessed.

Becca strapped on the helmet she'd been given and got in the car with her instructor who was riding shotgun.

"Buckle up. We'll be taking these corners really fast," he warned.

She frowned. "I don't get it. Shouldn't I be driving my own car for these lessons? I mean, if someone's going to try to run me off the road, won't I need to know exactly how my own car handles?"

He acted amused. "Let's get the basics down first. Then later, we'll switch to your own vehicle."

Whatever you say.

He pointed. "OK, start her up and keep both hands on the wheel."

Becca eyed the driving course with its cones and obstacles. She revved the engine. Wow, five hundred horses, nice. She could do this.

Two hours later, with the thrill of accomplishment surging through her veins, she thanked her instructor.

"Same time, Thursday?" he said.

"Absolutely." She glanced at her watch. Oh, darn, she was late for Arielle's school function.

Becca drummed her fingers on the steering wheel. Come on, change to green, would you? Green, green, green.

The traffic light changed.

She floored it.

Two minutes later, she raced into Arielle's school lot and screeched into a parking spot. She hated running late and of course things had put her behind, today of all days. She trotted into the school and found the auditorium. She'd made it.

"And that concludes our special program," the principal said. "Thank you, everyone, for coming."

Oh, no. She'd missed the entire thing.

Arielle crossed her arms and scowled at her from the stage.

This was not going to be a fun ride home.

Becca took the phone from the housekeeper, Shirley. The contractor was on the line. "I hope you have good news."

"We've uncovered some problems," he said. "The cabin needs a lot of work besides cosmetic stuff – new wiring, new plumbing. It's not going to be easy to get a backhoe in there."

"Do whatever you have to do."

"It might take a month."

Darn, she'd wanted to get Theresa up there sooner so she could spend a few days enjoying nature. Doc Juarez had said it would be helpful. "Please work fast."

"We'll get on it. Uh, on the plus side, we got the Jeep out. My buddy gave it a tune up, new tires and a new battery. She's set to go. Do you want it delivered to your house or taken back to the cabin's garage?"

The Jeep needed to be up there. It wasn't brand new but only had ten thousand miles on it. "Put it back in the garage, please. And thank you for all your trouble."

"Will do."

Theresa switched off the TV. Cooking shows. Reality TV. Nothing good was on.

She suddenly felt the urge to regurgitate and grabbed the bucket on her side table. Nothing.

The feeling passed.

Uh. This chemo. It was worse than the headaches had been. At least they had gone away after the surgery. With chemo, the effects lingered, only going away just in time for the next round.

Now, she just lay in bed in utter agony, trying to regain her strength, trying to have a smile for when Arielle came home from school.

She eyed her arms, skinnier than ever after the ravages of chemo.

Horrid stuff. Worse than death.

She picked up Arielle's picture. She was in her Brownie uniform, wearing a big smile with one missing tooth.

What would happen to Arielle if she *did* die from this cancer? No, stop thinking that way. She would beat this, had to make sure Arielle grew up with a mother.

"If it wasn't for you, kiddo, none of this would be worth it," she muttered.

The housekeeper peeked into her studio, phone in hand. "Sorry. There's a call for you."

Another interruption to her work. Just when she was on a roll.

Becca took the phone. She had no idea who it could be. Not many people knew this number. "Hello?"

"The Painter of Emotions, I finally found you." It was a woman, older sounding.

"Who is this?"

"Denise Schimmerwick. Becca, dear, you know that I'm a true supporter of the arts. I'm arranging for Nate Sheppard to come to town."

"The art critic? Really?"

"Yes. The Everest is hosting an event and I'm hoping Nate will see the value in opening his own gallery here."

"That would be a coup for Vegas." But that still didn't explain why the hotel owner was calling.

"He also needs to see that there's a thriving community of artists here."

Now it made sense. "You want me to attend?"

"I want you to host a social get together with him as the guest of honor. Now, I've got everything arranged – the Everest will provide the valet parking and cater the event, but I need an artist with a proper location."

Did she mean her *home*? "Surely there are other –"

"Mark Vranesh is still in Mexico, Nja is painting in the Caribbean and Alex Krasky is undergoing an operation. Other local artists have their little neighborhood places, teeny tiny homes." She huffed. "Honestly, I don't know why they can't live in mansions like everyone else who's successful, but, no, they prefer their comfy little shacks."

"Why not just hold it at the Everest?"

"I *told* you, Nate Sheppard needs to see that we have an artist community beyond the Strip."

"I really can't –"

"It'll just be one evening, a couple hours."

"Ms. Schimmerwick, I really don't think –"

"Call me Denise. We're going to be such good friends, you and I. I mean, I can introduce you to more art galleries than you've ever heard of. I'm on a first name basis with everyone, all around the world."

"My sister is not well, I'm not sure having guests –"

"Then an evening to take her mind off things is just what she needs. Now, Nate is only going to be here for three nights and the Everest event is Friday the fifteenth, so we'd better plan this for the following Saturday night."

It was a month away. "That's not much time."

"I told you, dear, I'll arrange everything. All you have to do is open the door."

Becca pushed back from her easel. Her paintings had been in flux lately, no doubt a reflection of her state of mind. Theresa's health, the sudden move, the news of Luke's wealth coming to her with its inherent danger, it was all affecting her artwork. Becca pulled back to eye her work in progress. Angst, uncertainty, they were intrinsically apparent in her strokes. She was the Painter of Emotions, all right.

The sun was just rising. She caught the aroma of the coffee the housekeeper was brewing. It smelled heavenly. She made her way down the hall and across the main room.

A man was coming down the main stairs. *An intruder!* Her heartbeat increased.

It was Dr. Juarez.

Hold on. Wasn't it a little early to begin a one-on-one relationship? Then again, why shouldn't Theresa have a life after that junkie husband of hers had made her life miserable? Plus, the doctor seemed to be an honorable man.

Becca moved to the bottom of the stairs. "Have breakfast with me," she said.

He blushed. "I was going to –"

"Sneak out? Not on your life. We're Trentons. We take in stray puppies, shoe the homeless and feed those we like." She took his arm. "Nice of you to make a house call, doctor."

Five minutes later, her private chef handed them their omelets.

"Tell me, Doc, how is my sister doing?"

"She was restless all night, not a good sign. I checked her vitals. They're OK, but I want to run some more tests."

So, Theresa wasn't out of the woods. She sipped her coffee. "I was thinking of taking her up to Mount Charleston, just to get away for the day. Is she up to that?"

"Sure. It would take her mind off her health." He looked up from his stabbing his next bite. "Nothing strenuous like hiking, though."

Mount Charleston was almost twelve thousand feet, maybe the thinner air could be a factor for her sister as well. "Tell you what, why don't you join us?"

He brightened. "Spend more time with her? Sure."

Maybe he was enamored by Theresa's status as a showgirl. Maybe he just liked tall, leggy ladies. Or maybe he truly liked who her sister was on the inside.

They decided to go on Sunday, his day off. Arielle could come along, too.

Becca saw him to the door. She put her hand on his arm. "Don't break her heart, Doc."

The doorbell at his brother's house rang. Marcus turned from the manning the bar, his job for the party. Whoever it was, they sure adhered to the "fashionably late" code of living.

His brother answered the door.

Marcus glimpsed a tall woman partially hidden by his brother. Long legs, model thin, and in a tank top and shorts. Wow, just look at those boobs.

She stepped past Winslow and now he could see all of the newcomer. Hold on, he knew that long red hair.

Shit. It was the driver in the convertible, the one who'd said that he needed to get a life. It was the same woman who'd accused him of running over the little girl who'd fallen on the bike. What was *she* doing here?

Winslow escorted the new arrival over to the bar and took the tray of food she'd brought. "This is Becca. Meet my bartender, also known as my brother Marcus."

She gave a start, then a half smile. "We've met, sort of."

"Good," Winslow said. "Then I'll go play host to the other gazillion people here." He excused himself.

Marcus gestured. "Your niece, she explained to you that she actually *fell* off her bike, right? That I was not the cause?"

"Yes," she nodded. "And I read the newspaper account of the fire. Look, I'm sorry. I was in mama bear mode, sure that you were some predator. The bike incident, I owe you an apology."

The "bike incident" but not their other meeting when he'd made her put up the top on her Jaguar. She obviously didn't realize who he was, that he'd pulled her over, argued with her and come "this close" to giving her a ticket Wait, that's right, he'd had his sunglasses and helmet on the entire time. She probably hadn't even been able to determine his hair color.

Winslow ducked back into the conversation as he whisked past. "She's an artist, just moved here from Europe."

"He makes it sound so glamorous," she said, waving his endorsement away. "I'm really just following my heart's desire. I think everyone should." She leaned forward like she wanted to confide in him. "Otherwise the world would be full of really grumpy people." She held out her hand. "Nice to meet you, Marcus, now that I know you're not a child abductor but actually a knight in shining armor."

She was being so breezy, so open and fun loving. Maybe she didn't need to be reminded of that traffic stop just yet. He shook her hand. "I'm Marcus."

She'd made a little shoulder shrug and it set her breasts jiggling. God, she must look awesome in a bathing suit. He tore his eyes away from her massive chest. "You like the outdoors, do you?" Maybe she liked hiking. Maybe she liked camping.

"I'd shrivel up and die if I was inside all the time. We have a family cabin on Mount Charleston. It's being renovated right now, and I can't wait until it's done so we can spend time up there."

So, she really *did* like the outdoors. "What part of Europe? Are you royalty?"

She laughed. "Hardly. I went there as an art student and had a really fantastic mentor. It's nice when someone who is accomplished steps up to help someone new to the business, you know what I mean?"

This girl certainly wasn't full of herself. She gave credit to others, appreciated the breaks she'd been given. She was truly a breath of fresh air in a town like Vegas.

She glanced around the room.

Marcus used the opportunity to check out her breasts. She could stop traffic with those things.

"Nice place your brother has."

"Huh?" His gaze shot back up to her face. "Uh, yeah."

"Do you live nearby?"

Sure, like he could afford a swanky place like this. "Not really. Can I pour you a drink?"

She leaned close and whispered. "Just pour water into a wine glass so it just *looks* like I'm drinking."

He smiled to himself as he poured her drink. This Becca was *so* unlike other Vegas girls. "Yeah, you want to be able to control your vehicle."

"As a matter of fact, I'm taking driving lessons."

He handed her the wine glass with water. "You don't know how to drive?"

"I don't know how to drive like a stunt man."

He had no idea what she was talking about. "And you want to learn those skills because …?"

She paused, acted uncomfortable. "Well, a girl can never be too careful."

Whatever that meant. Maybe she attracted men so unconsciously that they stalked her, followed her in their cars. She sure attracted him.

He glanced up.

Shit, Keith Uberhoff was approaching.

Marcus suddenly realized that he didn't want to share the attention of this girl. He wanted to keep talking with Becca one-on-one, learn more about her. He glanced at her chest again and melted. He'd like to do other one-on-one things with her, too.

Keith Uberhoff came up behind Becca. "So, Marcus, have you pulled over any more topless women in convertibles lately?"

Becca stiffened. "You! That was *you?*" Her eyes blazed across the bar at him.

Uberhoff turned to her. "Hi, I'm Keith. Have we met? No, we couldn't have. I'd remember eyes like those anywhere."

Marcus groaned. *Sure, like it was her eyes he was staring at.*

Keith took her elbow. "Let me steal you away from this ugly fellow. He'll bore you to tears."

She shot Marcus a look of contempt and linked arms with his patrol buddy. "Why don't you give me the house tour, Keith? I'm sure you'd be more forthcoming."

No, don't go. Let me explain.

Marcus watched his nephew, Timothy, cannonball into the pool. The kid was a regular fish in the water. He glanced around. Where was Becca? Holy shit, would you look at that.

She was just coming out of the pool house wearing a bikini no bigger than a band aid. There was no hiding her assets now, not in that tiny little thing. Becca had gorgeous breasts, full and sloped just the way he liked.

All the men at the BBQ turned to stare. Becca really *could* stop traffic.

If only he could redeem himself, get her attention, be the one who stood out in her mind, but in a good way.

In the pool, Timothy grabbed his buddy and they dunked each other, shrieking with laughter.

Marcus bit his lip. He had an idea.

Five minutes later, he sauntered over to where Becca was stretched out in a lounge chair. That body. Those legs. All that golden skin. She could be a goddess.

He squatted in front of her and cleared his throat. "I, uh, would like to apologize for the way I acted when I pulled your car over."

She lowered her sunglasses to peer at him. She was not smiling. "It's been said that we show our true selves when we hide behind masks of authority," she said.

Shit, she was going to cite philosophy at him. "I was in the wrong."

"Is that how you always are? Rude and obnoxious? Judging others without regard to the facts? Rigid adherence to rules when simple common decency would better serve the situation?"

Damn it woman, I'm apologizing and you're being a bitch about it.

"Look!" a little boy shouted. "Timothy's drowning!"

Becca gasped.

Marcus jumped up. "I'm coming, Timothy!"

He ran to the lip of the pool and dove in.

He grabbed the flailing Timothy and dragged him to the edge. Others helped the child out.

"Does he need me to do CPR?" Marcus yelled as he hoisted himself out of the water.

He risked a quick look around.

Where was Becca?

Had she seen him save him come to the rescue?

There, there she was, peering out above people, watching everything, eyes wide. She'd seen him make the dramatic rescue, right?

He knelt beside his nephew. "You OK, buddy?"

Timothy gestured him close and whispered, "When do I get my ten bucks?"

Becca arrived at the Moroccan Hotel and Casino with a painting for the Tip A Cop event. Inside, the Marrakesh Room was filled with people setting up the tables, arranging flowers, marking auction items.

"Becca, over here," Amelia Wutherbee called.

They air kissed and her hostess took the painting, holding it out before her. "Amazing. I just love your work. I hope it brings a gazillion dollars."

In New York or London, maybe. She wasn't sure Las Vegans were used to spending that kind of money. She followed her to where an easel had been set up. A placard read, "A painting by the renowned Becca, Painter of Emotions. Starting bid five hundred dollars."

She was right. Las Vegans weren't used to spending large sums of money. Oh well, it was for charity, plus, she wouldn't have to paint on stage tonight, wouldn't have to perform. "How does this work, again?"

"The dinner is nothing to rave about, but the fun is ordering the cops around. We have, like, two dozen of them. Every tip they earn goes to the charity, of course. They do this on their own time." Amelia smiled. "They fight crime by day and are forced to succumb to our commands at night."

"I'm going to like this."

"Come on, we've got an hour before things start up. Let's go get a foot massage. Andre has the most fabulous hands."

The Marrakesh Room, now dimmed, was bustling when they returned. Amelia hadn't been kidding. Andre truly *did* have the most fabulous hands. Becca found her seat at a table of ten. Only the chair beside her remained unoccupied.

"Sit right here." Her neighbor sloshed a drink her way. "Oopsies," the woman giggled.

Becca smiled. It seemed it was party time for the ladies. From the look of things, the women were already on their second glass of wine. Some of them had stronger drinks.

The lights dimmed. A cheer went up. Two dozen police officers took the stage. They were in uniform, no, not completely. They all had on uniform shirts, some tan, some blue, and their officers' hats, but they all wore black spandex slacks. *Nice.*

Amelia Wutherbee slipped into the vacant seat next to her. "Oh good, I didn't miss the show."

A throbbing disco beat came on the speakers. The women in the audience went into a frenzy, whooping and hollering.

One of the police officers was center stage, the others in a half circle behind him. He was grinning as he pulled his shirt from his pants and unbuttoned it, jiving to the beat.

Oh, my goodness.

"Take it off," a woman yelled.

He pointed at her and, grabbing each shirt panel, tore them open. He was buff, tanned.

Jeez, this guy should have been a Chippendale's dancer.

He removed his shirt completely, gave the ladies a body builder's pose and was rewarded with more shrieks and cat calls.

The next officer took center stage.

Becca sipped her drink and relaxed. Las Vegas could sure put on a show for the ladies.

After a third officer had done his mini striptease, the remaining officers removed their shirts at the same time. So much skin, so many muscles, she could get used to this.

She got Amelia's attention. "How can we tip them for stripping if they're all on stage, out of reach? Isn't the fun of Vegas about slipping a bill into someone's G-string?" *Oh, that sounded crass.*

"You're so funny, Becca," Amelia laughed. "They're going to be our servers tonight."

Even better.

CHAPTER TWENTY-FIVE

The emcee took the mic. "How about a big round of applause for our brave officers?"

The ladies whooped it up as the officers pulled their shirts back on and left the stage, waving goodbye.

"Let's not forget why we're here. All proceeds go to the Children's Foundation. They do such good work for the underprivileged. While the officers are getting ready to bring you your dinner, let's have a word from the CEO of the foundation, telling about all the programs that need funding."

A man in a tux took the stage and began a prepared speech.

Amelia turned back to the table and addressed the women. "Ladies, we have an international celebrity at our table. This is Becca, Painter of Emotions. She's donated one of her paintings for our silent auction. Let me introduce you to everyone, Becca."

The names came at her along with the women's affiliations. One owned a catering company, another had a slew of jewelry stores, yet another was the head of a publishing company.

A salad plate was slipped before her. "Thank you." She looked up.

A cop with dark chiseled features – oh, gosh, it was Winslow's brother, the one who'd saved the little boy from drowning – smiled down at her. His eyes held hers. "My pleasure, Becca."

His shirt was partly opened. My God, look at those pectorals. He had an airbrushed tan, all the cops did, but you couldn't airbrush on muscles like these. She hadn't noticed how fit he was at the BBQ. Now, she noticed.

Amelia nudged her. "This is Tip A Cop, remember?"

What? "Yes, that's right." She plucked a hundred dollar bill from her purse. Oh, Jeez, where to put it? Her face flushed red. She spotted his breast pocket and slipped it in. His chest felt hard as a rock, damn.

She sipped more wine and watched as he turned away – broad shoulders and a tight butt. Nice. He'd run into a burning building, saved two children and stopped to aid Arielle when she'd fallen on her bike.

OK, maybe when he'd pulled her over, he'd been having a bad day. She'd give him the benefit of the doubt.

She felt the wine give her a buzz. A crazy idea formed in her brain. Hmmm, cops were used to giving orders. Let's see how they did at taking them.

She caught Marcus' eye and tossed a utensil over her shoulder.

He watched it drop to the floor.

"Officer Meddevia? Could you bring me another salad fork?" She batted her eyes. "I seem to have dropped mine."

He gave her a saucy look and returned with one. "There you go, happy to help."

She rewarded him with another hundred dollar bill, down his pants this time. Her fingers lingered as their eyes locked. It was hard to breathe. She slowly slid her hand back out.

All the other women at the table looked at one another and tossed their forks in unison.

Marcus smiled. "Looks like you started a trend."

After the salad course, Becca lost her napkin. "Could I have another, Marcus?" She smiled sweetly at him as she ran a finger around the rim of her wine glass.

He brought her another and slipped it into her lap. His fingers slid against her thigh and lingered.

Oh, Lordie, he'd just reciprocated. Naughty.

Becca pulled out another one-hundred dollar bill. She smiled up at him as she tucked it deep down his waistband. "For your trouble, Marcus."

He bowed, giving her a long look. "Thank you."

No, thank *you*. God, this man was tormenting her.

Amelia broke in. "Did you see the items in the silent auction? Andre is offering a package."

Andre and his magic hands had something in the silent auction? She'd have to go bid on it. In fact, she should see what else was available while the salads were cleared.

Becca left the table and slipped over to the items up for bid.

Andre's package was pretty popular, a slew of women had bid on it. She upped the ante by another thousand dollars and went to add her name beside it, hesitated and wrote Theresa's name instead. Even if she didn't win, they could still go and get massages together, make a day of it. Her sister deserved a day of pampering.

Oh, look. There was the painting she'd donated. Five people had bid on it. The first name was a guy's. Funny, she didn't think any men were in the audience. She peered closer in the dim light at the name on the bid sheet.

Marcus Meddevia, it read.

The NHP trooper?

She turned, searching for him. There he was, across the room, removing plates from a table. She'd never guess that the NHP officer would bid on her painting. Artwork, Marcus – the combination just did not compute.

Maybe there was more to this man than she'd first thought.

Becca returned to the table. "Our hunky waiter bid on my piece," she whispered to Amelia as she took her seat. "But he only bid a thousand dollars."

"That's a lot for a police officer. They only make, like, forty grand a year."

That wasn't very much. No wonder he hadn't re-bid and upped the price. She caught his attention. "Officer Meddevia? There's no pepper." She pouted.

He gave her a knowing look, reached just beyond her plate to pluck it off the table. "It's right here by your water glass."

Becca breathed in his cologne as he slid it next to her plate. This guy was beyond hot.

"It was inches in front of you," Marcus pointed out.

"Why, so it was." She pulled out a one hundred dollar and slipped it into his waistband, letting her fingers linger even longer this time. Was she fooling herself or did he want this, too?

He shot her a look like he wanted to throw her on the table and ravish her. Oh, yeah, he felt it, too.

It was time to turn things up a notch. She turned to the other ladies at the table. "Girls, don't you think our server is overdressed?" She smiled at him. "You don't need that shirt on, Marcus. Take it off."

The ladies took up the call. "Take it off. Take it off. Take it off. Take it off."

He held his hands out like he was pleading for mercy. "Ladies, I mean, really?"

"Take it off. Take it off."

Marcus leaned into her and muttered. "I'm only doing this for you, Becca." His eyes held hers as he peeled back the shirt, revealing rock hard abs.

The ladies squealed in delight.

He pulled it from his shoulders until it was off completely as the ladies pulled out their money.

Becca looked up at Marcus as he draped the uniform shirt over her shoulders. "Just wait until I suggest you remove your pants," she whispered to him.

His grin froze. "You wouldn't."

"I might."

"You wouldn't," he repeated.

She pulled back in her chair and let her eyes travel down his body. "Don't tempt me." She took out a C-note and slid it down his pants, way down his pants. Becca let her hand linger there.

They locked eyes.

No one else in the room mattered.

God, she wanted this man.

A flash went off and they jerked apart.

Becca felt her face warm up. What had just happened? She'd never been so forward before.

He shot her a long look that said, "This isn't over."

Oh, yeah, he'd felt it.

Marcus moved off to get their desserts.

Damn, that man was hot.

There was movement along the wall. The silent auction baskets were being collected.

Wait. "Excuse me." Becca jumped up and hurried over to her painting. The highest bid was one hundred thousand. She scribbled down the final bid, two hundred thousand, and put it in Theresa's name. There, that ought to secure that she owned the painting.

Three days later, Becca's phone rang. "Hello?"

"It's Charles Shellenberger in Los Angeles. I was Luke's attorney?"

"Yes of course. I hope you'll forgive me for missing the reading of the will. My sister's been in the hospital."

"Understandable. I trust she will be better soon. I'm calling because my secretary has reported an unusual phone call. The man did not identify himself, but he inquired as to Luke's will and, in a crass manner, asked who gets his money."

"What?"

"Our firm did not divulge anything, of course, but it was so unusual, and in light of how he died, well, I thought you should be forewarned."

"I appreciate that."

"One cannot be too careful, my dear."

Marcus rapped on the Captain's door. "You wanted to see me?"

Captain Schiff looked up from his computer. "Ah, Marcus, come in." He reached behind a file cabinet and pulled out a rectangular package in plain paper. "This came for you."

Something was mailed to headquarters for him? That was odd.

The Captain gestured. "Open it."

Marcus found an edge on the backside and tore the mailing paper back. It was the frame for a picture. He freed it from the wrapping, turned it around and held it up. It was the painting from the Tip A Cop event, the one he'd bid on, the first to start the bidding. Others had signed up behind him, bidding more, way more. This didn't make any sense.

The Captain pointed. "You dropped the card."

He scooped it up and scanned it. "Thank you for supporting the children's event. I thought the painting should belong to someone who really seemed to appreciate it. Theresa Trenton." He looked up. "Who's Theresa Trenton?"

Captain Schiff shook his head. "Damned if I know."

She must be affiliated with Tip A Cop, on one of the committees or something. "I can't accept this. Do you know how much this thing brought in?"

"Paid for by someone with plenty of money to throw around, it seems." He shrugged. "It's yours now."

Marcus frowned. This wasn't sitting right with him. It had to be returned. Maybe motor vehicle records could lead him to this Theresa Trenton lady.

Luke was pacing outside her bedroom. Becca sat up in bed and rubbed her eyes. Her clock said three a.m. She slipped out to the balcony. "What are you doing here?"

He looked like crap, the stab wounds festering and his flesh rotting, but she wasn't going to tell him that.

"Don't go to New York City, Becca."

"I have to. It's a big show. Two thousand people." All her paintings had already been shipped to the hotel's event center.

"It's not safe. You'll be on Anthony's turf."

"I can't stop living, Luke. Painting is what I was always meant to do." How many times did she have to explain it to him? She could see the worry on his face. "I'll ask the hotel for extra security, OK?"

"Anthony wants the money, all of it."

"Maybe I should just give it to him, then, so I won't be looking over my shoulder all the time."

"Give him an inch, and he'll take a mile. He'll want the income from your art, too. For the rest of your life."

"What?" She pressed her hands to her temples. "This dilemma has to end. One way or another, it has to end."

The doorbell sounded. Becca set down her brush. Maybe Arielle's new bike was here. She'd better go see.

The housekeeper, Shirley, beat her to the door and opened it as she held back. Becca caught a glimpse of a tall man in casual clothes.

"Is Theresa Trenton here?" He held the painting from Tip A Cop.

She caught her breath. It was Marcus. "I'll handle this, Shirley." Becca stepped up. "Nice to see you again."

"Becca?" His jaw dropped but he recovered from his surprise quickly. "I, um, came to return this to Ms. Trenton."

"Theresa is my sister. Is there something wrong with the painting?"

"No, nothing. It's very nice."

So, he *did* like her work. She still couldn't equate a love of the finer things with a guy who could wrestle bad guys to the ground. "Please, come in." She led him to her studio. "If you like that, you might want to see these, my latest pieces."

He set down the painting and looked around at her work. "Very nice." Marcus turned to her. "There's been some mistake. This belongs to someone else. Mine wasn't the winning bid."

Her paintings touched people, struck a chord with them. Why wasn't it striking a chord with him? "Why don't you like my painting?" She had to know.

"I *do* like it."

"But you don't want it."

"Well, it's not that I wouldn't like to have it."

"But you do have it," she pointed out. "Now, you're trying to give it back."

He set his hands on his hips. "But I didn't bid on it."

"Yes, you did."

A hard look came on his face. "Mine wasn't the winning bid, woman," he said.

She liked the way he said "woman." Sexy. What would he say next? Me, cave man. You, cave woman. "Guess what? I decided it *was* the winning bid."

"Your sister bid higher than me."

"No, actually, I was the one who bid higher. I just wrote down her name."

He shook his head as though trying to make sense of it. "Wait. You bought your own painting?"

"Yes," she said, looking into his dark eyes, trying to read them. "Deliberately, so that you could have it."

He stepped a little closer. He was staring at her lips, which were almost even with his. "Why?" he breathed, maneuvering into her.

He was backing her into the corner, but she didn't care. He could back her off a cliff and she wouldn't care. This guy's animal magnetism was off the scale. It was hard to think with him so near.

"Why?" he repeated, softer this time. He moved a tad bit closer.

She barely found her voice. "You saved the boy from drowning, ran into a burning building. Then you gave up your time to be at Tip A Cop," she murmured. "You were funny, you were a gentleman" *And so freaking hot.* "I caught you blushing at one point."

"Well, you had your hand pretty deep down my pants -"

"Yeah, I was kind of bold." She wanted to be bold now, with him, right here. She lifted her lips to him. *Kiss me, Marcus.*

The intercom beeped. "Laurel?"

It was Theresa. Something must be wrong.

They broke apart, the spell broken.

"Yes, sis?"

"Can you come here? I don't feel so well."

Becca stepped away. "It's my sister, she was in the hospital."

Marcus nodded. "I'd better go." He turned to leave.

She scooped up the painting and followed him. "You forgot this," she said. "I don't take 'no' for an answer."

Marcus got to the foyer and stopped so fast she nearly crashed into him.

"Neither do I," he breathed.

His arm went around her, jerked her to him possessively. They were face to face, lips a mere inch apart.

CHAPTER TWENTY-SIX

His lips crushed hers, his mouth demanding, his tongue penetrating, searching.

She responded, hot for his kiss.

She dropped the painting, threw her arms around his neck. She wanted his hands on every inch of her, his lips on every inch of her, too. He was an addiction and she couldn't stop herself.

The kiss went on and on, hot, hard, demanding and oh, so sexy.

He broke it off, searched her eyes and breathed out like he'd just learned how. "What you don't do to me, woman." He turned and strode out the front door.

Becca grabbed the banister to keep her balance. *What a man.*

Anthony entered the New York art studio.

A man in a suit approached. The old geezer had on a bow tie. It was so old fashioned, Anthony almost laughed.

"May I help you, sir?"

"Yeah, yeah. I'm trying to locate an old friend, she paints."

"An artist, how lovely. Is she displayed here?"

Beats me. "Her name's Laurel Trenton."

"Trenton, Trenton, I can't say that I've heard of her, I'm sorry."

Shit, another dead end. "You sure? I've been to three of you art galleries and nobody knows who she is." Anthony gestured in frustration. "This is getting freaking annoying, you know?"

"I'm sure it is, sir."

Sure, like you with your stupid bow tie know what I'm going through. You don't have to answer to Uncle Sal.

The old man escorted him toward the door. "Not all artists are well known enough to be in galleries."

"Yeah, well, I got to find her."

The old man opened the door for him. "I'm truly sorry we can't help you, sir."

Becca glanced in the rear view mirror of the Jeep as she maneuvered it out of yet another rut. Maybe this outing wasn't such a good idea. The contractors had really dug up the road to the cabin. "You OK back there, Theresa?"

"I don't remember it being this rugged."

Yeah, well, they were kids the last time they'd all been up here. The back seat of the Jeep held her sister, Doc Juarez and Arielle, hardly any knee room, all squeezed together. Not good.

She glanced over at Marcus, sitting beside her in the passenger seat. "Can you take over driving? I think Theresa should sit up front. I prefer to walk." She gave him the key to the cabin. Becca caught his eye. "Be gentle," she mouthed.

He nodded almost imperceptivity.

"I'll walk with you," Doc Juarez said, sliding out.

The two of them watched as Marcus eased the Jeep along the rugged road, Arielle bouncing around the back seat.

She smiled at the doctor. "I couldn't help seeing you glued to your phone on the drive up the mountain," she said. Until the lack of cell coverage had killed it. "You're supposed to take a break from that stuff for twenty-four hours. It's Sunday, your day off."

"Actually, Theresa's latest numbers just came in." He hesitated. "We have to start another round of chemo."

Her heart sank. It was the last thing she wanted to hear. "I thought she was doing better."

"She's recovering from the surgery well, that's true." He looked grim. "But disease cells spread, and you almost never know where. I'll be telling her tonight."

When they got to the cabin, Arielle was playing at the water wheel, pushing dried leaves along the miniature pool, no more than three feet wide and a couple feet deep at the bottom. Even if she fell in, all she risked was getting wet.

Becca heard Marcus and Theresa inside. "So, let's see what the contractor's been up to."

The kitchen was mid remodel. No sink. No appliances. "Please tell me the toilets flush," she muttered.

"They do, I checked," Theresa answered. "I told Marcus how to turn on the lights."

Yeah, the electrician needed to do more work and had told her to use the circuit board down in the basement until then.

Marcus entered from the other room and caught her eye. "About time you got here, slow poke."

Well, someone was feeling cocky.

He hefted on his backpack. "Ready for our hike?"

"Sure. Ready to be left in the dust?"

The two of them reached the top of the mountain about fifteen minutes later.

Marcus stopped, arms akimbo, as he looked around. "What a view."

It was time to bring up something that had been bothering her. "I need to apologize to you."

He shot her a look of confusion. "What for?"

"The school told me you were set to do career day and my bicycle donation kind of, well, postponed that."

He shrugged. "The kids benefitted, which was the main thing."

That was gracious. "I'm going to do a 'paint with me' program before school ends. Say, maybe we could piggyback. You could ride in on your motorcycle and I could help them paint you."

"You like helping disadvantaged kids, do you?"

After learning all the good Josephine did for orphans? "I confess, I enjoy helping them partly because it makes me feel so good. Is that wrong?"

He smiled. "I'd like that, the piggyback thing." He breathed in the mountain air. "It's so different from Vegas up here."

"You haven't seen the best part." She led him past the trees and pointed.

"A cave, I would never have guessed." He strode closer and peeked inside. "It looks like it's big enough for two." He took her hand, led her inside, lost his backpack and pulled her into his arms. "All we need is a storm to strand us for a few hours."

He felt so good, so strong. "I'd feel safe with you with or without a cave."

"That's because I'm the man, your protector."

Yeah, Luke had said that, too. But with you, I like it.

He smiled. He had a great smile.

Becca stared into his eyes. "Another confession. I liked kissing you in the foyer."

"I don't know," Marcus said, shaking his head seriously.

What?

"It wasn't my best effort."

He was teasing her. OK, two could play this game. "Then, maybe I should give you another chance."

"If you insist."

She slipped her arms around his neck. "Oh, I insist."

His lips were suddenly on hers, searing hot, his tongue probing.

What a turn-on. She responded, unable to resist. The way he held her, so sure, so manly. Becca gave into his demanding kiss, lost in the utter sexual command he held over her. No man had ever kissed her quite this way before. It was heady.

Marcus pulled back, seemed to catch his breath. He bent in for another taste.

She met him with sudden abandon. A flash of desire raced through her. She clutched him, crushing her body to him. He could take her right here, right now, and she wouldn't be able to say "No".

He slid his hands over her clothes, grabbing her buttocks, squeezing her breasts.

It was hot, so hot. "Marcus," she breathed. She arched her back to press her breasts into his hands. God, she loved having these huge mounds, loved having a hot guy like Marcus run his hands over them, knowing he wanted them exposed, it was beyond sexy.

He yanked the tail of her shirt out of her jeans and ran his hands up underneath. They seared her flesh.

Becca reached between them and began unbuttoning his shirt, yanking it open. Those pecs! Those abs! "You have on way too many clothes, Marcus."

"You, too."

He kissed her hard again.

Her senses came alive, a flash of desire streaking straight through her core. To hell with it, she couldn't stop herself. They should be naked, in each other's arms right now. She caught his eye. "I want to do more than just kiss you, Marcus."

He let out a groan and began tearing off his shirt even as his lips stayed locked on hers.

"Aunt Laurel, where are you?"

Shit. It was Arielle.

They broke apart and scrambled to pull their clothes back into place.

"Over here, honey," she called, tucking her shirttails back down her jeans. Now, all she had to do was act normal. Sure, if only her loins would stop aching for this incredible man.

Back at home, Becca pushed her dinner plate away, hardly touched. "Arielle, why don't you go see if your favorite show is on?" She looked over at Doc, nodding almost imperceptibly. The ball was in his court.

He cleared his throat and took Theresa's hand. "There's no easy way to say this, sweetie. I got your test results this afternoon when we were on the way up the mountain. It looks like we didn't get all the cancer."

"What? Are you sure?"

"I ran them twice."

Theresa flinched and searched his eyes. "Chemo?"

He nodded. "The 'aggressive' chemo this time."

Theresa gestured helplessly. "I can't afford any kind of healthcare. My insurance coverage has maxed out."

Becca leaned forward. "I'm your health insurance, sis. I'm here for you and Arielle, whatever you need."

"Thanks, Laurel." Her lip quivered. "Chemo? Do I have to? I've heard such horrible things."

Doc Juarez looked into Theresa's eyes, intent on her. "Listen to me. Everyone reacts differently to it. You're in great shape from your job, you eat healthy foods. All that could make the difference for you."

The tears welled up in her sister's eyes. "I'm going to lose my hair, aren't I?"

Doc shrugged. "I don't care. We've got to get you well, so that you and I and Arielle can start our lives together."

Theresa nodded and slipped into his embrace and the two of them held each other tight.

Gee, it looked like three was a crowd. Becca pushed her chair back and tiptoed away. She felt a sense of peace. Doc had automatically included Arielle in his plans, like it was a given. No doubt about it, Theresa had found a great guy.

Marcus picked Becca up at a quarter to six. She was in jeans and a tailored shirt that showed off her great figure. "You sure it's not too early for dinner?" He said as he held open the door of his Mazda.

"Are you kidding?" she said, laughing. "I'm starved."

Not many women would admit such a thing, let alone so openly, but Becca wasn't most women.

"Don't forget, I get up at four in the morning to paint."

Shit, that was right.

The Mazda started with a protest and he revved the engine before starting out. He'd spent all afternoon cleaning it. He wanted to make a good impression.

Marcus headed for the pizza joint that one of the guys at work had recommended. "How's your sister?"

"I've been in video consultations with top specialists around the world. They say Doc Juarez is doing everything right. But let's talk about you. What led you to be an NHP officer? I mean, that's a pretty heavy decision."

She wanted to hear about his life, really? "In school, I was the one to stand up to bullies. It just seemed right."

He found himself telling her more, it was easy with such an attentive listener.

At the restaurant, Marcus finished his last slice of pizza and sat back, satisfied. Becca had eaten almost as much as he had. There was nothing fake about this girl. He'd found himself telling her about his life, his views, even about Suzie and how she'd gotten the four wheel drive SUV before he'd had a chance to take it up to Mount Charleston.

Somehow, with Becca, even talking about Suzie's infidelity had lost its sting. It just didn't seem to matter, not anymore. And that felt good. Marcus gestured to her plate. "Had enough?"

She patted her stomach. "Had too much."

"Good, let's go work it off. Ever shoot a gun?"

An hour later, they left the paintball arcade where they'd run around the mazes, ducked behind barriers and shot off round after round with only safety goggles to protect them.

They got back to his car. They were both covered in paint splatters, but Becca had gotten the worst of it. You wouldn't know she'd been the loser by the way her face was lit up.

"That was so much fun," she said as she slid into the passenger seat. "I would never have known about this place if you hadn't taken me here."

God, he wanted to kiss her. Instead, he shut her door and hurried around to his side. If only she didn't have to get back home so early. He knew a spot that overlooked the lights of Vegas, a spot where they could park and not be disturbed.

He turned the key.

Nothing.

Shit, not now, not on this perfect date. He gave Becca a little smile and tried it again. Still nothing. His face heated up. "Um, know of a good mechanic?" *Jeez, that sounded lame.*

"I think your starter is shot."

She knew about stuff like that?

Becca pulled out her cell phone and dialed. "Hi, we need a tow truck."

Anthony strolled into the affair and grabbed a wine glass off the reception table. He took a sip and made a face. "This all you got, sweetheart? Nothing harder?" These art functions were pretty upper crust affairs, but they didn't know shit about how to throw a party.

"We need your name sir. Please sign in on this sheet," the young woman at the table said.

"I don't need to sign in, I'm invited by the artist."

"Which artist?"

Shit, there was more than one at this hoity-toity shindig? He turned to Frankie, brought along to help "convince" the host to find out where Laurel Trenton was. "Can you believe this? They say they don't know me?"

Frankie shook his head. "Freaking unheard of."

"Look, sweetheart," Anthony said. "I need to speak to someone in charge at this joint. Who would that be?"

"The host? He's with the senator right now. But, um, the art critic is Harold Deller."

"Fine. Deller, smeller. Point him out."

Deller was across the room, a small man, balding, with glasses hallway down his nose. He blinked in surprise when they approached. Maybe he thought they should be in tuxedos like everyone else. Forget that shit.

"Deller, right? We need to speak with you in person," Anthony took his elbow and found a small room off to the side.

"What, what's this all about?" Deller stuttered.

Good, he was already sensing trouble and feeling fear. "Listen, pal, all we want is information. I need to find this bitch, er, artist." He pulled out a picture. "This is Laurel Rebecca Trenton. Trenton, like the city. Blonde, gray eyes, crooked nose."

"I don't know her."

"She paints."

"Does she? I've never heard of her."

"Oh, come on. All you artist types know one another." He grabbed Deller's arm, tight. No more kidding around. "I need to find her, do you understand me?" He leaned in close.

"Yes, yes, I understand." The guy was shaking now.

Anthony smiled. He had this guy right where he wanted him. "Tell you what I'm going to do. I'm going to give you a couple days to make some calls, put out some feelers. I know she went to some art school here in the states, somewhere east of Ohio, I think. You find this gal and then you and me will talk again."

He stepped aside.

Frankie moved in close and Deller shrank back.

Anthony looked down on the shrimp of a man. "Understand?"

"Y-y-yes."

"Don't disappoint me." He gave the little guy a shove. "I know how to find you."

He and Frankie strolled out. He was closer to locating Laurel, he could feel it. They passed a promotion flag in the lobby. It promoted the next event. "The Painter of Emotions."

"Your uncle Sal is really pressuring you for the three million, huh?"

"He'd be pressuring me even more if he knew the deal was for, like, ten times more."

Frankie stopped in his tracks. "You shitting me?"

Anthony gestured for him to keep moving. "Not that I'd tell him that, of course. And neither will you."

"Of course."

Good ole Frankie, he could always count on him.

CHAPTER TWENTY-SEVEN

Marcus stood at attention in Captain Schiff's office.

The Captain was not smiling. He slammed a newspaper on his desk. "Did you see this?"

Marcus cringed. It was a photo from Tip A Cop. In it, Becca had her hand down his pants, way down his pants, and he had a shit grin on his face like he was encouraging her to stroke his –

"It's utterly disgraceful," the captain said. "Do you know how much heat the department is taking for this?" He began pacing.

Marcus fought for something to say in his defense. Nothing that would make a difference came to mind. "I'm sorry, sir."

"Sorry? *Sorry?* My wife is all over my butt, day and night, wondering what kind of deviant you are, what we're really doing all day long. And the department is on my ass because it was *me* who insisted you be in at the event. 'Our big hero.' You turned it into a freaking *sex orgy.* The whole town is in an uproar."

Oh, sure, when he'd run into a burning building, not once but twice, he'd been the hero. "The women were drinking and got a little carried away. What was I supposed to do? Slap my cuffs on them?" From what he'd witnessed, they probably would have liked it, a couple of them, anyway.

"Don't get cute. I'm under a lot of heat, here, Marcus." He stopped pacing and gestured helplessly. "They want your badge."

What? They were going to fire him? His blood boiled. "You can't let them do that, Captain. I'm the best NHP officer in the division. Why, just look at my call records, my performance reviews. I've devoted my *life* to this job."

"Sorry. Those are my orders. Hand over your badge. You're fired."

Becca raced into the nearly empty school parking lot and screeched to a stop. Shit. It was ten minutes after school got out.

Arielle was waiting just inside the doors, arms crossed and a scowl on her face. "You're late."

"Sorry, sorry."

The receptionist pushed a sign-out sheet at her and held out a pen. "Sign here." The penalty sheet for parents and those who were trying to be parents. Hers was the only name. How had Theresa, essentially a single parent all those years, done it?

Becca ushered her niece out the front door. "Shall we have the chef make your favorite meal tonight?"

"I don't care."

"I know, we can rent that new movie you wanted to see."

"I don't care."

"Maybe you should invite a friend for a sleepover this weekend."

Arielle shrugged.

They got to her car and strapped up.

Becca didn't like Arielle's sullen attitude. This was about more than being ten minutes late. She tried again. "We can go out for a spin on your new bike. I'll ride beside you this time."

"I don't care."

"Honey, what's wrong?"

Arielle looked down into her lap. "I heard Dr. Juarez talking to Mommy about her disease."

Shit. She'd overheard that conversation? "Just what did you hear?"

"Mommy's going to die, isn't she?"

Jeez, she'd overheard the bad stuff. "Oh, sweetie, we're doing everything we can to see that she gets better, everything." She reached over and gave her niece a hug. "I promise you, whatever needs to be done to get her better, we're going to do it."

She just hoped it was enough.

Becca entered the gallery at the Everest Hotel. Denise Schimmerwick was there, her jewelry clinking as they air kissed. "Oh, good, you brought the one I like so much."

"It's a giclee."

"Whatever, dear. It'll sell. Let's decide where to hang it."

They rounded the wall. The corner setting had been changed. Becca stopped. "What's this?" There was dramatic lighting, subtle music.

"We decided your art warranted more 'atmosphere.' Do you like it?"

It was different, certainly. "I would never have thought of it," she said. Vegas sure had its own way of doing things.

Marcus was leaning on her car when she exited the Everest. He was so decent, admirable and upstanding. What was he doing here? "Done fighting crime for the day?" she said as she approached.

"Why are you at the Everest?"

Jeez, he was sexy. "I had to deliver a painting."

"I thought maybe you were consorting with questionable characters."

"No, I only do that when I'm with you." She slid into his embrace. "I'm going back up to the cabin today. Care to join me?" *And do unspeakable things to my body while we're there?*

He kissed her. "Go back to the cave? Sounds good."

"It'll be too dark by the time we get up there. I had satellite TV installed. We'll be just in time to watch the Dolphins football game."

"A woman after my own heart."

She pressed her lips to his, a sultry kiss, then pulled back. "I need you to help me with something before we head up."

"Name the time and place."

Wow, a man who took orders, she could get used to this.

Marcus shot her a quizzical look as she pulled into the Jeep dealership. What were they doing here?

They parked and got out.

"Did the Jeep break down? I was as careful as I could be, driving Theresa in and out."

Becca waved away his concern. "This is the favor I need from you." She pointed. "I think it's that one."

The maroon one? "You mean you bought another Jeep? Why?"

"Because the one Grams bought is really for two people. The family is bigger now and needs a full back seat."

It must be nice to be rich.

"I was hoping you could follow me up there in it."

Whoa. Drive a brand new Jeep, put it through its paces? Such a chore. "OK, I'll do it. But you'll owe me. And I demand payment in kisses."

She considered his offer, eyes shining. "Why, officer, you drive a hard bargain."

Wait until you see how hard.

Twenty minutes later, they left the highway at the Kyle Canyon turn-off. The Jeep was humming like a dream. They started to climb. Marcus stayed behind Becca's luxury car. The Jeep was fighting the reins, wanting to break free and really tackle the road.

There was no oncoming traffic. He swung into the passing lane and hit the gas. He passed Becca with a little wave. *Sorry, sweetie, but this horse wants to run free.*

The Jeep ate up the pavement, taking the curves with precision. It was exhilarating stuff. He arrived at the cabin's garage and got out to wait for Becca.

He couldn't shake the hold she had on him. And it wasn't just sexual, though he'd certainly tossed and turned enough, hoping she'd invite him into her bed. No, there was more to her. In the past few weeks, they'd ridden the rollercoaster on the Strip, gone target shooting at the gun range, attended a baseball game and worked out together in the weight room. Each had ended in a make out session that left him wanting more.

Maybe being back here at the cabin would be the night she'd come to him. He sure hoped so. Cold showers were getting old.

She wasn't far behind and pulled up next to him. "Thought maybe you were making a break for Canada," she said as she got out. "How was she?"

"Eight cylinders? You kidding me? No comparison to my poor little Mazda." He'd been tempted to put the little car up for sale after getting the starter fixed, but it was kind of hard to afford a brand new vehicle when you didn't have a job.

Becca popped open the trunk and began transferring their belongings.

"Let me get that," Marcus said, taking a canvas sports bag from her. Other women would probably have brought roll–along luggage. Suzie had brought nail polish, for goodness sake. Not Becca, she was a realist and this was the forest.

The new Jeep packed up, he took the wheel and they started out for the cabin.

He had to tell her. "I have a confession to make."

"Been robbing banks again, have you?"

"I've been fired."

"What?" Her shock was genuine.

He pulled the Review-Journal article out of his pocket and passed it to her. "Seen this?"

"I don't get the paper," she muttered as she scanned it. "I can't believe they fired you. Over this? I thought this was Vegas, party town, anything goes, what happens here stays here."

"The mayor said some strong words about it, what with me being a public servant and all."

"The mayor spoke out against it?"

"Apparently, this went to CNN."

"Maybe Anthony Amalfitano saw it," she muttered. "Great."

The fireplace crackled, but she barely noticed. The Chargers had just missed a field goal. From twenty-seven yards out, no less. Unbelievable. Becca scowled at the TV. "I can't believe my team lost."

"Well, it wasn't for lack of you shouting what they should do," Marcus pointed out.

"Very funny." She chucked him in the shoulder. "Do you want more to drin-?"

He threw up a hand. "Shh."

"What?"

"Something's outside."

Was it Anthony? Oh, God.

Marcus reached in his bag and pulled out a handgun. Damn, it was big. "Stay here."

No, she wasn't staying there. She was going with him, where there was a weapon to keep her safe.

He turned out the lights and hurried to the door. She shadowed him. Becca glanced out the window. There was enough moonlight to see fairly well.

He stopped and she bumped into him.

Marcus sent her a silent, exasperated look.

She sent him one back. So there.

Marcus cracked open the door and peered out, then ducked outside, motioning for her to stay close.

She tiptoed behind him as he moved stealthily forward. What had he heard? She was desperate to know. Was it a person or a bear, a big huge bear, looking for his next meal?

Mr. Bear could be lurking right behind that tree, or that one over there. Shit, he could be anywhere. Maybe following Marcus outside hadn't been such a good idea.

There was a scurrying sound going off in the woods. Marcus stood up straight. He clicked something on his gun. "Coyote."

"Oh." Better a coyote than a bear.

He pulled her to him and held her in an embrace. "Scared, huh?

Only like, to death. "Concerned," she admitted. His arms felt so good, so strong. His body fit into hers and Becca pressed into him, her nerves coming to life, demanding. She lifted her chin and moaned.

His hands ran over her curves. His lips were on hers, exploring, hesitant, asking for permission.

Like she could say no. She broke from his kiss and looked into his eyes. "Take me to bed, Marcus."

CHAPTER TWENTY-EIGHT

They tumbled into bed, yanking at each other's clothes as they kissed. He wanted her so badly, he gave up trying to free himself of his pants. Her globes looked golden in the low light, golden and inviting and, oh God, those nipples. They were exposed in all their glory, and they were his. His mouth was on them in a nanosecond, sucking the dual trophies, consuming them.

Becca moaned beneath him as her nipples hardened.

The flash of urgency in his pants demanded attention. He had to get these trousers off. He jumped up and danced them off his hips and down his legs until he could step out of them. Damn, get off.

His underwear went next.

On the bed, Becca was shimmying out of her clothes.

She was gorgeous, long and lean and he wanted those legs locked around him so bad he winced. "You're incredible."

Becca crooked a finger at him. "Come here," she said with a naughty gleam in her eye.

His knees were like jelly. This was it, the consummation of all those shared looks, hot moments and deep kisses. He couldn't get back into bed fast enough.

"I want you to kiss every inch of me," she breathed.

Fine with him. He began at her neck and moved his way down her body, licking those globes, those hot nipples, moving down to her tight, flat stomach before finding her target spot.

Becca moaned with pleasure at his tongue fest. "Me, too."

She swapped her position and soon she was pleasuring him the same way. This girl was incredible, a golden goddess.

After a while, she broke off.

What? No, don't stop.

Becca gave him a naughty look, took the top position and lowered herself onto him.

Oh, God. He felt her wet walls accept him as he slipped into her. How long had he waited for this moment? He guided her hips, moving with her. She felt amazing, utterly amazing. His hands roamed all over her incredible body. *Becca, Becca, oh God, you're everything I dreamed you'd be and more.*

Becca moaned, closed her eyes and rode him, slow at first, then harder and harder.

They moved faster, the heat escalating with each thrust.

He ground into her, wanting to dominate every inch of her.

It was just … too… good.

"Here I come," he gasped and his body exploded.

Becca made the scrambled eggs. The new cabin stove worked perfectly.

There was a rap on the kitchen window.

It was Luke. His skin was rotting off of him in chunks, large areas of his skull and jaw bones visible.

Poor Luke. It had to be painful to hang on, being in limbo like this.

"Laurel, can you hear me?" His voice was muffled by the windowpane. His jaw bones clattered when he talked.

"Luke, are you all right?" He looked terrible.

"Laurel, don't go to New York City. Please."

"I have to. It's a big chance to get my art out there."

"It's not safe."

"I'll be fine."

"No, things are happening. You'll be in danger."

"I'll be careful."

"Cancel it. You'll be on Anthony's turf and he's -"

"Everything's all set up. I can't pull out now."

Something knocked into her hand. Becca gasped and sat up in bed.

Marcus stirred beside her. He'd turned over in his sleep.

It was dark. The clock read three a.m.

Becca laid back down and stared at the ceiling. The visitation had seemed so real. It was comforting to know Luke was still trying to look out for her, but he had to understand that she wasn't going to let herself be intimidated by some goon from his past. She'd take precautions, arrange for her hotel room to be in a different name, but she'd be damned if she'd be forced into seclusion.

"I have to go to New York, Luke," she whispered to the night. "A person isn't truly living life if they're living scared."

Becca eased the new Jeep along the dirt trail, back to the cabin's garage. "If you're not with the NHP anymore, why do you still carry a gun?"

"It's mine. I have all the proper permits, if that's what you're worried about."

Worried? With the noise outside the cabin, she'd been worried. When Marcus had pulled his gun and gone after the culprit, she'd been glad he was armed. "If I asked you to be my body guard, would you?"

His hand went to her knee and that spark of desire shot through her again. As many times as they'd made love this weekend – in front of the fireplace, out in the forest, inside the cave – she couldn't get enough of him.

He gave her a saucy grin. "Believe me, there's nothing else I'd like to do more than guard this body of yours."

Agreed, but this wasn't the time to jump each other, as nice as that would be.

She told him about the art exhibit in New York. "I'm a little apprehensive about going." OK, she was a *lot* apprehensive about going. Saying that she wouldn't live her life scared was easy when you knew you were safe. Well, she felt safe with Marcus at her side. "Anthony Amalfitano wants to find me and there's nothing like drawing attention to my whereabouts with a splashy event."

"You know, it's thought that Amalfitano associates might have interests in Vegas."

Her stomach lurked. "I'm not safe here, either? Now I really need protection."

Marcus looked deep into her eyes. "I'll be your body guard," he promised. "Day and night."

They reached the garage and transferred their belongings to her car.

Marcus opened the garage doors and eyed the interior space. He frowned. "It'll be tight, fitting this bigger Jeep in here with the first one," he said.

Becca shook her head. "Only the new one is staying up here," she said and held up the keys to the original Jeep. "I was hoping you would take ownership of the two-seater."

Theresa sat in front of her makeup mirror and tried not to dwell on how weak she felt. She tipped her head and inspected her scalp. "I'm losing more hair," she told Diego.

He toweled off from his shower and stepped over to kiss the top of her head. "It'll grow back, don't worry."

She wished she was as sure as him. "You're into bald women, are you, doctor?"

"Only if that woman is you." He got ready for work. "Your next round of chemo starts in a couple days."

Oh, God. Did she have to? "Same dose?"

"Yes. Are you up for it?"

Like she had a choice. She had to beat this cancer, couldn't leave this world and make her daughter an orphan.

Arielle's face came to mind. Right now, her daughter was having an overnighter at a friend's house while her Aunt Laurel was at the cabin. But her sister had a life of her own, was required to jet off to art events, hold exhibits and rub elbows with high society. There was little room in her schedule for a child.

"Darn, I left my shaving cream at my place again," Diego said. He turned to her. "As nice as your sister's house is, and believe me, I love the convenience of having a personal chef, but maybe you and Arielle should move in with me. It's closer to your infusion center, closer to the hospital for me and it'd save me time, running back and forth. Plus, I'd get more sleep."

She'd been so focused on her own needs, she'd completely ignored his. Fighting traffic to come out to Summerlin must be like going to a hotel every other night for Diego. She'd never meant to inconvenience him. It just seemed "right" to have him here, monitoring her health, comforting her. How selfish she'd been. Theresa nodded. "I'll tell sis we're moving in with you."

Anthony sat behind the wheel of his car, munching an order of chicken wings. He spotted Harold Deller. It was about time the art critic emerged from the building. "Come on, Frankie." He licked the sauce off his fingers and tossed the rest of the food out the window.

Let some poor schmuck working for the sanitation department clean it up. He and Frankie jumped out of the car. "Hey, Deller."

The shrimp practically jumped. He stood there, quaking on the sidewalk.

Anthony sauntered up and threw an arm over the little guy's shoulder like they were pals. Sure they were. "We meet again."

Frankie stepped around to stand behind their prey. "Hope you have the information we want," he whispered in Deller's ear.

The art critic nodded, still shaking. "Laurel Rebecca Trenton paints under the single name of Becca. She's called the Painter of Emotions, very big in Europe."

Ooh, Europe. How hoity-toity. "Where in Europe?" Anthony asked.

"Marbella."

"Mar what?"

"It's on the Costa del Sol."

"Speak English to me, would ya?"

"Spain."

"I'll have to get a passport." Shit, like the feds would let him have one with his record.

"She's not there anymore," Deller said. "But she's got an exhibition here in the city and it's this weekend."

That's right. He'd seen the posters for it. Talk about his lucky day. He could hug this guy, even if the little shrimp *was* afraid of his own shadow. "Good work, Deller."

He'd found her, finally. Laurel Trenton, now painting as this Becca person, had better cooperate if she knew what was good for her.

CHAPTER TWENTY-NINE

Becca rolled her luggage out to the driveway, cell phone to one ear. "I'd love to come see you and the baby, Josephine. I'll check my calendar and get back with you. Bye."

Marcus pulled up in the Jeep, right on time. He hopped out and kissed her. "I missed you."

Yeah, he could have stayed with her at the mansion, but wanted to get moving on his job hunt instead. Now that Theresa and Arielle had moved in with Doc, the house seemed huge, silent and way too big.

Marcus grabbed the luggage from her and steered it to his vehicle. "Let's take my Jeep. We don't want your car sitting at the airport for three days."

She used her cell to bring up the house alarm system application and secured everything – air conditioning, door locks and video surveillance system. She slid into his passenger seat and turned to him. "You brought your gun, right? You can protect me if Anthony shows up?"

He patted one side of his chest. "Don't let me forget to tell the flight attendant that any air marshal on the flight needs to know I'm on board. Part of keeping you safe is keeping those around you safe, too."

Becca smiled to herself. Yeah, he was the right man for the job, all right.

The limo delivered them right in front of their New York Hotel. The doorman hurried to open the passenger door. "Welcome to the Neapolitan," he said.

"Thank you." Becca accepted his hand and stepped out. The bustling sounds of New York hit her ears.

"Your name, mademoiselle?"

Huh? What one had she used? "Ann Jones." Let Anthony try to track her down with a name like that.

The doorman spoke into his collar, made sure Marcus was out of the limo and then hurried up the steps to open the front door with a flourish. "Your luggage will be taken to your room for you," he said gesturing them inside.

Marcus handed him and the driver each a tip and took her by the elbow. Such a man. Becca stood a little taller.

The lobby was posh, filled with flowers in impossibly big vases and adorned with copies of famous Roman statues. A thirty-ish woman in a suit, sensible heels and a hotel name tag hurried up to them. "Mr. and Mrs. Jones, welcome to the Neapolitan."

Becca flicked a look at Marcus. Maybe he wouldn't appreciate being labeled a married couple, but it was part of her disguise. No, he didn't seem overly concerned.

"I'm Cindy, your concierge. Everything has been arranged just as you requested. Let me show you to your suite."

The elevator whisked them up to the twenty-fifth floor and a private entrance. Double doors opened to a foyer, then the main room. Becca stepped over and looked out. What a stunning view of the city. She could feel the vibrancy even from up here. It made her want to get out her brushes and capture the feeling.

Behind her, Cindy was chatting up the hotel amenities – pool, workout facility, personal spa services, and a chef should they wish to entertain. "You'll also find –"

Marcus interrupted her. "Is that the only elevator to get up here?"

Cindy hesitated.

Becca turned to look at her. The question seemed to have stumped the woman.

Cindy recovered her composure. "We maintain a private one for guests," she said. "Only your key card will allow it to operate."

"What about the maids? Do they use that elevator?"

"Sir?"

"And how many exits are there once we're on the main floor?" Marcus asked.

"The front doors are always open," Cindy said uncertainly. "Do you have an issue with stairs? We have handicapped capabilities for our guests who –"

"How many security people do you have on your night shift?"

"I've only been here three months. I'll have to check, Mr. Jones. Perhaps if you tell me all your questions, I can find out the answers and get back with you."

A bellman arrived with their luggage. "Where would you like these?"

Marcus gestured to the corner, went to tip him and hesitated. "How long have you worked here?"

"Six years, sir. I was a porter before being promoted."

"You probably know this hotel inside and out, the employee tunnel network, loading docks, all that. Yes?"

The bellman nodded. "Pretty much every inch of it, sir."

"You're just what I need," Marcus said. "Cindy, I'm going to steal this young man away from his post for the next half hour while he gives me a back-of-the-house tour." He pulled Becca aside. "Stay here. Don't leave the room."

After the door closed behind them, Becca turned back to the view. Somewhere out there was a man who was determined to get her, but he'd find it hard to even get close to her with Marcus at her side. Her heart soared. What a man she'd found.

The exhibition hall was humming with voices as she stood backstage. There was electricity in the air, she could feel it. New York wasn't like L.A. with its laid-back vibe, or Paris with its sophistication. No, New York City was always abuzz, moving forward with unbridled intention, with an urgency that said, "Just try and stop me, world."

She grabbed Marcus' hand and squeezed it, eyes bright. "Can you feel it?"

"Feel what?"

"I've got to paint this, right now." Where was the stage manager, Stephen? There he was, talking to some lighting tech. She hurried over. "Stephen, I've got to get out there. Announce me."

"But you're not due on stage for half an hour."

He didn't feel it either, didn't understand how creativity worked. In thirty minutes this sensation would dissipate. "Announce me, now."

Stephen shrugged. "Artists," he muttered and went to the sound board. He turned a dial, hit a button and picked up the microphone. "Ladies and gentlemen, welcome to a very special evening ..."

She winked at Marcus, then swept out onto the stage.

There was applause.

Her earpiece clicked. "Your mic is live," Stephen said. "It's all yours."

"Hello, everyone. It's fabulous to be back in the city that's so full of energy and vibrancy, it makes all other cities jealous. I look out over this hall tonight and I see that same energy reflected in you. What a special group you are." Becca approached her easel and supplies. "Shall we get started?" She took a seat.

Stephan hit the music and a throbbing beat filled the room. People began to dance.

"That's right, this is a party, get into the beat," she urged them.

She picked up a brush and threw on the colors that called to her – periwinkle, turquoise, midnight blue. "Night time is when this city comes alive," she said. "It transforms into a magical place, pumping with energy, vibrating with a sense of urgency. I know you feel it, too."

The cityscape began taking shape on her canvas, towers looming and bustling streets below.

She pulled back. There, the foundation was made. Sparkle, it needed sparkle. Gold and yellow followed. "What's a city without glitz and glamor, huh? You know New York has plenty of both."

Anthony hit the dashboard with his fist. Of all the freaking nights for there to be a multi-car pileup, it had to happen tonight. "This road is a parking lot, for Christ's sake," he seethed. He wished there was something he could punch.

Frankie gestured helplessly. "Sorry, boss," he said. "The traffic report said everything was clear before we left."

Yeah, and if he hadn't banged Maria two extra times that evening, they would have had an earlier start. But she was so damn hot, his dick couldn't resist. Now, he was paying for having a good time. Shit, Luke's millionaire girlfriend was right within reach and here he was stuck in traffic. Of all the luck.

"It's a two hour affair," Frankie said. "We'll just be later than we'd figured. It'll work out. Everything will be all right."

"Who are you? Freaking Dr. Phil?"

Becca signaled Stephen and set down her brush.

He didn't miss a beat. "It looks like the Painter of Emotions is finished with yet another masterpiece. And it was painted right before your eyes. You were part of the experience. Let's take a look, everybody."

The crowd looked up at the monitors. Jaws dropped.

Becca felt the sense of amazement radiating off them and threw open her arms. She wanted to hug them all in one big embrace. "I call it, 'City of Vibrancy' because that's how I see your fabulous town."

There were cheers and applause.

She nodded, beaming. Good, they understood. They got it. New Yorkers weren't standoffish, weren't conceited. They had heart and soul and here it was, on display tonight.

Stephen took over in his TV voice. "Remember, half the proceeds will be donated to the children's cancer hospital. We all want to help the kids, right?"

The crowd cheered.

Stephen continued. "Now, while you're bidding, Becca has another special attraction. Two ladies from our invitee list have agreed to be her living easels. This has never been done before."

Becca almost laughed out loud. Of course it had been done before, but she appreciated him ad-libbing.

"She'll use their energy as her inspiration and paint directly on them, creating one of a kind outfits for her new Xavier Fashions line."

Two women joined her on stage, both in simple white dresses, sewn up by her Long Island contact. They were in their forties with at least one facelift each. They hadn't just agreed to be her living easels, they'd each paid twenty-five grand for the privilege, a drop in the bucket for them, no doubt, and well worth the privilege of saying, "I was the inspiration for an outfit by Becca, Painter of Emotions."

Becca had them stand and face her, then stepped back to assess each of them.

The one on the left was beaming, excited. "I see effervescence in you," she told the woman. She would use a fuchsia color as the basis for her.

The one on the right was – whoa, this woman was calculating, devious. One didn't have to be in tune with their intuition to pick up on that, no sir. It was written all over the woman's essence.

"Now, in you, I see –," she hedged, wondering how the heck she was going to phrase this. "– a true sense of purpose." *Who will stop at nothing to get what she wants.*

The devious woman smiled.

Thank goodness. Becca cued Stephen to begin the bidding for the painting. "Let's get started, shall we ladies?"

Anthony braced himself as Frankie hit the brakes and the car screeched to a stop.

"You can't park here, sir," someone called out.

"Blow it out your ass," Anthony yelled as he hopped out.

"Sir, you have to move your car or –"

He strode over, got in the guy's face, inches away. "Or what? You're going to make me?"

The guy backed down.

What a schmuck. He and Frankie hurried inside. It was like a frigging convention hall, banquet rooms everywhere. Becca, Painter of Emotions, where the hell was the function?

"Look." Frankie pointed to a sign down the hall. "There." They raced toward it.

"Wait," Frankie said, stopping him. "How are we going to do this?"

"What? We nab her, tie her up."

"In front of everyone? We have to get her to leave with us quiet like."

She couldn't raise a ruckus if she was unconscious. "I can knock her out."

No, that was no good. "And carry her out in front of everybody? No, she needs a reason to go with us willingly."

He was right. They needed a plan. He thought fast. "I'll say there's an emergency, um, that her mother is in the hospital and she needs to come with us."

Frankie grinned. "You're a genius, boss."

They ran up to the banquet room and barely avoided being hit by the doors being thrown open. Men and women decked out in party outfits poured out, laughing, chatting, confetti in their hair.

Anthony stopped one of the men. "Where's Becca, the painter gal?"

"The artist? She left, like, ten minutes ago. Great event. You should have gotten here earlier."

Marcus slid his arm around Becca. The woman was sitting in their hotel room, doing her banking in the nude. She had no idea the effect such a thing could have on a man.

Well, he was about to show her. "Come to bed."

First, she'd worked out with him, wearing a tight spandex top that had nearly caused him to drop a free weight on his foot. Now, she was lounging around naked after her shower.

Maybe he should scoop her up and just toss her on the bed, caveman style. Then he'd jump on top of her and –

She gestured for him to give her a minute. "The limo driver that drove us here from JFK. How much did you tip him?"

Huh? His inner caveman hesitated. "Fifty. Why?"

"And the bellman who showed you the back hallways, how much did you give him?"

"A hundred bucks." He paused. Was that being cheap? This was New York, after all, where everything cost an arm and a leg. "You think I should have given him more?"

"No, no, I'm just figuring out what I owe you."

He pulled back. "Owe me?" Becca made it sound like he was some contractor on her payroll. "You don't owe me for those tips."

"Of course I do. You wouldn't be here if I hadn't asked you to come with me."

Surely, she was joking. "I wanted to come with you." Heck, he wanted to spend every moment he could with her.

Becca twisted in the chair and smiled up at him. "I wanted you here, too." She turned back to her calculator. "To protect me."

Wait a minute. She was obviously looking at this as a business transaction. He saw it as much more than that.

His phone buzzed. Not now.

Shit, it was that new detective agency where he'd applied. "I need to take this." Marcus stepped into the other room. "Hello?"

"Marcus, your credentials checked out with flying colors. We'd like you to join our team and work for us. You said you'd be on the East Coast this weekend."

"Yeah, I'm there now."

"When will you return to Vegas?"

"We leave tomorrow, early morning." The first nonstop of the day had been Becca's idea. She'd figured that anyone who was a hood wouldn't be up at the crack of dawn, a line of reasoning that made him chuckle. But, hey, maybe she had the right idea. "We land about noon."

"Excellent. Can you come into the office that afternoon, say three p.m., and sign some papers? We already have a client who requires your services."

That was fast. "Sure."

When he made his way back to the bedroom, Becca was writing a check. She tore it off and handed it to him.

Three hundred fifty dollars and no cents. "What's this?"

"Reimbursement for all the tipping you did."

Like he was some lowly servant, there to be ordered around? Like he was no better than an employee of hers? His face grew hot. "Shit, Becca, what are you doing?"

"I'm paying you back for everything."

"Stop." She didn't get it, didn't get that he was here for her of his own volition, that he'd follow her to the ends of the earth if there was any chance something would happen to her.

"Don't insult me like this." Yeah, his voice was getting loud and harsh and he was barking at her, but he couldn't help it.

She reached for the hotel bathrobe and pulled it around her like a shield. "I'm not insulting you."

"The way I see it, you are." He paced. "What's next, are you going to hand me a paycheck for my hours?"

Becca glanced at her checkbook and flinched.

Shit. He grabbed the checkbook and scanned the pay register. There it was in the notation: Marcus Meddevia – doorman/limo/bellman tips. The next line read, Marcus Meddevi – bodyguard services. "What? You were going to *pay* me for my hours?" He threw the checkbook down and raked his fingers through his hair. "I don't believe this."

"You wouldn't be here if not for me."

"I *told* you, I wanted to be here."

"You said that after I asked you to come. Besides, why wouldn't I reimburse you? You're out of work."

His blood boiled. Oh, so now he was a charity case? Was that how she viewed him? "I don't need your money, woman." He was out of here.

"You're an officer of the law. I asked you to look out for me in that capacity."

He grabbed his suitcase. "I don't need a freaking job handed to me, damn it!"

Becca hurried over, looking clueless. "Marcus? What are you doing?"

What did it look like, Becca? He threw his clothes in. "I've had enough of your insults. I'm leaving. You can get back to Vegas without me."

Becca tipped the Las Vegas cabbie generously. After all, it was doubtful he'd find a fare from Summerlin back to McCarran airport. Tipping, that was how that horrible argument with Marcus had begun.

She'd spent the rest of her time in New York crying in her hotel suite, wishing Marcus would stride into the room and scoop her up saying he'd been a fool, had blown up over nothing.

She would have forgiven him instantly

Just as bad, she'd been startled at any little noise, sure that Anthony was going to barge in behind the maid or be waiting for her the moment she stepped out. What should have been a night of bliss spent in Marcus' strong arms had been, instead, utterly miserable.

The cab pulled away and she rolled her luggage to the front door of her mansion.

Her phone rang. It was Denise Schimmerwick.

Becca tried to make her voice upbeat, like nothing was wrong. Sure, nothing was wrong. She'd only lost the only guy who accepted her for who she was. "Hi, Denise. I just got back to town."

"You haven't forgotten about our little event at your place next weekend?"

The one she'd gotten roped into? It was next weekend? "How could I forget?"

"My husband has a number of oil barons flying in that weekend and their wives all go stir crazy at the hotel." She laughed. "You can only get so many back massages, or do so much shopping before it gets boring, right? Anyway, I get to play activities coordinator and find things for them to do, so I'm adding them to the guest list. Just wanted to let you know."

"Well, OK. I'll have to alert the guards at the entry gate. How many more people are we talking about?"

"I won't know until they get here. Maybe fifty or sixty."

"Security will need their names."

"Names? You're joking, right? These are high rollers, Becca. They buy a Rolls-Royce at the snap of a finger." Denise chuckled. "They're not going to have some wanna-be cop decide whether they gain entry or not."

"But –" *You're asking me to open my home and I want it to be secure. There's a killer after me.*

"They fly here in their own wide body jets." Denise rang off.

Wide bodied jets? And here she'd thought Josephine's eight-passenger Learjet represented the epitome of wealth.

Maybe she'd sell more paintings at this event than she'd anticipated. Her mind went into task list mode. She'd have to order more giclees, have the seamstress on Long Island to sew up a couple more dresses as blank canvases. The glitter confetti Stephen had suggested for the New York event had been a hit. She needed to find a Las Vegas company that could provide that.

Becca opened the front door. Her footsteps echoed on the marble floor. She winced. The silence was deafening. If only Theresa and her upbeat nurse were here, laughing in the kitchen. If only Arielle could be heard dunking basketballs in the pool.

If only Marcus was walking toward her with his strong arms out, saying, "It was all just a misunderstanding. Let's make up."

Yeah, if only.

Anthony flicked through the menu on Frankie's cell as he waited in the car. There was one message. He hit "play." Uncle Sal's voice came on. "Thanks for alerting me, Frankie. I'll deal with him personally." Why was Frankie talking directly to his uncle? That wasn't the way things happened in this business.

Frankie returned and slid behind the wheel. "Here's your coffee, boss."

"So, what did you go talk to Uncle Sal about?"

"Huh?" Frankie shrugged. "A guy was giving me grief about paying on a loan, you know?"

He slapped his face, hard. "You're my underling. You come to *me* with those things, understand?"

"Sure boss, sure. It won't happen again."

Better not.

Becca left her house. The Jeep she'd given to Marcus was parked in her side driveway.

Her heart leaped at the sight of it. Marcus was here, but ... where?

The street was empty. All was quiet.

There was a note under the windshield wiper. She hurried over, yanked it out and unfolded it.

"Becca – From the moment I met you, I knew there was something different about you and you stuck in my mind. When I got to know you better, things just seemed to click between us. You were everything I wanted. Every day, I couldn't wait until I saw you again."

Me, too, Marcus. She kept reading.

"I really thought we had something, but I was wrong. Obviously, I'm nothing but a charity case to you. Take the Jeep back. All it does is remind me of you and what I thought we once had. - Marcus"

She wanted to cry. No, this wasn't the way it was supposed to be. It was all a misunderstanding.

If only she'd heard him pull up, she would have run out, told him how miserable she was without him, apologized for whatever she'd done to make him think she didn't care about him.

She tried his number. It rang and rang, then went to voice mail – just like the gazillion other times she'd tried to reach him.

Becca disconnected. She had to face it, she'd lost him, the man who held her heart, and it was her own damn fault.

CHAPTER THIRTY

Theresa opened the door and brightened. "Sis, what are you doing here?"

"Doc didn't tell you that I'd called?"

"On surgery days, his mind is so busy, he forgets messages like 'Laurel's coming over.'" She ushered her in. "Coffee?"

"Are you doing OK? Feeling better?"

Like chemo was something you just bounced back from. It left her weak and unable to eat. "I'm getting through it. One day at a time." *Like an alcoholic.*

"You're wearing one of the wigs I got you. Cute. Did it all fall out?"

She wanted to see the fabulous result of chemo? Sure, why not. Let her sister see how she was an egghead now. Theresa slipped the wig off. "What do you think?"

"You could start a new fashion trend."

Ha. Leave it to her sister to be funny. She tossed the wig aside. "It slips off half the time. I hate using the glue." She poured out two cups. "How's the inspiration been lately, famous Becca, Painter of Emotions?"

Laurel sighed and accepted the coffee from her. "Don't ask. Marcus and I had a misunderstanding and all my paintings are sad and tortured."

Ouch. "Sorry to hear that. What happened?"

They talked about the trip to New York, the argument and the note he'd left on the Jeep. Poor Laurel, her heart was really hurting.

"I don't know if we'll ever get back together."

She needed a hug. "Listen, Laurel, I have a favor to ask. Diego has scheduled me for a new procedure. He thinks this could accelerate my healing. But I have to be in the hospital. Could you take Arielle for a couple weeks?"

"Of course. We'll do our nails, have a pajama party. She can dress up for the little get together that I'm hosting."

The weight that had been parked on her chest lifted. "Thanks, Laurel. I knew I could count on you."

Anthony waved off the doorman of the Everest Hotel. What? He couldn't open his own door? He stepped out into the Vegas sunshine. It had been raining when he left La Guardia.

The front desk had a cute clerk, blonde, pixie-nosed with big blue eyes. She beamed. "Welcome to the Everest where we go to the highest heights for our guests."

Really? Maybe he could entice her up to his room. "You got a reservation for –" Shit, what name had he used to avoid the notice of the Nevada Gaming Commission?

Denise Schimmerwick stepped up. "Anthony, welcome. My husband will be so happy to see you again." She turned to the pixie-nosed clerk. "He's in the Peaks penthouse."

"Ah, yes," the clerk said, clicking something on her computer. "Your room is fully comped, Mr. Stewart. Have a fun expedition climbing the heights of gaming fun at the Everest."

Denise Schimmerwick steered him to the side. "I have to get going. Donald, here, will help you." She handed him over to a bellman. She went to leave and turned back. "You know, you're uncle is expected."

Uncle Sal was going to be here? Funny he hadn't mentioned it, but then, it was not unusual for him to check up on their interests in Vegas. "Yeah, yeah, whatever."

Anthony smiled as the Everest's stretch limo was waved through the security gate. In the car with him, a couple of high rollers laughed and drank champagne. Let them get the party started early. Too bad that their hostess would not be in much of a mood to join in, not once she caught sight him. And by then, it'd be too late.

He glanced out the window at the mansions on either side. Luke's girlfriend sure had moved up in the world since the Close Call had brought her millions. Now, all he had to do was convince her to part with those millions. The Glock semiautomatic in his pocket would help persuade her.

The limo rounded a corner. There were a bunch of cars being valet parked up ahead. He rubbed his palms together. This must be the place.

Marcus strolled over to his desk. He'd always thought being a detective would be invigorating, exciting. Nothing was exciting without Becca. He thought of her a dozen times a day – her laugh, her smile, her perfume. But then he'd remember the way she'd treated him and it hurt, hurt deep.

He scanned the computer printout someone had left there. Shit. Anthony Amalfitano had come into town today? And his uncle, too? He turned to his colleague. "George, when did this alert from McCarran's Homeland Security office come in?"

"Couple hours ago. Is it important?"

"Could be." He'd bet his last dollar that Anthony was staying at the Everest. Damn those Schimmerwicks. He'd always had a feeling that they'd been involved in slimy dealings, just when Vegas was in the process of cleaning up its image. Now, with the gaming commission a client of this new detective agency, he could investigate them, dig into what they'd been up to all these years.

Marcus grabbed his suit jacket. "I'll be at the Everest, checking their surveillance video." He wanted to know everything the Amalfitano family was doing, and warn Becca if Anthony headed toward Summerlin. He owed her that.

Anthony nursed his scotch on the rocks. It wasn't like the shit he served in his strip joint in New York. But then everything was high class out here in the suburbs of Vegas, especially in this ritzy neighborhood.

Just look at this mansion. The damn ceilings had to be twenty feet high and pillars were everywhere. He should have a place like this. Too bad Little Miss Painter of Emotions wouldn't be able to afford it once he got control of her bank account. He smiled. He couldn't wait to see the expression on her face when she learned what he planned.

She was across the room, shaking hands, making nice with her guests. There were so many people around her right now, he'd have to bide his time to catch her alone.

But it would happen, oh yeah, it would happen. He sipped his drink and kept watching.

Marcus had the Everest security chief run the digital recording again. Denise Schimmerwick had personally greeted Anthony at the front desk. *Personally,* like he was some kind of honored guest, the low-life schmuck. "And he checked in under the name 'Stewart'?"

"Yes sir."

"Let's see where the cameras pick him up again."

"I believe he left with Mrs. Schimmerick's high roller group." He advanced the tape. "Yes, you can see him right here, getting ready to leave."

Sure enough, there was Antony sliding into the stretch limousine with some other people. The time stamp said it had been half an hour ago.

Marcus turned to the security chief. "Where were they going? Do you know?"

"There's some art event, a local painter, fairly new to town, who's doing a live demonstration," the security chief said.

New to town? Live demonstration? His heart stopped. "Do you mean Becca, the Painter of Emotions?"

"Yeah, that's the name. It's a private affair at her home in Summerlin."

Shit. Anthony was at Becca's event? In her house? This was not good. She was in danger. He had to get there, had to stop Anthony.

Marcus turned on his heel and ran.

Becca stepped away from the easel and set down her paintbrush. It was done, complete. The painting had practically created itself, a jumble of color, images conjured up from her turmoil of emotions since Marcus had stormed out. She studied it – "Lost", she would call it.

The attendees applauded.

"Bravo," Denise Schimmerwick said using the DJ's PA system. "Can you believe we saw her do that right before our eyes? Bravo, bravo."

Becca bowed. As quickly as the painting had come together, it had taken its toll on her energy, her psyche. She needed to take a break, splash water on her face. "If you'll excuse me."

She threaded her way through the crowd, nodding to those who congratulated her. It was funny how she could be surrounded by so many people and yet feel so alone. If only Marcus was here to share this with her.

She would paint the two women's white outfits after the painting sold. She heard Denise begin the bidding. Becca climbed the stairs to her bedroom.

Anthony snapped to attention. This was the moment he'd been waiting for. Becca-Laurel-whatever name she went by these days was heading to the second floor. And she was all alone. Perfect.

He set down his drink and slipped out of the room to the foyer. At the bottom of the stairs, he caught a glimpse of his prey as she disappeared off the bridge.

He hightailed it up the stairs, feeling the thrill of the chase, and pulled the Glock out of his pocket. In just a moment, she'd be all his.

A cheer went up in the main room, the painting must have sold. The disco music started up again, a dull vibration up here. Perfect. Becca could scream and no one would hear a thing.

He rounded the corner. It was a bedroom, as big as the one he had at the Everest.

Water was running in the en suite. Maybe she was showering and he'd see her naked and all soapy, like those nudie magazines did sometimes. Yeah.

A little girl appeared off to the side.

Anthony flinched. "Where the hell did you come from?"

"The servants' stairs."

"A back way, huh?" It could provide the perfect way out. "And how many servants are there, little girl?"

There was movement.

"Twenty," Becca said, suddenly appearing in the en suite door. Her eyes were locked on his semiautomatic.

Arielle shook her head. "Six and you let them all go, remember?"

Anthony smiled. Leave it to a kid to tell the truth. He almost laughed. This was too easy. He waggled the gun at them. "OK, both of you, lead the way downstairs. We're going to take a little drive."

Becca balked. "I'll do whatever you want, just leave Arielle here."

"Are you shitting me? She's my insurance. With her along, I *know* you'll cooperate."

Marcus sped up to the security gate, the undercover town car's emergency lights flashing. The guard hit the gate switch and waved him through. He hit the accelerator.

With all the precautions Becca had taken to find a gated community and install a top-notch security system, none of it mattered if you invited the lion inside your net of safety.

He screeched to a halt outside Becca's mansion, shut it down and killed the lights. He jumped out and the sound of pounding music emanating from inside hit his ears. It wouldn't be playing if Anthony was holding everyone at gun point. He had to get inside, find Becca and get to her panic room. George was just a few minutes behind and would arrest Anthony.

The garage door powered up. Anthony was there. Something in his hand gleaned – a gun- and it was pointed at –

Becca! Shit, she was being held hostage. All her driving lessons, all her hours at the gun range wouldn't help her now. She looked scared as heck.

Marcus yanked out his handgun and ducked behind his vehicle. All he needed was one clear shot.

Anthony shoved Becca into the passenger seat of her car. He shook his finger at her, seemed to be warning her of something.

Inside, the music paused.

Good, he could hear them now.

Anthony slammed the car door. "Cooperate or I'll kill you," he warned.

Marcus took aim. *Not if I kill you first, you son of a bitch.*

Anthony stepped back and there was movement behind him. Shit. Arielle was there. What the heck? He had them *both* hostage?

Anthony was talking. "– get to know one another better at this little cabin of yours. Thanks, kid, for telling me about the place."

So, she and Arielle were being taken to Mount Charleston, far from town, where they'd be isolated, where cars like this one from the detective agency couldn't go.

Becca's Jaguar started up, shot out of the garage with a tweak of its tires and roared off.

Rain was threatening. It would be a downpour on the mountain. He'd need a four-wheel drive vehicle.

Wait. The two-seater Jeep was parked on the side of the garage, right where he'd left it.

Marcus ran over and yanked opened the driver's door. He felt around in the dark. Where were they?

His hand found something hard, metallic. Thank goodness. The keys were still where he'd left them.

Standing in the doorway of the cabin, Becca clutched Arielle to her as Anthony stepped inside where it was pitch black. She had to think of something, had to get them out of this situation. If they stayed here, they'd be completely under his control. Her mind raced.

Anthony had the keys to her new Jeep, and she had no idea how to jumpstart it, so that was out.

They could run to a neighbor's, but the nearest place was a vacation cabin three or four miles away and there was no guarantee anyone would be there to let them in.

There was the sudden sound of the kitchen table legs scraping on the floor. "Ow," Anthony said and cursed.

He knocked into other things, books spilled, a lamp smashed. A whirring sound started from the other side of the structure – the water wheel. He must have hit the wall switch to activate it.

"How the hell do you turn on the damn lights?" he yelled out to her.

They're on a separate circuit, you idiot. "The contractors have been turning the power on and off as they renovate," she said loudly. "Maybe they left it turned off."

Becca leaned down by Arielle's ear. "Don't move," she whispered. There was a flashlight kept in the kitchen drawer, not ten feet inside the door. She hoped this idea worked, for both their sakes.

CHAPTER-THIRTY-ONE

Becca tore off her high heels and tossed them aside. She couldn't risk them clicking on the floor. She tiptoed inside. Her hands felt along the kitchen counter. Four drawers in - one, two, three, here it was, this one. She eased it open. Not a sound. Thank goodness for modern cabinetry. She'd opted for soft-closing type.

Farther inside, Anthony crashed into something else. "Can't you people keep a clear path to walk through this freaking place?" he muttered.

Becca felt the flashlight and snatched it up.

She dashed back to the door and pressed her hand to Arielle's back. "Run."

They hightailed it down the drive path. Thank goodness Anthony hadn't gotten the lights to come on. Otherwise, their eyes wouldn't be adjusted to the darkness. The trouble was, his were adjusted, too.

It started to rain, not a light rain, either.

There were car lights bouncing up ahead, headed their way.

Shit. It had to be the Uncle Sal fellow who Anthony had called on the way up here, telling him where they were headed. Her heart pounded even harder.

She glanced back at the cabin. They'd only gotten about seventy-five feet down the dirt drive, if that. It was not nearly far enough. Becca grabbed Arielle's hand. "This way."

They crashed into the brush. Oh shit, Anthony could probably hear them. He'd come running out and be on them any minute. "Stop. Crouch down. We've got to be quiet."

The rain pelted around them, coming down harder now.

Arielle whimpered. "I'm so scared, Aunt Laurel."

Me, too. She put her arms around her niece, felt how fragile she was, and held her as tightly as she could. "I know honey. You've got to be a big girl, OK?"

Becca shivered in her evening gown and wished she had a coat. The mountain was getting a real soaking.

She could hear the four wheel drive kick in as the vehicle spit back mud. "Don't look into the headlights," she warned Arielle. "Close your eyes."

The vehicle rolled past them, not ten feet away. *Please don't let the headlights hit us, please.*

As it rolled past, the moonlight caught the emblem on the side: The Everest.

What the heck? The hotel was loaning its vehicles out to thugs? Hold on, what had Marcus told her? That there was still an underground element in Las Vegas. Yeah, and it was being fostered by Denise Schimmerwick and her husband.

Becca swallowed hard. She'd been duped by Denise into having an event at her home, into having her so-called high rollers traipse past security. What an idiot she'd been.

The Everest's vehicle pulled up to the cabin and stopped. An older man got out, his features stark in the glare of the dome light.

Anthony came outside, clearly visible in the headlights. He gestured. "I'm surprised that you're here."

"Frankie's on his way, too."

Becca's heart stopped. There were more thugs coming? She glanced down the path to the road. They'd be spotted for sure if they tried to escape that way.

Anthony looked smug. "Uncle Sal, you sure you want to be here? I mean, it could get messy. I'm not sure how much it'll take to break her."

"That's part of the fun. Where is she?"

"Huh?" Anthony's head turned this way and that.

Becca gave a slight snort. *You idiot, we're long gone.*

Anthony started in one direction, then another. "She was just here."

"Calm down. Let's look inside before we go running all over the woods," his uncle said.

She waited until they disappeared inside. Time to move. They had to get back to the path that led up the hill so they could cross the peak to intersect a different road. "Try not to make a sound. Let's go."

They headed out. She hoped this worked.

Marcus raced the Jeep up the mountain road in the rain. He was halfway there, would have been there sooner if the Jeep hadn't needed gas. Lights were flashing up ahead. Road construction maybe, no, those were police lights.

It was a road block with police cars parked at a ninety degree angle to the road. OK, this was a minor hiccup. He'd show them his ID, explain that he had to get through.

Marcus pulled up and powered down his window. He squinted at the bright flashlight beam that placed on his face. "I'm on official business, have to get through," he said, holding up his badge.

"I'm sorry sir, flash flood. You'll have to turn around."

"I'm on official business."

The officer looked closer at his ID and raised an eyebrow. "For a detective agency?"

"Look, two people have been kidnapped."

"Nothing's come over the radio."

Becca could be being tortured while this idiot talked. He had to get to her. "Look, just let me pass. I'll explain later."

"I'm sorry, sir. The road is out."

"Fine. I've got four wheel drive. This puppy will go through anything."

"I'm sorry sir," he said, moving his hand to his sidearm, "I'd lose my job if I let you past."

Lose his job? Becca and Arielle could lose their lives. His fist pounded the steering wheel. *Think, think. There has to be another way to get up that mountain.*

Becca's bare foot slipped in the mud. She caught herself and held up the hem of her gown, trying not to step on it.

She looked through the rain. She and Arielle were finally at the top of the mountain. Better, no one appeared to be following them.

She stepped carefully. It was rocky up here.

"I'm cold," Arielle whined.

The poor little thing had been a real trooper this whole trek. "We're almost there, sweetie."

Damn this gown, it was tripping her up. Becca gathered up the hem and tied it in a fat knot just below her knee. There, now it was up and out of her way.

They kept climbing. It was tough without shoes, with a child, tough in the dark and knowing they were being pursued by crazed killers. How had it ever come to this?

She stepped on a pebble and winced. Her foot was already throbbing from tripping over that unseen root. "Look, there's the cave. We can get out of this rain."

They dashed inside. She flicked on the flashlight, risking that Anthony and his uncle would never see it. "Go to that corner over there." *Where Marcus and I made wild, passionate love.*

Her chest clutched. *Marcus, where are you? I need you so badly right now.* She had to stop thinking that way. It was up to her and her alone to evade Anthony and get them to safety. Had they lost them?

Arielle curled up in the corner. Poor thing, she'd been through a horrible ordeal.

They couldn't risk hiking in lightning. Becca collected about two dozen baseball-sized rocks and stacked them by the cave's opening. She sat down beside them and peered outside. She'd pelt anyone who came close.

Anthony played the flashlight on the trail. Damn, he hated rain. Vegas wasn't supposed to have rain, but this damn mountain was getting drenched.

A helicopter flew overhead, passing the peak. Probably some television traffic reporter telling drivers to stay off this freaking mountain.

"Look, a track," Uncle Sal said.

Anthony hurried over to him. "Where?"

"There."

His flashlight caught the footprint – a bare footprint. Becca had chucked her high heels by the cabin door. It had to be her track.

Anthony's shoulders relaxed. It looked like the mud was going to lead them right to her. If he wasn't so wet, he'd find it funny. Right now, he wanted to wring her neck with his two hands for making him track her down in this shit weather.

Oh, yeah, as soon as Luke's sweetheart was back in his clutches, he'd extract his revenge on her, but good.

Marcus jumped out as soon as Keith Uberhoff set the NHP helicopter down.

"You sure you don't want me to be your back up?"

It was tempting. "No, Keith, I need you to bring reinforcements," Marcus shouted above noise of the swishing blades.

"OK, but you got lucky with this break in the weather. Otherwise, I couldn't have helped you. If it starts raining like a bat out of hell again, this puppy will be grounded."

Shit, like he didn't have enough problems. Marcus flicked up the collar of his suit jacket and set out. If he rounded this peak, then he could catch the trail by the cave.

His foot slipped. Damn this rain.

He rounded the peak.

There was a light, faint, but definitely a light. It was coming from the cave, not a camp fire, but a flashlight. Someone was up here. Was it a hiker who'd been caught in the rain? It didn't make sense that it would be Anthony.

He approached with care, trying to get a glimpse of who might be inside. A thought struck him – if it was a hiker, maybe he'd have boots to borrow.

The light went out.

So much for having the advantage. He'd have to show his hand. "Hello, the cave. Who's in there?"

A dark figure appeared in the cave's mouth. "Marcus? Is that you?"

Holy heck, it was Becca. "Sweetie?"

He ran to her and she met him in the rain, launching herself into his arms and holding tight, like she never wanted to let go. So, she'd missed him, too.

She snuggled into him. "You're here."

"I'm here," he murmured into her hair. It felt so right to have her in his arms again.

She pulled back to look at him. "I've been miserable without you."

It was a state he knew well. "I've been a certifiable wreck, can't think, can't sleep." What a fool he'd been to storm out of that New York hotel room, to leave her there unprotected, not when she meant so much to him. He ran a hand down her face and suddenly realized she was wet, and she was in a slinky evening gown, no doubt freezing. "You're getting soaked, come on." He led her into the cave.

"Don't step on Arielle," Becca said, flicking on a flashlight. "Anthony held her at gunpoint."

The low-life lout. Marcus flexed his fists. Just wait until he was face to face with Anthony. He'd gladly settle the score.

Becca clicked off the light.

He pulled her into his arms and held her close, as her arms slipped around him in return.

"I'm sorry, Marcus," she said as she hugged him. "I should have seen things from your perspective, realized how it would have looked to you, paying you back for those tips. I was wrong."

"No, it was my stupid pride. I blew everything out of proportion." His lips sought out hers and pressed into them. She was his woman and it was his job to protect her. Marcus broke off the kiss. "We've got to get you two off this mountain, Becca, get you away from –"

"Anthony," some man called out. "Look, there's a cave up there. I think I found them."

She sensed Marcus scooping up Arielle.

"We've got to get out of this cave," he said, stepping up beside her to peer out.

Surely the cave was safer than the forest. "But this is rock. It'll will stop their bullets."

"Yeah, but I only have this one gun. Six bullets."

Six? Only six? Anthony had a semi-automatic pistol. She yanked on his sleeve, urging him forward. "We've got to get out of this cave."

"Ready? Hold onto my suit jacket so I know you're right behind me. Here we go. One, two, three."

They dashed out.

She glanced around. Where were Anthony and his uncle? Their voices had sounded close, but who could tell in this muffling sprinkle of rain?

Marcus sprinted toward the thickest part of the forest. Thirty more feet and they'd be there.

She stepped on a rock. Ouch, damn it. *Keep moving. Keep moving.*

There were shouts behind them. "There they go."

A bullet rang out.

Becca ducked instinctively. *Shit, we're being shot at!* She tensed, waiting for the bullet to hit her.

Nothing.

Marcus ran into the woods. A branch slapped back at her. She'd take a dozen branch slaps if it meant not taking a bullet.

Arielle woke up. 'What's going on?"

"Shh, sweetie," Becca whispered. "We have to be super-duper quiet. Can you do that?"

They kept running.

There were sounds of footsteps pounding up behind them.

Oh shit, they were coming closer.

"Quick, behind this big tree," Marcus said, grabbing her shoulder. Becca pressed her back into the trunk and risked peeking out. Nothing.

There was muffled talking. They were making a plan. Maybe a third guy had joined them. Maybe there were now three guns, out numbering their one.

Marcus set Arielle down. "My NHP partner, Keith, airlifted me up here," he whispered. "He'll be flying back with more men."

She'd never heard sweeter words. "We'll be saved."

"Well, as long as it only sprinkles. The copter can't fly in a torrent."

As if on cue, the rain came down harder.

No!

CHAPTER THIRTY-TWO

"Right there," Anthony said to his uncle, pointing through the woods. "I thought I saw movement." Shit, this was taking too long. They had to find Becca, the stupid bitch was making him run all over this freaking mountain, ruining his shoes, his evening clothes. It was going to feel so good to watch her suffer while he pried off her fingernails one by one. He'd teach the little kid a lesson, too, just for kicks.

But why Uncle Sal had joined him up here in the mountain was a mystery. He usually kept his nose clean when it came to jobs like this. Sure, way back in his heyday, he'd handled plenty of uncooperative people. But these days, his uncle took it easy, let his associates do the dirty work while he raked in the dough, living the good life.

Well, fuck his uncle. With Becca's millions secure in his pocket, *he'd* be the one living the good life.

His uncle nodded. "I saw it, too. Let's fan out and surround her and the kid."

They approached the tree, thirty feet apart, guns out.

Becca gasped. "Don't shoot." She clutched the little girl close to her.

There was a guy with her. And – shit - he was armed, pointing his weapon at him. Oh, yeah? "Drop the gun, mister, or I shoot the kid."

The big guy hesitated, then relaxed his grip. The gun thudded to the ground.

Where the hell had he come from? Then he remembered. The helicopter, had to be. Anthony gestured with his chin. "Kick it away."

His uncle came up around the other side of the tree, his own piece drawn. "Good work, Anthony."

Damn straight it was good work. "Who are you, mister?"

"I'm a detective."

Like that was supposed to impress them? Anthony shrugged. "We don't need him. Right, Uncle Sal?" He raised his gun.

Becca moved her body to shield her companion. "If you kill Marcus, which one of you is going to carry Arielle?"

She had a point. *He* didn't want to carry the kid and his uncle sure as hell wasn't going to jump to the task. "OK, you live," he told the big guy. *For now.*

Uncle Sal raised his own gun. "But you don't, Anthony."

There was a blast and pain like he'd never felt before in his shoulder.

Becca screamed.

What the hell?

His uncle had just shot him.

"Uncle Sal, what are you doing?"

His uncle stepped closer, the gun pointed at him. "You should have thought things through before crossing me, Anthony. Did you think I wouldn't find out?"

The second blast hit him in the gut.

Fuck, it hurt. His knees gave way and he dropped to the ground. "Uncle Sal, I was going to tell you, honest."

"This woman stands to earn closer to a hundred million, Anthony, and you told me ten. *Ten!*"

Frankie must have ratted him out to his uncle. He'd kill him if he ever saw the punk again. "I can explain."

"I groomed you and this is how you pay me back?" Uncle Sal's eyes blazed. "You frigging piece of shit."

Another shot. The gut again. Shit, this was beyond painful. This was it. This was how he was going to die.

Anthony rolled onto his back. The tree limbs above him shimmied in a gust of wind. He could see every raindrop as it fell toward him like it was in slow motion.

A woman, Becca, appeared above him, knelt over him. What was she doing? Playing Nancy Nurse?

"He's hurt bad," she cried in slow speed, her words like molasses. "We've got to help him."

Anthony closed his eyes, the image of her above him still in his mind. This was it. He was done. *Just take me, Jesus.*

Marcus carried Arielle down the mountain, careful not to slip in the mud. Beside him, Becca eased along, the hem of her gown caught up in that funny knot she'd made.

He could feel the gun as though it was pressed in his back, even though Uncle Sal was a good twelve feet behind them. Keith wasn't coming back with the helicopter, not in this downpour. It was up to him to do something, anything. He found Arielle's ear. "If we get to the cabin, can you get to the road, find a neighbor and get help?" he whispered.

She nodded in earnest.

"Good girl."

Whether she called for help or not was irrelevant. He needed her to get away from Uncle Sal so there was one less target for the goon to shoot.

He glanced over at Becca, picking her way down the trail. Why had she played Nancy Nurse back there with Anthony? He *knew* how much she loathed the gangster for killing her high school sweetheart. It didn't matter at the moment. Right now, they were in deep trouble.

He had to distract the man behind them somehow, charge him and wrestle that gun from him.

The cabin came into view.

"No funny business this time," Uncle Sal said. "Turn on the lights."

"It's a circuit in the basement," Becca said. "I have to go in this door here." She pointed.

"Then do it."

Becca shot him a sideways look. She was going to do something.

Marcus set Arielle down on the ground. "Get ready to run," he whispered.

Becca entered the dark basement.

The seconds ticked by. Silence.

Behind him, Uncle Sal rocked from one foot to the other. "What's going on in there?"

Still silence.

"You'd better not be trying anything stupid," the gangster called out. "I'll come over there and just start shooting."

Still silence.

Becca began screaming at the top of her lungs.

Uncle Sal hurried past him.

Marcus gave Arielle a nod. "Run!"

He launched himself at the older man, tackling him to the ground. *The gun, the gun, had to get the gun.*

They rolled as they tussled. Damn, the old guy was stronger than he'd imagined.

The gun discharged, the bullet ricocheting off the rock foundation.

Uncle Sal pushed him into a tree stump. It tore into his ribs. Shit.

The old guy regained his feet and turned, the gun swinging his way.

Oh no, you don't. Marcus kicked out, brought him down.

He smashed his fist under the old guy's chin and grabbed his arms.

He knocked the gun away just as Becca appeared in the doorway. She'd been brilliant, ad-libbing with that sudden, disconcerting scream. "Thought you hurt my woman, huh? You piece of shit."

He snapped cuffs on the old geezer, hard, to really let him feel what it was like to be in the grasp of justice.

Uncle Sal squirmed as he was forced to stand up. "I should have killed you up there by the cave, you and the kid both," he wheezed, sitting up.

Marcus bit his lip. It was so tempting to kick the crap out of this guy.

Shots rang out from the woods.

Shit.

Anthony was stumbling down the path.

In front of him, Uncle Sal fell back, mouth open, eyes staring up at the sky. Blood began staining his shirt front.

Anthony had just killed his kin, a totally defenseless man. And now they were back in the clutches of this psychopath. Shit, this thing wasn't over.

Becca ducked as the bullets flew.

Marcus fell to the ground, clutching one knee. "Ahhh," he moaned.

"Yeah. Hurts like hell, doesn't it?" Anthony taunted him. "Guess you won't be coming to the lady's rescue any time soon, will you?"

"You son of a bitch," Marcus seethed.

Anthony kept the gun trained on her, lurched closer and reached down. "Fooled you," he laughed. He tossed away the gun he'd just used.

Becca stared. He'd shot his uncle with Marcus' revolver, then shot poor Marcus and emptied the chamber – six bullets. She could have beaten him to Uncle Sal's automatic if she'd realized. Instead, she'd frozen. Stupid, stupid, stupid.

He trained his uncle's gun on her.

She backed away from him. He wouldn't hurt her. He needed her. But he could hurt Marcus. Her lover meant nothing to this deviant from society. She had to draw him away from Marcus at all costs.

Anthony headed toward her, gun out.

She edged around the back corner of the cabin. She had to get him talking, get him to follow her. "I don't know why you brought me up here, Anthony. All you had to do was tie up Arielle and take me to a bank. I would have transferred my last dollar to you."

He stumbled after her. "I'm not stupid. You can make bank transactions by phone these days."

"There's no cell service up here," she told him, speaking above the creak of the water wheel as it turned. "No phone service of any kind at the cabin."

He hesitated, looking stunned.

Good, she'd penetrated that tiny little brain of his.

He advanced on her. "So I'll take you where there *is* cell service."

"Nope, has to be done in person," she said. "The money's in a Swiss bank account. I stipulated that they can't release my funds any way but in person. You see, Anthony, you can't kill me, you can't even *harm* me. Even if you escort me, people at the bank would see my bruises and become suspicious."

"I'm still going to make you suffer. I'll shoot you in the hip, the shoulder, some inconspicuous area like that. You'll live, but you'll suffer. And I'll still get my money. I didn't struggle down off this freaking mountain to give up now."

He was going to shoot her. He was determined, that was clear. Well, then, there was only one thing she could do. She backed up some more. *Come on, come on, a little bit farther.* She maneuvered to the back corner of the cabin. She had to make sure Marcus wouldn't be hit by a stray bullet.

Anthony lurched toward her again. Uncle Sal's gun wavered unsteadily in his hand. He'd probably lost a lot of blood. She'd thought he was near death when she'd knelt beside him up on the mountain top.

They were on the far side of the cabin now. Marcus was out of danger.

Keeping her eyes on him, Becca bent down and fished in the skirt of her evening gown, just below the knot she'd made.

There it was, Anthony's gun, caught in the folds. Thanks goodness Uncle Sal had been distracted when she'd played Nancy Nurse. She clasped the cold metal in her hand behind her where he couldn't see it.

He grinned. "You can show up at the bank with injuries. I'll make an excuse, tell the employees you were in a car accident. Happens all the time." He raised his gun a leering look in his eye. "Right now, I just want to see you suffer."

A bullet whizzed past her.

She whipped up the semiautomatic, aimed and fired, center mass.

Bam.

Bam.

Bam.

Bam.

Anthony jerked with each hit. Blood gushed from his chest. He looked surprised and staggered backward into the water wheel.

The motor groaned as the wheel churned. Anthony's lifeless body was scooped up in one of the troughs, hanging there like a rag doll as it was lifted up and over the top of the arch.

Arielle ran up to her and threw her arms around her. "Oh, Aunt Laurel, I was so scared."

"It's all right. It's all over." She crouched down and hugged the little girl tight.

The water wheel creaked, the motor straining as it lifted Anthony's body, still snagged, to the top of the arch and back down again. Becca shielded Arielle from the sight. "Let's go help Marcus and get him to a hospital."

Becca dabbed more paint on her latest work. Her newest pieces had been fueled by the emotions of many factors – Theresa's improving blood work, Marcus' rehab advancements for his shattered knee, Arielle's coming to terms with the kidnapping.

Movement at the window caught her eye. *He was here, in the daytime? And she wasn't dreaming? Wasn't meditating?*

Luke was out on the patio. He was all skeleton, but she'd know him anywhere.

She hurried to the French doors and stepped outside. She hated seeing him in this state. It had to hurt. "Are you all right?"

Luke nodded.

Sure, he was. "You don't need to visit me anymore, Luke," she said gently, taking his hands in hers. Who cared that he was a skeleton? He'd been human once. "Go and be wherever it is that you're supposed to be in your realm. I'll be fine in this one."

"I know." He nodded. "Marcus is a good man."

"So are you."

"But I'm on this side. I can only do so much to ensure that you're safe."

Didn't he realize how much he *had* done? How he'd warned her, guided her? "Anthony is dead, his uncle, too. They can't hurt me anymore."

"Marcus will recover. He's going to ask to marry you, you know."

She'd suspected as much. "We'll see how it goes."

"I won't be visiting you anymore. He's your protector now." Luke paused. "I ... wish you both the best."

There was hurt in his words. She knew he'd wanted to be the one true love of her life.

She leaned forward and kissed his cheekbone gently. "Thank you, Luke, for everything."

She watched him disappear. "You were a wonderful protector," she whispered after him.

* * *